Within the void of spac,
and although painfully   .
Searching the deepest,   -
every galaxy — every p.

Tiny particles of disruptive energy shabbily ripped through the fabric of time and space, superabundant with bleakness and greed, existing only to satisfy its hunger to grow — to survive. It always found its nourishment, be it in vast areas or tiny cracks in the vacuum, it mattered not.

It became stronger, sluggishly overcoming, like a fire that tries to ignite in the dampest of lands, destroying — until its prey succumbed to join the throng. It knew nothing of peace and love, it knew nothing of kindness and compassion, nor did it ever know how to live without causing pain and suffering to all other life forms; it always took, and kept on taking, without hesitation nor consideration.

The mass had evolved billions of years ago and was named by those of the purest light. Though it's not, and never would be worthy of an identity or title, it's ancient, dark and dangerous — simple, yet soul-destroying. It was birthed purely through persistent cruelty and unrestrained behaviour from all life forms across the cosmos, and along with dire emotions of distress, anguish and hurt, intense negative energy had spawned. The woe and disdain manifested into an entire entity with an acute awareness of its own.

Life forms lived in fear and uncertainty as they struggled to survive in worlds ravaged by negativity. Atmospheres were filled with the stench of hurt, death and darkness; the voices of those suffering echoed continuously.

In many of the once-thriving lands, wherever they may have been in the universe, now stood as mere shadows of their former glory. Broken and stained with the innocent despair of the fallen.

Hatred and animosity ran throughout the galaxies as different life forms harboured deep-seated grudges and prejudices against one another. The history of these realms was marred by centuries of conflict and betrayal, fueling a never-ending cycle of torment and revenge. The inhabitants were divided by their differences in beliefs and fueled with hostility, as they glared upon each other with disdain.

Love, kindness and compassion became extremely rare commodities, forever overshadowed by the presence of negative traits.

Positivity radiated pure light, resilience, and a belief in the inherent goodness of life, to illuminate the path towards progress and success. It fostered a sense of gratitude, enabling life forms to appreciate the beauty that life still had to offer. It was a force that uplifted spirits, encouraged growth, bringing a sense of hope and new possibilities. Moreover, it created a ripple effect and tried to spread its contagious energy to all those around. However, sometimes this became a tremendous feat as the dark side was never far away, consuming those who let it.

The areas that held the light shone with passion and tried to grab hold of glimmers as they passed by, so that they may join with the positive, but there was little that could be done in such negative turmoil.

Dark energy was a formidable opponent, capable of sowing seeds of doubt and, in turn, possessing the same traits as any other energy. Negativity loomed with its dark clouds, casting doubt and fear upon all.

Because Like attracts Like.

THE ARC

LAURA COSBY

Published in 2025 by Laura
The Arc Copyright © 2025 Laura Cosby
ISBN 9798316732579
Lauracosbyauthor.co.uk
All rights reserved under International Copyright Law.
Contents and/or cover may not be reproduced in whole or in part without the express written consent of the publisher.
Names, characters, places and incidents are either products of the author's imagination or are used fictitiously.

For my sister Becky.
Thank you for being you.

Love & Light.

Chapter One

Year 2243

Becky

After witnessing a colossal explosion, Becky was left terrified. She picked up her pace hoping to find an area to hide and settle down for the evening; it was dangerous for anyone to be alone, particularly this late at night.

She pulled her weathered overcoat snug to her body and with that continual sense of urgency, she hurried down the street, where the scars of war were deeply etched.

Becky passed bodies sprawled on the remnants of buildings. Some leaned against the walls, their faces dazed and lifeless, like discarded rag dolls left by careless children; they seemed to blend into the background as if they were mere props in a horror film. Other figures darted and weaved, desperately trying to evade danger. With each passing second, their need to escape or hide became more urgent.

She could feel eyes watching her; she glanced at their owners, ensuring her gaze did not linger enough for them to approach her. She had no intentions of stopping and no idea how to help anyone anyway. She could see their mouths moving in desperation amid the noise, clearly wailing — their facial expressions contorted, pleading with anguish. But Becky's instincts had kicked in; she felt her core wrench, urging her onward to find safety, always tense and ready to fight or flee at a moment's notice.

The sound of war and terror ricocheted through the air. Blaring lights and thunderous noises from battered Army vehicles, both on the ground and airborne, glared and hammered in all directions; she simply couldn't understand why the Armed Forces weren't trying to save people like her. Maybe the gang members they were fighting were making it too hard for them.

She was amazed that she was still alive! All day and every day, each step Becky took was thought through, and as precise as it could be when navigating this maze of danger.

Beams of light pierced through the darkness nearby, illuminating the surroundings, casting long shadows, some moving, some not. Clouds of dirt and debris mixed with rain danced around, impairing her vision. It was like peering through foggy windows, ones that she couldn't wipe clean with her hand. Struggling to make out any shapes or forms left her feeling disoriented and vulnerable, plunged into a world of further darkness.

Her legs carried her towards the nearest abandoned building and, seeking to take refuge within the crumbling walls, she slipped into its darkness. Now concealed within the shadows like a lost ghost, she held her breath, waiting for dangers to pass by and airborne vehicles to fly overhead. Becky covered her ears; her hands shook with cold and terror, but they were firmly placed.

There was an odd calmness to this solitude, eyes open, ears shut — an air of serene peace. Tranquillity bathed the outside conflict in a haze of slow motion and blurred lines, and somehow muted the continuous ruckus further, dulling it to a muffled fog...just like…

An unpleasant memory came flooding back…sticking her tiny fingers into her ears as a child. It stilled the scary noises and helped her drop to sleep amid the fighting and loud, uncouth visitors that would call to the underground shelter to see her mother and father, on a regular basis. She shook the thought away; it was a lifetime ago now.

Becky released her ears and shuddered. The peace that her plugged ears had brought her, stopped.

She turned to peer through some broken bricks. Her eyes swung wildly from left to right and noticed someone running towards her; she shrank back into a corner, making herself as small as possible. She watched on, as the figure rushed into the building. It was a woman; she whimpered and didn't even notice that Becky was standing there in the darkness, just feet away. The woman scurried past, continuing straight through and out the other side, and was shot down in an instant.

A deep, primal, gripping sensation in Becky's gut prompted her up; her instinct had spoken again. Seizing the moment, she made her way out of the building to stand amid the carnage, unsure of which way to turn; her anxiety was always set on a high level, to which her heart protested daily.

On the war-ravaged street, distant explosions and echoing cries from those who had not hidden well enough disturbed her greatly. The darkness had been her ally, and she'd hoped it would continue to do so.

The chilly wind found its way to her body, cutting into her brow, whisking dark hair about her face in twirls, and knotting it to resemble a deserted bird's nest — a storm was settling in, the heavy rain turning to sleet. Her ears were becoming painfully numb; how she wished she'd still had the woollen hat. It was pulled from her head a few weeks before in the night. She'd been unceremoniously dragged from her slumber just in time to see a female stumbling away, clutching a child. The woman had stopped briefly, turning to make eye contact; she'd placed the hat on her daughter's small head.

Becky had let it be.

The sound of people shouting nearby brought her from those thoughts — she quickly gathered herself, hunched her shoulders and pushed on. Murky, freezing air caught on the back of her throat with every breath, leaving a thick metallic taste, the taste of cold death and dust.

On turning the corner, her heart stifled — she'd collided with someone; they'd knocked her meagre bag to the floor. Becky's hands shot up in defence. With the lack of visibility, it was impossible to gauge the person's intentions or even see their face. She teetered on the spot, leaving her bag on the ground.

The man shivered.

"Sorry." Dark hair escaped from the hood of his sweater and whipped in circles over his eyes. He was underdressed for the weather conditions and kept his back curved as he prepared to face the biting winds from the next street. He bent to retrieve her bag and handed it to her gently.

She took it cautiously, snatching it at the last second.

Before rounding the corner, he turned back sharply.

Becky's body jarred; she warily eyed him as he pointed.

"Don't head that way, love, guns are out real bad tonight; it's not safe anywhere!" He had no response. "You did hear me, right?"

She nodded slowly, head low, eyes watching him steadily.

He continued, "It's sketchy. The Army's about again in the droves, the sky is alive, it's bright with lights round there…don't seem too bothered where they're shooting either!"

She nodded again.

He paused, then turned away.

Becky watched him disappear, vanishing through a curtain of sleet.

She started off, first crossing the road, scrambling on rubble, around abandoned vehicles, dead bodies and discarded items, and over to the opposite corner of the street.

She stopped in utter fear; the pit of her stomach felt heavy, like cement had cured there. From close behind came vicious shouting and ear-shattering gunshots. In an instant, she'd slammed her cold hands over her ears again and lumbered forward, pressing the front of her body against the building, and froze.

Thinking better of it, she carefully turned so her back was on the wall and slid herself along it, tears seeping from her eyes; the pressure of the brick on her body was not comforting. She spotted a burnt-out van nearby, abandoned and left — rammed into a building long ago. Becky's chest ached with fear and threatened to burst at the sternum, but then an idea came to her. Perhaps she could hide in the van, squeeze herself in the footwell, and be undetected.

After lurching towards it, she was there in no time. Becky blindly fumbled for the latch, only to find the door partially open anyway, with enough room to curl her fingers around to pull it further open. She yanked it with all her might — her eyes alert for the owners of the guns.

She mumbled to herself in panic.

With one last hefty pull, the door creaked open. She placed her hands on the seat to haul herself up, ready to dive into the passenger side. But became motionless, stifling the cry that pushed hard on her lips.

Sitting slumped together, propping each other up, were two bodies gaping at her. Their jaws hung low, their cheeks drawn and eyes dull, misted by death. Gunshot wounds had torn through their bodies, leaving vicious holes; their blood blackened and crusted with time. Curled neatly at the woman's feet, was a dog with the same fate.

She recoiled and scurried back to the corner again and leaned forward to look around the building. Her breathing was uneven. Plumes of white mist left her mouth and drifted off around the corner as she peeked.

Gangs were rushing out from the side streets, soldiers hot on their tails. Through the sleet, Becky could just make out the figure of a person lying on the ground, his hood spattered in dark red, now resting on his back; his hair becoming dampened and flat, while a pool of blood gathered beneath his body. Beams of blue light rained down on him. It seemed he had lost his life to save hers, and her heart burst with sadness at the knowledge.

But she'd been seen! Her breath had deceived her, given her away; she covered her open mouth as tears welled, threatening to breach her lids.

"Oy, you! Stop where you are; we are armed!"

Time was of the essence. It was run or die. She ran.

She'd done nothing wrong, just tried to survive, yet no one else knew that. In the eyes of the Armed Forces, she was possibly a gang member or criminal, and in the eyes of the gangs, she was someone to rob, attack, an outcast or just someone to kill — either way, a young innocent victim.

She glanced up as a vast number of lights swooped above her. She covered her ears again; she needed to find a safer place.

She could hear dogs barking in the distance — another danger. Stray dogs almost certainly packed together, becoming a formidable enemy, hunger driving them forward. She didn't relish being eaten alive.

To her left, a defeated building had finally given up and was crumbling, sending plumes of its own debris into the already unclean air. Becky ran faster, just as a huge dirty grey wave of it came rushing up to engulf her. Half blinded by the grit she floundered over uneven ground; clouds of musty brick dust filled her nostrils and stalled her lungs. She panicked, stumbled and fell, but made herself get up — to keep moving forward.

Lone dogs and scraggy cats careered here and there. Rats scuttled on tiny legs, although some were undeterred by the commotion and carried on eating, burying their faces into whatever they could find. People ran, pushing and shoving in their haste to find cover. Some just stood amid the carnage, dazed, defeated and accepting their fate, while others staggered in a drug or chemical-induced state — they reminded her of zombies; the old stories of the undead unnerved her to the core.

Becky nearly fell again as a man ran past her; he took a rifle from his waist. She recoiled, a whimper escaped her lips, begging him not to shoot her; she cried and clasped her hands as if in prayer. But he started shooting upwards; aircraft flew overhead, shining their lights to the ground and glaring on those below.

He had just enough time to tell her, "Get outta here kid! Hide!" Because a volley of single shots showered down from the aircraft, the man was killed instantly and fell like a sack in front of her. Becky was dumbstruck that the bullets had missed her completely; a wave of panicked relief washed over her — she backed up with an intense will to survive. She took her opportunity and jumped over the body — then fled as fast as she could.

She ran on in terror, arms flailing, checking above and behind her with every stride for pursuers, but she fell forward; her right arm was now trapped beneath her body. She sobbed, tired and broken.

Becky managed to lift her head from the dusty ground; her vision spun in jagged circles, and her head hurt. Bile rose to her throat with the harsh sting of acid, and rubble stuck angrily into her ribs. She rested her chin on the bricks, exhausted.

Was it worth the struggle?

Should she just lie still and die?

Becky hauled her arms from under her body and rubbed the grit from her eyes, but instead pushed more into them. She felt her eyes begin to water, which slowly flushed them out just enough to see an open area up ahead and to her left. A gang of weapon-wielding thugs were goading someone; they swung their arms high, hitting a dark shape. Muffled insults drifted over to her on the vicious wind.

She lay silently amongst the debris like a baby fawn having lost its mother in a desperate need to be unseen and survive. Becky crawled painfully towards a partially erect wall for better cover, though she tried not to lean against it; one small touch and it could fall directly on her.

Tears washed the grime from her face in angry streaks as she dared to steal a glance at the victim. How she wanted to help, but she couldn't bring herself to reveal her hiding place and most certainly didn't want to watch the attack. Turning away, she dipped her head in self-shame. She got to her feet and went on slower, staying in the shadows, close to buildings. Her knees and hands were raw with grazes, and the gash on her forehead bled down to her mouth. Gripping her sore ribcage and keeping low, she was soon out of sight.

Tired and almost defeated, her ankle throbbed wildly, crying out for rest. She held a broken handgun at her side as a deterrent. She'd found it smashed up in a pile of rubbish one day while looking for anything that might be of use to her; no one could tell the barrel was split, the grip was partially missing, and the trigger nonexistent. It had been useful a few times before now, but only for close contact encounters. One night, months prior, she'd been searching for her friend, when a drunk approached her. He'd slurred something unpleasant, and stumbled towards her, then, before she could get away, he'd fallen onto her, pinning her against something. His breath had been rotten and stale; he'd then tried to force a kiss from her. She quickly fumbled in her pocket for the broken handgun and shoved it to his cheek.

He laughed at her.

That made her mad.

Without hesitation, she shoved the barrel into his mouth, pushing it deep into his throat; he fell backwards, gagging, and with a sickening crack, hit his head on rubble behind. She ran, never knowing if he'd ever got up.

Becky finally found a spot in an alleyway; she knew it well and hoped her street friend Dawny would be there too. They had been friends for two years and had nothing really in common, just friendship and trust — the rest of their lives were, and had been, pitifully sad and painful, but their friendship made up for some of it.

Old Tom was there, although barely visible and could easily be missed if one wasn't looking. He was fast asleep under heaps of damp cardboard and rags, slouched against a pile of worn blankets; his little dog snuggled up under his owner's threadbare coat, only the very tips of his fluffy ears on show.

No sign of Dawny yet, she thought to herself.

She tucked the broken gun back into her bag and tiptoed down the alley a little further to find her spot. A recess in the brickwork gave enough shelter for her; she was only a small-framed girl.

With her breathing settling a little, she began rubbing her foot, hoping to ease some pain, but the dull ache persisted. At least she had a decent pair of socks on — stolen from a dead man's feet, and her cheerfully coloured wellies helped support her bad ankle.

After dumping her bag on the spot she'd chosen, she examined her sore hands and knees; she knew they were badly cut, but it was too dark to see exactly how much. So, she crept off to gather pieces of rubbish from further up the dank alleyway. The stench of urine was strong, but she was undeterred.

Wiping away the settling snow from a bin nearby, she found some smelly material, along with the odd blood-stained item of clothing; anything to cover and hide herself with. It would have to do and went back to the wall; she didn't want to die in the freezing conditions tonight. However, there had been times when she wished that she'd slip away in her sleep, unknowingly and pain-free, because this was no place to be alive.

Just as she reached for something to cover her face, the moon peeked from behind a war-tinged cloud, illuminating the alley a little more. She'd cowered at first, thinking it was aircraft spotlights. But at that moment, Becky noticed a little flash of colour nestled on the wall that she was about to bed down against. Her eyes widened with wonder as she reached to touch it.

A small plant had found a crack in the brickwork and was peeping through; it had been the first piece of green she'd seen in a very long time. One little piece of pure magic still trying to survive in this god-forsaken place, just like everything else.

Becky shoved some debris from under her; it clattered, and she became still, hoping no one had heard. There was a sound to her right, she gently moved forward to see — it was just Tom. Not wanting to speak, she carefully leant backwards, dragged something over her head from the pile of oddments and settled down amid the rest of the rubbish, where she promptly fell asleep.

Old Tom had stirred; he'd heard her pushing some tins about on the ground. He lifted the rubbish from his head and craned his stiff neck down the alley. Just her Wellingtons stuck out from the brickwork.
"Sleep well, little Becky Red..." he whispered, "...may tomorrow bring us all good fortune." He knew deep down that this would never happen.

It was in the early hours that Becky was woken by the terrible metallic scraping sound again. It penetrated everywhere and everything, every time it happened — and everyone simply called it, 'The Noise'. Nobody had ever had an explanation as to what it was, and no one seemed to care. It was like a prolonged wail, engulfed with anger, pain and grief all at the same time. When she was a small child, she'd imagined it was an enormous monster, scrambling its way up from deep under the ground to feed greedily on the humans. Sometimes she still believed it, half expecting a grotesque creature to scoop her up, and swallow her whole.
  Becky tried to stay warm; she wriggled her toes and hugged her body, then snuggled down in her pile, to sleep once again.

In the early morning, Tom was woken by Bob.

"Morning old boy, I hope I didn't squash you again."

The little dog barked as he tried to escape the warm confines of Tom's jacket.

"Oh yes, I see what you mean, Bobby boy." Old Tom spluttered and coughed hard; he clasped his chest; the little dog scrambled out successfully and shook the sleep from his fur.

"Well now, the snow settled a bit, didn't it, boy!"

Bob ran in circles, nose sniffing, pushing it through the snow; he then whined.

"Shh, you'll wake our little Becky Red," insisted Tom. He leant forward carefully and peered up the alley to see her. He twisted to touch and soothe his back as it protested the movement.

"Oh, I can't see any bright red wellie boots, Bobs. Looks like she left before the snow hit too hard. Dawny must have found her and taken her off to somewhere better." He patted the dog on the head and brushed snow from his snout. "Come on, let's find a bit of food from somewhere!"

It was still very early when Tom had gathered his bag and trudged up the alley towards the street; his little dog sniffed the ground at his feet. An aircraft flew overhead. Tom stopped, coughed deeply again, and watched as the helicopter rattled by.

"Come on Bobby boy, let's get going," he said, slowly stretching out his crooked back, but he stopped.

On the opposite side of the road was a dark bundle of what looked like material. Old Tom's eyesight was poor; he opened them wider as if to make his vision clearer, then squinted hard; his skin wrinkled and creased like old parchment. He could make out a human form lying curled on its side.

"Hey, you! Who is that?" he called across. There was no reply. He sniffed and walked cautiously over. The snow clumped on the end of his holey shoes; he stopped again just before the curb. Bob sat beside him. It was indeed a person huddled on the ground.

Tom glanced to his left and right. There weren't too many people around at this time of day, all still in hiding perhaps, which is why he thought it odd to find someone here out in the open; it was rather a dangerous area to be sleeping rough.

He went closer. "Hey, you..." he started, but gasped. This made him cough again. He lost his balance and staggered backwards onto the road, landing on his back. He groaned in pain and stayed there for a few more moments, unable to strain himself up. Tom rolled carefully to his side and hitched to one elbow; this was when he saw the blood seeping into the snow. He stared in disbelief for a moment. The cold and wet seeped through his sleeve, chills crept up his arm to his shoulder like jittery icy fingers, and then penetrated his thinning skin, but he hardly noticed.

He shifted himself up a little more and shuffled closer on his rear. Tom recognised who it was. He couldn't hold back the sorrow and cried softly beside her.

And as 'The Noise' reverberated around him, echoing through the streets of London, he said,

"Dawny, I hope you rest in peace, little flower. Where is Becky Red...?"

Chapter Two

Suze

Day 1

Suze grabbed the soft duvet and hitched it up snugly under her chin. With a sleepy groan of satisfaction, she turned over to lie on the other side, content with the warmth.
 Burying her head into a sweet-smelling, clean, puffy pillow, she closed her eyes, settled, and lay there for several more seconds before she dozed off again.

Lights swoop on the ground and shine in her eyes, people shouting, running, and crying, an uproar of explosions, crumbling buildings, blood, and death. 'The Noise' is there; the intense sound penetrates her soul and makes her want to cry out in despair.
 Gunshots deafen her, and now a continuous ringing is overwhelming her hearing.
 She can feel soft fur — her face is wet...the black, war-ridden sky above her, moves in turmoil.
 Someone is speaking to her, but she can't make out what they are saying, just soft lips, moving slowly, forming silent words; she tries to reply, but can't.
 Now, she is being lifted. Her arms and legs are falling, dangling beneath her torso as her stomach bends upwards and her back curves, her chin is facing the sky towards airborne vehicles. She is panicking; she tries to move, but her body feels paralysed, she is numb with fear.

She can taste the saltiness of perspiration on her top lip; her heart is thundering heavily, threatening to break through her ribs.
Now she is dropping abruptly; an intense whooshing stills the ringing in her ears. She is screaming for help.
She is now lying on her back and is searching for her sight; she sees nothing, feels nothing — there is nothing, just the dark.

Suze jolted awake, her legs spasmed as if she were falling down a hole.

She looked around.

She could see a heavy, wooden wardrobe standing against flowery wallpaper, a curtain moved gently in the breeze from an open window, and a dresser stood just below it. She blinked rapidly in agitation; her nerves did not want to settle.

She sat up rigidly in the bed, rubbed her eyes vigorously and waited for the blur to cease and her vision to adjust.

Where am I? Am I still dreaming? she thought.

Suze looked slowly back and forth and all around; she was in a room, a room illuminated by a golden haze. Small dust particles glistened as they floated freely in the beams of sunlight that cascaded through the open window in great shafts.

She pinched herself. It hurt. She moistened her dry lips with a roll of the tongue and swallowed hard.

There were two doors; the one to her right was obviously an exit, and the other to a smaller room that jutted out in the far corner. The floor was made of dark wood, and in the centre, a green patterned rug spread neatly out.

Quietly raking shaky fingers through her tangled blonde hair, she felt confusion and panic sweep over her like a flood of dirty water. Suze sat bewildered. Fear crawled eagerly in her stomach. Then, as she realised this might not be a dream — that fear started to wriggle up her throat, like millions of spiders scurrying to escape through her gaping mouth. As she tried to make sense of this, she remembered she'd been running for her life amid lights, people…and then, trying to get to the bridge for safety. She had wanted to be with people she knew. Except all she could remember was running, shouting, screaming, blood — and then, then nothing…she simply couldn't remember.

Suze had a disconcerting thought and touched the bed sheets; she'd unconsciously stopped breathing. Swallowing back the bile that had risen — she gagged and gingerly lifted the duvet.

To her surprise, she was still fully dressed in dirty, worn jeans, a jumper and a denim jacket; a thinly knitted scarf hung at an angle on her right shoulder. No signs of struggle or, more importantly, no signs of constraints. It was unexpected, but she was satisfied she'd not been hampered with.

Just as her thoughts changed to ponder where the dog was, she heard mumbling coming from somewhere, people clearly in mid-conversation. She grabbed the duvet in both hands, pressing it on her lips to muffle the involuntary gasp and stiffened, straining to listen.

A door opened somewhere in the building, it hit a wall with a loud thud, making her jump — Bailey's head appeared at the end of the bed, and promptly went to her for his morning fuss. She was entirely relieved to see him but hoped he wouldn't start his usual morning greeting of whining and jumping about like a goofball, so she scratched behind his ears, to which he melted and gently rolled to his back for a scrub on the belly.

The voices were getting heated; Suze could hear

pushing and shoving. She briefly thought about escaping through the window, easy enough — it was open after all, but getting the dog out would be a different story; she couldn't leave him. Instead, she stared at the door as if it would help her ears work better.

She strained to hear an argument unfolding behind the closed door. The muffled voices grew louder, filled with anger and frustration. Then the real shouting started. Her mind raced, trying to piece together the fragments of the conversation; her stomach churned with unease as she listened.

"What do you think you can do to me, mate? If you even dare come near me, I'll..." said a female. Rushing footsteps boomed across what sounded like a wooden floor.

"What is this? Hey, steady on lady...where did you come from? When the hell did you get here?" asked an agitated male. "I never touched you! How did **you** get here?" he repeated.

"Stop talking!! I know where I came from, you scruffy little man! I wanna know why you brought **me** here!" the female bellowed. "Did you drug me? How dare you just pick me off the bloody street! Now get outta my way, Dingbat...move away from that door! I'm leaving!"

More fumbling, more mumbling, someone knocked something over, and it clattered loudly. Suze's heart palpitated; she didn't know what to do or where to turn.

More loud confrontation.

"Ok...steady on lady, I was just going out there myself!" There was high anxiety in the man's tone. "I didn't drug you, and I'm not going to hurt you...hey, watch what you're doing!" he grumbled sharply.

Suze heard another thud.

"Then move! Before I remove you! Quick!" The woman's instruction was so savage that Suze imagined

venom seeping through her teeth and down her chin.
She then heard a sharp slap and stumbling feet.
"Owww! Jesus! Wait I...!" remarked the man.
All went silent after a door slammed shut.

Suze quietly pushed the sheets away from her body. She noticed her shoes were still attached to her feet, frayed laces tied with the double bow as she always did, then swung them out of the bed; it creaked as she stood and to her utter disbelief, Bailey barked.

Standing stock still, Suze waited to see if they'd been heard.

They had.

Heavy footsteps came closer and closer.

The door swung open forcefully, crashing against the wall, causing Suze to jar.

In the doorway stood a man, his eyes wide with shock and confusion. His brows furrowed, forming deep lines on his forehead as if trying to make sense of an unexpected sight. His mouth hung open, speechless, as he took in the scene.

After recovering from his initial shock, the man's confusion quickly turned into frustration. His voice filled the room, echoing loudly as he demanded answers.

"What the...? Who are **you**?" he flustered loudly. He was touching his face; the right cheek was fiery red and had a welt on it the size and shape of a handprint.

"Who the **hell** are you?" Suze retorted, screwing her face up. "What's going on? Where the hell am I?"

She deftly leapt over the dog and steadily walked backwards towards the open window — feeling blindly on the dresser behind her for a weapon. Her fingers tapped hard on the wooden surface until she grabbed something; she brought a book titled 'Earth' up in her right hand and glared at it...

Terrific! For God's sake!

She shifted it from hand to hand; jutting her chin, she tried to look threatening.

Bailey sat up and barked loudly, startling the man. He jolted, clasped his chest, and bent over, panting hard. Suze smirked at his hysteria.

He expelled a sharp huff and looked up at her. "Phew, it's a Golden, huh?"

Suze didn't accommodate his question.

"What you gonna do with that?" The man gestured to the book, "Hit me with it?" He looked around nervously, then at the dog.

She was quick to shut him down, "You must be Dingbat? Don't come near me! Or I'll slap the other cheek! REALLY HARD…and yes, with this book!"

He was tall, skinny, and untidily dressed in grey joggers, a navy blue hoody and trainers that had seen better days. He lifted his arm, pushing the thick, dark hair away from his eyes; his lashes flickered rapidly.

"Listen…" Dingbat started, but Suze very quickly interrupted him, and he visibly stiffened. She tried to keep her voice firm, loud and steady, but it wobbled a bit.

"**NO!**" she bellowed, "Don't talk to me, don't even **look** at me…I'll jump from the window, just get out!" She glanced briefly out the window to her right. Her mouth fell wide open; she looked like a goldfish in a bowl. Then she snapped back to the man, shuffled on her feet and waved the book.

"…It's a hardback!" Suze turned her eyes to the open window and took in the view with bewilderment.

Dingbat followed her gaze. "I know, right!" he said.

"What is this? Where am I?" Suze demanded again.

Bailey barked, bringing Suze from her confusion. Her head whipped back to the man, who just stood there — his eyes dropped to the floor; he shoved both hands deep into his pockets.

"I dunno what this is..." He shrugged. "If you're going, don't leave that here." He pointed to the dog, "I'm allergic to the hairs."

"You shouldn't have kidnapped us in the first place, you arsehole!" she hollered. "And why would I leave him with you, or anyone!"

"I didn't! ...I don't even know how **I** got here, let alone **you**!" he said, exasperated. "And if you're leaving, there's no need to jump from the window, I found an exit fifteen minutes ago..." He then paused, noticing the dog had become interested in him.

He trotted to Dingbat and sat at his feet, waiting for fusses. Dingbat stared at him momentarily, frowned, and then continued...

"I'm just as confu...no...stay, back...**SIT**!" When the dog didn't receive the attention he'd hoped for, he lunged forward. Suze watched with a wry smile as Dingbat was pushed against the wall with a thud; Bailey nibbled the dark stubble under his chin, while two giant paws rested on the man's chest.

"Oh my God, no, please, lady, get it off! I'll be sneezing..."

She made Dingbat wait a short while, letting her dog smear his sticky drool.

"He shouldn't hurt you **too** badly," Suze paused, then added "...I'm not too sure what he'll do if you try 'n' hurt **me** though mate! Don't come any closer!" she finally told him.

Dingbat then said, "I don't want to hurt you! And...he's just a Golden, he wouldn't hurt a fly. Anyway, I can't come closer even if I wanted to; this mutt has me pinned to the door!" His eyes shot to Suze, and he quickly said, "Not that I want to come any closer. I'm not the bad guy here, I didn't kidnap you!" He pushed the dog away at last, rubbed the back of his head, and looked at Suze.

Her belly turned over in reaction to one of his comments; she lifted her book a little higher.

He put his hands up in defence. "Look, I just woke up, about thirty minutes ago, some mad woman just tried to damn well kill me!" He watched as the dog slowly retreated, returning to Suze.

"You did huh?" she asked, puzzled. After all, she had heard the confrontation when she'd woken. "Where is she now then?" Her eyes narrowed with suspicion.

"I dunno where she's gone! That's the truth; last I knew I'd fallen asleep on a street in Westminster! Or had tried to!" he remembered.

"Westminster, London? That's a lie!" Suze said hotly.

"It's not a lie, it was just crazy last night again, and now this..." He waved his arms about in a disorganised circle.

Suze recalled the night before, "That's funny, I…"

But before either of them could say another word, someone obtrusively entered the building not too far away.

Dingbat turned so sharply to the impending footsteps that Suze didn't know whether to hit him with the book now or wait to see if she should hit someone else with it. Her chest felt like it had been wrapped in a rubber band and she found herself moving to stand behind him, only so that whoever was coming would get him first.

He then muttered, "Oh shit, who's this?" They both backed further into the room. Suze realised at this point that Dingbat was just as terrified as she was, but she wasn't going to take any chances.

A shrill woman's voice echoed. "DINGBAT? Where are you, lad?!"

Dingbat shuddered and backed up. "Oh no! It's her!"

"Don't come too close, I'm warning you mate!" Suze

hissed tightly; she didn't feel comfortable, but at this moment, they both seemed to be in the same danger.

"I am just as confused as you are…" He sneezed. "…And I suppose **she** is too!"

"Who is…?" she started, but there didn't seem to be any point in continuing. Suze waited, shaking behind him, book in hand. She could feel her muscles twitching, her heart rate and breathing hadn't slowed down since she'd opened her eyes, and she was now getting ready to run — somewhere.

They were both alarmed and staggered backwards when the woman, dressed in black, stomped noisily into the room — unartistic tattoos ran down one arm and up her neck. Her coppery-coloured hair was shaved on one side, while the rest hung in a disorderly fashion on the other.

She was squinting and briskly rubbed her eyes with the backs of her hands. Her whole face was enraged; she was breathing heavily, and perspiration was forming on her brow. She brushed some debris from her hair, which fell to the floor, and then rubbed her shin, never noticing Bailey.

"Bloody hell! You're back?" Dingbat sputtered. Suze partially lifted her book; she'd now decided she could hit 'copper lady' over the head with it as well, or instead of even.

"**I sure am back, Dingbat**! Where the hell am I? Tell me now, before I wring your neck to the thinness of a pencil!" The woman ripped off her shabby, black, puffy coat and slung it on the floor, before frantically rushing forward. She placed both hands around his neck and then tightened her grip just enough so he could still speak.

"Wasn't the slap enough?" she seethed, pressing her lips together, while shaking his neck back and forth.

Suze's eyes widened in disbelief; she let out a wheeze;

the situation had left her momentarily speechless.

Dingbat squeaked something inaudible.

The woman growled, "I can't get out! Tell me which way is out, **now**!" Her top lip was tucked up and spittle sprayed in his face as she spoke. Her twisted mouth then snapped to Suze, who flinched at her discoloured teeth and unsavoury breath.

"If I don't get the answers I need from him in a minute, you're gonna be next, sweetheart!" Her grip tightened further; Dingbat groaned some more. He tugged at her wrists so tightly that his knuckles were white.

Suze touched her neck at the very thought. A golf ball-sized lump had suddenly emerged in her larynx; she swallowed it back hard, realising she hadn't been breathing again for a while.

Stuttering, she told the mad woman, "I...I don't know."

The woman was the same height as Dingbat, slightly broader, a bit stockier and much more ferocious looking.

Suze briefly glanced at her faithful pet, who'd quietly climbed onto the bed, dragged copper lady's black coat up with him and was chewing the collar. Suze almost died inside as she watched him pull the stuffing out.

Never count on a Golden for protection!

The woman continued to tighten her hands around Dingbat's neck. He was trying to talk, but only a few choked grunts escaped between his thinned lips. His airways wouldn't allow much more than that; his cheeks were getting redder and his lips bluer.

"**WHO ARE YOU**? Why have you brought me here? What the hell is all this?" She kept her eyes on Suze, whilst tightening her grip on Dingbat once again with small twists of the wrists and the odd shake.

"Suze...my name's Suze," she answered quickly. "I don't even know him! I didn't bring anyone here; I didn't even bring **me** here!" She was nervously fiddling with the book, turning it over and over.

Dingbat croaked something.

Suze choked, "I think he's trying to talk... You're going to kill him at this rate, and we'll never find out how we got here." She was trying hard to stay calm and hold on tight to the hardback, not that it would be much use against her, she'd decided.

The mad woman frowned, then said, "Don't think you're going to bring down my defence pretending you no nothing...so you can take me unawares — torture me, murder me, cut me up into tiny pieces and bury me in this god damn..." Her face was bright red. She looked puzzled for a moment then added, "...there's trees...! I can't find my way out! Because of the trees!"

Suze thought it better to put the book back on the dresser. She was starting to feel a little worried for the man they called Dingbat; he sure as hell hadn't done any harm to anyone yet, and she didn't want to see another dead body.

"Let go of him!" she pleaded as calmly as she could. "Neither of us knows what's going on here. Just let him go!"

The woman twitched as Suze placed the book down.

"What were you going to do with that **Suze**? Throw it at me?" She smirked and loosened her grip a bit. Dingbat's knees began to buckle immediately, he took a small, tight breath. Then she completely let go, allowing him to fall in a crumpled heap on the floor.

Suze watched him go down like a rag doll.

"No, I was going to hit Dingbat over the head with it; it's a hardback!" she muttered, feeling stupid.

"Get up Dingbat," said the woman, hauling him up by his clothes. She realised he had no strength in his legs and let him go again, he landed with another thud. "If either of you makes one move, I'm going to flatten the pair of you, do you understand?" She jabbed her finger in Suze's face. "So, let me get this straight, blondie. You have just appeared here, like me, yes?" She threw her head back and gave a quick guttural laugh.

"Yeah, I guess!"

The mad woman wasn't laughing anymore; her sour face said, "What about him? I suppose he just appeared outta thin air too, eh?" Strands of her coppery hair were now stuck to the sweat on her forehead.

"So he says," replied Suze, then added, "I suppose so…whatever **that** means." She was wringing her hands together; nerves were getting the better of her. She glanced back out the window, wondering how the hell the trees got there, too.

Dingbat coughed and spat on the floor.

"Why don't I believe you?" sneered the fiery woman.

Dingbat sputtered. "Well, just tell me how the hell **you** got here then lady?!"

"**I don't know**…Dingbat!" she roared, shoving her face in his.

Suze shuffled on the spot, then offered feebly, "I just woke up in here, Bailey too." She watched Dingbat slowly hitch himself back to two feet, clutching his neck.

"Who the bloody hell is Bailey?" the woman grunted, then looked at Dingbat and slowly said, "Is it yooooou?"

He coughed before answering, "No, no. It's Max, I'm Max."

Finding some courage, Suze asked the woman. "Who are you?"

"What's it to you?" she replied, her face contorted. Suze repeated her question bravely, looking the woman straight in the eye.

She scowled at Suze; her left eye twitched. "Nina… If he's Max, who's Bailey?"

Suze hesitantly pointed to her Golden Retriever on the bed, who had managed to silently rip the coat to shreds. "He's there."

The dog looked up from the carnage on the bed, a small amount of coat padding was stuck under his top lip.

"Goddammit! My coat!" wheezed Nina.

Suze clasped her face; she was terrified and quickly stammered, "Nina, I…I'm so sorry! He chews things!"

Nina pushed away the hair that was sticking to her face with the palm of her hand.

"He's a beut, what the hell have you done to my one-and-only coat — you big donkey!" She let out a raspy laugh that was hard to decipher. The tough woman, who had scared the living daylights out of them moments before, was now crouched over Bailey making a huge fuss of him, scrubbing his belly, running her fingers through his fur, picking bits from his jib; she swore loudly as she tried to flick the damp padding from her fingers.

A dog always softens an angry heart.

Nina seemed distracted, so Suze felt brave enough to ask,

"Did you go outside Nina? I heard you arguing with Max. All I can see is trees, I don't understand — where's all the..." She trailed off and turned to push the window further open.

Nina got up, "Bugger, I'm covered in fur!" She brushed herself down, to no avail; the creamy fur remained stuck to her black leggings and holey black sweatshirt. "Yeah, trees, trees, and more bloody trees! **No way out**, is there Max?"

Suze spun back around. "…the trees, where did they come from?"

"Nina, what do you mean there's no way out?" asked Max, now partially recovered from his strangulation.

"Listen Dingbat..." Her soothing doggy voice had vanished in less time than it had arrived.

"It's Max!" he told her carefully. He was a bit worried about saying anything to Nina or even being pleasant to her, but realised if he didn't, they were never likely to resolve their whereabouts or anything else, for that matter.

"**Max**...the door is open, go find out!" Nina insisted.

He sneezed.

"The trees, where did they come from?" Suze repeated her question.

Somewhere in the vicinity, a very loud, very cross male voice bawled several unrepeatable words that permeated the building — along with the persistent banging on a door.

The trio froze, ceasing arguments and altercations in an instant — in the silence, they eyed each other trying to figure one another out, while listening to the yelling.

Chapter Three

Ben

"Hello? Who's there? You wait til' I get my hands on you!" came the voice.

Max groaned, "Oh no...not another one!"

Suze reached for the book again.

"Don't bother with the book **Suze,** for God's sake, it might be a hardback, but it's a bloody thin one...let's go, come on, you two go first!" Nina ordered with a wave of her hand. Suze momentarily looked at the hardback, opened the drawer, tossed it in, and slammed it shut.

Feeling confident, she said, "Why should I go with you, Nina? **You** go first!" Nina turned back, rushed forward and was in her face as quick as a blink.

They were nose to nose.

"Look, blondie..." She shoved her finger in Suze's face again. "I've no idea how I got here, or who you two are, so I wanna keep you **both** in my sights. I also wanna stop that bonehead banging on the door before my brainache comes back. Now are you coming with me or not?"

With that, they slowly left the room. Nina behind, Bailey followed, with Suze's scarf held firmly in his mouth.

All four walked cautiously through the door to the next space and stopped in a hallway.

There were six doors in all, which included the room Suze had woken. All doors were white, with a silver doorknob — but only five had a number at the top; the hallway walls had the same pale, delicate, flower design as in Suze's room, number five.

Set between rooms 1 and 2 on the opposite wall was a large window; it was a misty, cloudy white, with small dark streaks running through that looked like veins. Suze gingerly touched it with her fingertips; it was warm.

She peered closer through the window; she could just make out a small courtyard area. One wall was covered with a plant clinging to it and on the opposite side, huge water butts with drainpipes leading from the roof down. Nestled in the middle of the patioed area was just a table and chairs; thankfully, no abductors or gunmen were in sight.

A male voice continued to shout and thump the door.

"Bloody well let me out, right now! I'm a master of martial arts, I'm an important person! I'll kill you with one hand!"

"Shut up!" bellowed Nina, stepping forward to be at the door when it opened. "Not on my watch mate!"

Max sneezed again. Pointing to room number two, he said. "I woke up in there, just before I met Nina." He elbowed Suze's arm, startling her. She looked him up and down and brushed his remnants from her body.

Sheepishly, he put his hands up, "Sorry, sorry, I'll move away."

"Oh, will you just **shut up,** too Dingbat," Nina snarled at him.

"It's Max, Nina…" he huffed.

They shuffled down the hallway a bit further.

"Who's out there? Let me out right now!" wailed the furious man from room number three; the door vibrated as his banging continued.

Bailey barked.

"Get yourself out, you idiot! The door isn't locked!" Nina shouted over the thunderous noise. She turned to Suze, her eyes squinting amid the commotion, "Mine wasn't locked. Was yours?" She gestured to room number one with a flick of the hand.

"No," she replied, "I don't think so. He just came bursting in. Did you unlock it, Max?"

Bailey barked again.

Max sneezed again. "No Suze, I didn't lock or even unlock your door for crying out loud, mine wasn't locked either!" he said defensively, wiping his nose, which, along with his eyes, was getting redder by the minute.

From behind the closed door came, "If that barking mutt attacks me, I'll kill it with my bare hands, do you hear me? Let me out!"

"It's just a Golden Retriever, mate." Max sighed.

"Will you stop thumping that blasted door and open it?" Nina bellowed, picking the odd hair from her top.

There was a short silence until the doorknob began to twist. The door was set ajar, then stopped. Just at that moment, when the trio wondered if it was an invitation to enter the room, the door swung open violently, hitting the wall and making them all jump. The young man inside did nothing but launch his fist at the nearest face. But the only impact made was in Max's hand, who'd clasped it tightly and was now grinning.

Nina was not only surprised but thankful; she didn't relish swallowing any teeth.

"Why, thank you, Max!" she said far too politely while eyeing the man. "Big mistake, Bonehead! You're in for it now!" Nina made straight for him.

But the dog saved a full-blown fight from occurring; he was so pleased to see yet another person, that he dropped the scarf, excitedly bundled through three pairs of legs, nearly pushed Nina over, and bounced up to the man's chest; Max's grip was suddenly yanked away. The dog toppled the man onto his back and pinned him to the floor.

Suze rushed in and tried to pull her hefty dog from the

new guy's chest.

Nina stopped her, "Hang on lady! He clearly could be the bad guy!" She held Suze's arm tight.

"Yeah, and so could **you** Nina! Now get your nasty hands off me!" she retorted, ripping her arm from Nina's grasp.

"It's gonna kill me! Get him off me — before he eats my face!" Bailey lay on the man, licking a new chin.

Suze pulled her dog away and calmed him with an ear scrub. A few moments later, he sat panting next to her.

Nina stood upright with her arms crossed firmly over her chest. "Get up lad!" she ordered.

He wore dirty combat trousers, with a very faded and worn brown leather jacket and a grimy white T-shirt under it. The boots he wore were too big for him. His hair was a mass of brown curls, and the top was partly held back with a band. He didn't look like a 'master of martial arts' to them. He sat up, eyeing the dog.

Max leant forward and offered the man his hand — after hesitating for a moment, he accepted it, soon to be on his feet again, brushing the dog hair off his t-shirt and wiping his wet chin.

"ARH, my nose!" said the man, "He's broke it. I'm bleeding!" He patted the tip gently and winced.

"No, he didn't! Besides, you could easily have broken mine!" Nina told him.

The guy grinned.

She shot him a dirty look. "I would've thought you'd have been a bit quicker anyway, Bonehead — martial arts and all that!"

The man smeared a bloody red streak across his cheek with the back of his hand; he wiped it on his combats, sniffed, then said, "What's going on here? What do you want from me? Don't kill me, I'm a good fighter!"

"No one wants to fight you..." Suze told him, glancing

quickly at Nina… "At least I don't think so…"

Just then, Nina pushed her out of the way and grabbed the man by the collar with both hands.

"Who are you? Tell me right now, or there will be big problems!" she told him.

He immediately whipped his hands under and up through Nina's arms, releasing her hold, then took a Kung Fu stance, and wobbled.

Nina laughed in his face.

"Nina really…is there any need for that? We…" said Max, rubbing his itchy nose with the palm of his hand.

"…Shut up Dingbat," she scowled and turned to Bonehead. "Answer my question..." she hissed, "…and stop standing like that; you look like an idiot."

"Well now, let's see…" he said sarcastically. After holding his pose, he continued, "…I don't bloody know what I'm **bloody well doing here**! I opened my eyes to banging 'n' shouting…and then I…wasn't where I **was** anymore!" He looked down in confusion, then sharply back at Nina. "How's that for an answer?" A line of blood trickled down to his top lip as he slowly bent his elbows, firmly placing his arms in front of him, then whipped them round in circles, off to the sides and back again — his knee shot up and back, resting quickly at the rear; he stood there bouncing gently on his toes.

"Oh, come on mate," Max said, "what sort of a move was **that**?"

Nina was livid, "You're certainly not a master at it! **Who are you**?!" Her voice broke with the volume. "**And on the streets**? **I'm surprised you're still alive**…"

Ben's face grew angry. Nina enticed him closer with her fingers so she could punch him swiftly on his already damaged nose.

"Let's be having you mate! I'll beat the truth right outta ya!" she bawled, jabbing one fist into the palm of her other hand.

The dog started barking at Bonehead.

"Oh, shut up, you flea-ridden mutt!" he exclaimed, lifting his arm to swipe the dog.

"Don't you **dare do that**!" Nina growled, edging nearer.

"And why not lady? Who's gonna stop me?" asked Bonehead defiantly.

With that, the dog circled and ended up behind his Alpha; Suze stood firm, now with her arms folded on her chest. "Me!" she told him.

"Not if I get there first!" Nina remarked, launching her punch. She proudly caught him on the chin, sending him flailing back once again.

"Woah, now!" Max frowned at Nina. He staggered between them, arms spread out to create a gap — his hands planted firmly on their chests.

"Get off me Dingbat!" she warned.

"...Nina! My name is MAX! Just stop this! Step back." Without hesitation, he pushed on her shoulder. "And while you're at it, close your loud, continuous mouth for one short, goddam moment!" He then turned to help the man from the floor again, adding, "That goes for you too mate!"

Nina grumbled quietly.

They all stood watching each other.

There was a moment of tense quietness until the new guy lashed out again!

But Nina knocked him out with a swift jab.

They stared at him on the floor, Bailey sniffed him.

Suze blinked wildly but said nothing.

"Ohh, what have you done, Nina!" exclaimed Max.

"What an arsehole! There's our man! There's the abductor!"

Max nudged him with his foot; he was at least

groaning and coming round. Max hauled him up and sat him slumped against the bed.

Suze stiffened. Anger, fear and frustration boiled like a pot of stew left unattended on a stove — and although she tried to keep it under control, keep her mouth shut and the lid tightly sealed, the pressure was mounting. It was only a matter of time before her boiling point would peak, and her anger would erupt…

"RIGHT!" she bellowed, causing the others to flinch. "Enough! For Christ's sake! Firstly…" She turned to Bonehead and pointed her finger straight in his face, "…don't **ever** touch my dog with anger, or **mine** will surface!" She then addressed them all. "Arguing and beating each other to death won't get us anywhere… We're all in the same situation, what the hell that **is**, we don't bloody know! There's no need for bickering, shouting, and swearing, and just so you know, my dog does not have fleas and is not a vicious wild animal that wants to eat your blasted faces! Do Not Hurt Him!" She walked purposely through the group, pushing them apart even further, then turned back, adding calmly, "So, if we could all start acting like grownups, that would be much better, please and thank you!"

They stared at her; she thought she might have said too much and suddenly wished she'd kept hold of the hardback and her mouth closed.

"Jesus. Take a breath, Suze," hissed Nina in disbelief.

After a brief, anxious moment, Max turned to the new guy, sighed and said, "Anyway, I'm Max, this is Suze, and Nina — you've already met Bailey."

"And you are?" Suze asked the man, feeling relieved that Nina hadn't lumped her one as well.

"Confused. Names Ben." He pushed himself up and flopped on the bed, frowned, and then frantically felt about frantically on the covers around him as if searching for something. Got up, fell to his knees, lifted the sheets, and peered under the bed.

"What are you doing?" Nina scowled.

"Did you take it?" he asked, jumping up.

"Take what?"

"My gun!" he replied, jutting his chin at Nina.

"You've got a gun?" Suze stammered, stepping back.

"Apparently **not now**!"

Nina stepped forward, "Listen, I had a metal bar tucked in my jacket last night, and that's gone as well! You got that instead?"

"No! You're insane! Why would I want a bar if I've got a gun?" he growled at her.

"Can we all just bloody well calm down?!" Suze shouted.

Max sneezed again, then said, "Look, there's a kitchen through the end door, let's go and talk like civilised people, work this out, and, see if there's food in the cupboards, coz I'm starving — before **they** get back, lock us up and starve us some more…work out a plan of attack," he said and went to turn, but stopped because Nina's shrill voice sounded out like a siren in the fog.

"Oh, what a great thought that is **Max**, now that we are all **friends**!" She flicked her arms up in annoyance and led the way, then added, "Cover your snotty nose too, I don't want your stinking little germs!"

"It's an allergy to the dog! Plus, you said we can't get out of those bloody trees Nina! We need a plan!" he insisted. "And…**you've** lost your bar, and **he's** lost his sodding gun!"

Unwillingly and sluggishly, they followed.

Ben mumbled, "Course we can get out! You said the room doors weren't even locked."

Nina stopped and turned to him, "We have apparently, all spontaneously arrived in this building in the middle of

a forest, numb nuts!!"
"Nina, please!" croaked Suze.
Ben bravely stood his ground against this tyrant, "Oh sod off Nina! Spontaneous my ar…" he paused, "…what? Wait…did you say forest?" Then he laughed loudly in her face, "You really are crazy…"
Nina was about to lump him again just then. Suze was stumped; she didn't know what to say or do, but thankfully, Max spoke.
"All of you, **STOP**! Nina, allow me." Everyone stopped where they stood. He turned to Ben. "None of us know why we are here, or how we got here, ok?" he told him. "Now let's go this way and find food, and sort out a blasted plan, shall we? No one is out there yet…I have been as far as the door in the kitchen! And yes, there's a forest!"
Suze decided to support the most sensible person.
"Good idea Max," she agreed swiftly, calmly bundling through the small gap between them, to defuse more rising heat, "Come on let's go, but we need to be careful, someone might be on their way back." She ruffled Bailey's head, which he thought was a game and started nibbling at her fingers.
"I need a stiff drink. Those trees…" started Nina, shaking her head, then had a thought, "…No, wait. Shhh, wait Suze… be quiet…hang on a minute, go carefully!" She joined Suze at the front.
"Nina?" shouted Max from behind, he pushed his way past Ben to reach her.
"Shhh…keep your bloody voice down, will ya?" she hissed.
"Yep, sorry, ok." Joining her at her side, he whispered, "What about the trees Nina?"
"Well, why are they there for a start...?"
Max thought for a moment, then said, "Where's the

path? There must be a way leading...out?"
By now, they'd all stopped in the hall.
Nina was hesitant. "Then go find it. I ran that way, through the trees..." She swung her arm off to the right.
"And?" Max prompted.
"And no path...and the forest, it closed in on me," she continued quickly. "So, I ran that way instead. I had to jump the branches!" She pointed forty-five degrees to the left. "The same thing happened, so I came back to kill you! And then found her as well." She thumbed Suze.
Ben piped up, "Don't tell me...the branches bent down and attacked you like man-eating monsters. I'm sure they never used to be like that!" He laughed loudly at his own joke.
"Shhhh, for Christ's sake!" Suze hissed.
Ben shrugged it off. "Well, they must have heard us all by now, anyway!"

They slowly made their way down the hallway, turning carefully to the right into another room. Max was first to turn the corner, soon followed by the others. They stood warily at the entrance, expecting to see a group of face-covered baddies awaiting them, guns poised, knives and ropes in their hands.
Bailey ran straight in and flopped to the floor, panting.
They entered the room slowly and steadily, dispersing to check the corners. Nina tried the door to the right; it was still unlocked and opened easily. She closed it quickly again, then turned the key — now it was locked.
The kitchen was a large space, almost homely looking. Wooden cupboards lined the walls to the left and right, from top to bottom, and a ceramic sink sat under a large

cloudy window which glistened as the sun shone through it, sending shards of light across the room. To the right of this was a huge wood-burning stove with a vent hood, and to the left of the sink was a large fridge, which looked out of place. A chunky wooden dining table with five matching chairs stood in the centre of the room, beneath a crisscross wooden beam structure rising to the shallow roof.

On the left-hand wall and at the end of the cupboards was an archway leading to a medium-sized conservatory; in it, a cane sofa and five chairs, all adorned with seagrass cushions. Rugs of the same material lay on a stone floor and poised in the front-right corner, a telescope.

Tall, wide windows surrounded three sides, the middle one with a door set in it, giving a spectacular view of the gardens; the ceiling overhead looked like another stunning sheet of veined glass.

Ben pressed his nose against the glass and blinked hard. "There **are** trees…" He turned slowly to face the others, who stood there watching him with their arms folded and eyebrows cocked.

"Didn't you already see them from your window?" Nina asked him impatiently.

"No, I was busy, banging on the door."

They remained quiet for a while, taking in the new area. All in all, it was a one-floor building with five bedrooms, a hall, a kitchen, and a conservatory.

After gathering their senses, Nina offered to keep watch for anyone approaching, circulating the windows and doors every few minutes, while they found food. She went to the conservatory door and turned the lock.

They'd found plenty to eat in the kitchen cupboards. Herbs, loaves of bread, eggs, lentils, and chickpeas, all set in little wicker baskets — practically everything they wanted or needed was lined up and neatly displayed. The fridge was stacked with mushrooms, salad, vegetables, berries, and other fruits. Fresh bottled water, orange juice, tomato juice, and milk. Even five bottles of wine, three dry whites and two fruity reds.

"Unreal!" Ben blurted, happily cracking open a bottle of red.

They busied themselves for the next half an hour or so, keeping watch, quarrelling and disagreeing, while preparing a salad, topped with just about everything they could find to enhance it. Never in their entire lives had they seen food so fresh or so colourful.

Max had discovered a huge bag of kibble in one of the bottom cupboards.

Suze watched him. He'd found a bowl and scooped a generous portion into it, placed it near Bailey, who ate hungrily, then filled a bowl of water from the tap and set it next to the food — all without even asking her; she was grateful for his kindness.

Later, the mood changed again. There had been no sign of returning abductors for what seemed like hours, the arguing had almost ceased; they now sat around the large wooden table, chatting, discussing what to do next.

"My nose feels sooo much better already," grinned Ben, his cheeks redder than his nose.

Nina glared at him with glazed eyes. "You're still an arrrrse hole."

Suze started giggling.

"It's the wine, Ben, you just drank a whole red!" slurred Max, then added, "So Ben, I have an easy question. You were on the open streets? Or did you have a community?"

"And you lot haven't drunk any at all!" he bawled back. After a pause, he managed, "In London." They were all deep in thought for a moment, watching him, and then he continued.

"I was so hungry I was looking for food, the streets were just chaos. I travel alone…like being my own boss, but I do hunker down with the Underground community. It's full of homeless people — we don't do the open streets, it's structurally safe as well," he said, lifting his eyes, then belched. "I was safe in there ya know! Not now!"

"Not what?" asked Max, slowly circling a tipsy finger.

"Safe!" spat Ben.

They continued to watch him thoughtfully, all asking themselves the same questions.

Suze said, "So, where are we now do'u think?" She studied their glazed eyes and bewildered faces. No one could muster an answer, perhaps the effects of alcohol.

Then, Max said thoughtfully, "Nina, were you homeless too by any chance? You did say something about being 'picked off the street.'"

"Yeah, I was actually, open street, London, I was on my way toooo…errrm…" she paused, unable to recall, "…somewhere. Something kicked off, I heard gunshots, loads of noise 'n' lights everywhere again. I didn't wanna get involved…just decided to scoot off the other way, lots of people running about. I remember my eyes hurting." She touched her lids and checked her fingers for blood.

"You?" Ben laughed in distaste, swinging an invisible bar at Nina. "You didn't want to get involved?" He checked his glass; it was empty. So, he reached for another bottle.

"Oh, shut up Ben, you drunken fool!" Max warned and snatched the bottle away before he got to it, then asked, "Suze?"

"Mainly Westminster…on the outskirts before that though…me and Bay were alone," she trailed off, rubbing her face, trying to remember the moment, the people, the noise, the smells.

Max frowned slowly, burped and offered, "Same, Westminster, living on the street, heading for an underground community too, in fact," he said, nodding at Ben. "It was a strange night." He stared lazily into space.

They sat in silence.

Suze was hiccupping.

"What about family? I don't have any to speak of…" Max offered with a slow head shake, looking around the table.

"Nope," mumbled Nina, exaggerating her shoulder shrug. She was slumped forward on the table, her forehead resting on her hands.

Ben shook his head, "Noooope." Then rested it gently on the tabletop, too.

"Me neither…" Suze changed the subject because there was nothing left to say for now, "…look, I need to let doggo out."

Bailey had been snoring loudly beside her but was now getting a little unsettled and walking in circles near the glass door of the conservatory.

"Jesus, I'm sooo pissed," she announced, getting up, rubbing her forehead.

"What's he got in his bloody mouth?" Ben asked her; he leant so far back on his chair that it nearly gave way, but he corrected it just before it toppled.

"A tea towel," she replied matter-of-factly.

"Riiiiight. An' what's he gonna do with **that**?"

"He's a Retriever Ben, he'll do that, ya know…carry things…off," Max told him, pointing his finger again.

Suze slowly nodded at Max in acknowledgement.

"But isn't he supposed to 'retrieve' it, not steal it?"

"Does it even matter Ben?" Nina huffed loudly, watching the dog claw at the door.

Suze placed her hands heavily on the table, wobbled a bit, but managed, "We alllll need to go out there!" Then pointed for far too long, "He really needs a pee — all together though, watch each other's backs, don'tu agree?" she slurred, waiting for replies; since none were forthcoming, she spat, "Welllll?"

There was an awkward silence as the others looked at each other with vacant eyes.

"Forget it, I'll go on my own, you're a useless bunch of…" She quickly ended the sentence without finishing it, remembering she'd told everyone to stop insulting each other.

"…I'll go with you Suuuze," offered Nina, standing unsteadily.

Suze nodded.

"I agree with you, we should **all** go out," Max said, getting up too quickly. He leaned on the table, waiting for Ben to copy.

Ben grumbled; the wooden chair scraped noisily on the kitchen floor as he stood.

Everyone made their way to the conservatory door and hesitated, peering curiously through the cloudiness of the windows; it hampered their view a bit. The dog began whining behind them, which prompted Suze to unlock and open the door. He dashed past them all without hesitation, dropped the tea towel he'd been carrying, sniffed the air, circled, and dashed off out of sight.

From the safety of the inside, they gawped quietly at the enormity of the 'new tree' scenario; it was a vastness of green. Their eyes steadily explored the lush landscape. It was as if the world had transformed into paradise.

Max sneezed and, along with Ben, ventured haphazardly to the edge of the decking outside, where they teetered curiously.

Nina remained still, watching from the door while holding the frame for support. She blinked rapidly, looking for any kind of movement, people, aircraft — listening in the disconcerting quiet for the sound of weapons and screaming.

Suze was in between, bent forward with her hands on her knees, swaying. Then, carefully went out to the decking to join the fellas.

They briefly noticed the dog appear, then vanish again; the sight before them was far beyond what they had anticipated.

Nina staggered out.

All four pivoted slowly, realising the entire house was indeed surrounded by trees. None of them had seen a healthy tree or one blade of grass in their lives; all had been destroyed by war and climate change decades and decades prior.

Towering trees rose towards the sky; their branches reached outward like arms as if to welcome. Delicate saplings, still in the tender embrace of youth, swayed gently in the wind, their slender trunks bending and flexing.

"And this is the danger, Nina?" Ben butted in, disrupting their thoughts, slapping his hands on his thighs and ribbing with laughter.

"Shut up Ben!" He didn't hear her. "Where's doggo Suze?" Nina's brow creased with concern. Suze felt a pang of anxiety in her stomach that twinged enough for her to soothe it with her hand.

"He'll be back soon enough Nina." She'd practically

raised him and knew him well. Nina straightened her back and stood tall, then Suze asked her, "Are you worried about the tree thingy?"

"They are **trees** Suze!" she reminded her. "**Look, treeees!**" She spread her arms low and wide.

"Yeah, I know, a bit unsettling. But they're so pretty!" She gazed with a cheesy grin.

Nina nodded in agreement, "I shat myself to be fair! Who wouldn't?" she whispered, "The trees, they just…closed in on me like massive living gates, I had to jump the branches. Look, they scuffed my legs!" Nina balanced on one leg unsteadily and pulled up a legging to reveal red marks on her shins, which had clearly bled a little.

"It's freaky alright, not only that they attacked, but that they are, **here!**" Suze touched her arm. "Bailey's ok, look," she assured, pointing. Nina managed to keep her eyes straight and follow Suze's finger. There was the dog, his straggly, feathery tail stuck in the air amid some greenery like pampas grass, which only meant one thing: he was digging.

They all made their way down to the grassy lawn. Max bent forward and touched it with his fingers. Curiosity got the better of him, he had to smell it, so he dropped to his knees and shoved his nose in; the scent of grass filled his nostrils. The rest couldn't help but copy, all falling clumsily to their knees, running their fingers through the blades, relishing in the new sensation.

They took deep breaths, savouring the earthy fragrance; it was a sensory overload, and they had never smelt anything quite like it before.

The sun was shining intensely down on them; wispy, white clouds hung suspended against the pale blue. A silvery haze danced in faint swirls across the sky, like a fading aurora borealis.

Suze noticed Nina had seen it too, so she said, "What is it?" She shielded her eyes from the brightness. "It feels like summer Nina…"

"Yeah! Makes a nice change at least, if only we knew where we were, and how we got here, **and** how safe we are now!" she replied, sniffing. Her brows furrowed at the soft light display high above their heads, and was just about to comment on it when Ben's slurred voice broke another peaceful moment.

"Welllll, since we are out here, wherever the hell **here is**, we might as well find a way through this monstrous forest." He looped his arms around in the air, then clumsily folded them over his chest while still kneeling.

"Good luck with that!" Nina shouted over, getting up, "I already told you; you can't get out of this easily..." She prodded at the trees, "…goes on and on and bloody on!"

Suze had wandered a few feet away. Her Nanna Edie would have loved it here. She'd been sixty-seven when she had died; she'd a vast knowledge of plants and taught Suze what she knew by drawing pictures of trees, herbs, and other plants on the dusty ground with a stick. It was a game really. Suze would guess the names; Nanna's smile would light her whole face, telling Suze she'd got it right again.

The smell was intoxicating, mint, rosemary, thyme, sage and basil, all jammed the beds just to the left, and all drawing her closer. It was a far cry from London fumes, fights, death and bleak madness. She was so armoured by the display that she couldn't help but touch it, running her hand through each one, making the air erupt with sweetness. She was stunned to find a huge Aloe vera plant rising with pride from the beds. Suze spun around to take in the entire view.

The house was set in a large clearing, the decorative garden surrounded it, and fifty meters or so away was the forest tree line. Amid the green flourish of herbs stood an array of roses, bushes, reds, pinks, yellows, and oranges. She took a deep breath and inhaled the pure, fresh aroma; it danced right up her nostrils in a colourful melody, filling her lungs with scented movement.

This all must be a dream, she thought. *How can this possibly be?* She didn't want to wake up. *No wait…we are all hammered.*

She watched the others, no sign of the dog, she noted. Nina was standing precariously on one leg again, her hand on Max's left shoulder, showing the boys the marks on her shins.

Suze called to them, "Someone has been taking care of this; someone must live here… They might come back any minute!"

Her eyes swooped back to the beautiful garden. The grass was thick and green everywhere, smaller shrubs filled other areas, all planted with precision, creating a sea of different shades.

"Just look at the size of those! I've never known they grew so tall!" she yelled, pointing to the forest. They were vibrant, alive. "No, never! Are those Palm trees?" she gawked, astonished, "Where in the hell are we?"

But then, in her peripheral vision, something caught her eye. She tried to focus, but her alcohol consumption was hampering her quite a bit. She blinked and gazed with purpose through the tree line deep into the forest and stopped abruptly, instantly rooted to the spot.

Jesus Suze…you must be soooo leathered! She told herself.

"Guys, can you see this?" She glanced at them; it was kicking off again. Nina was in Ben's face muttering something, her finger was extended precariously close to his nostril, clearly another altercation.

"You lot stop arguing! Get over here now!" she yelled,

watching the spectacle in the trees.

Someone was approaching at last.

"Don't get too close **Suuuuuze**, I haven't ever seen a proper one before, but I hear they are now **monster trees** and attack humans!" Ben sniggered; he paused, straightening himself up. "Jesus! Are those Balm trees over there?" He wobbled a bit. "I used to hunker in Cornwall by the coast when I was eighteen. I saw a few; they didn't have as many hangy bits, though! And they were all brown…"

Suze turned to Ben, looked him straight in the eye and said, "You're bladdered! They're Palm trees, not Balm trees!" Her eyes rolled in exasperation.

Ben sighed, "That's exactly what I said, Palm trees!" He frowned as if wondering what she was talking about.

She stared back at him, bewildered, before continuing, "Past the Palm trees Ben, do you see those in there? Look again!" she insisted, pointing to the forest.

Squinting, he said, "Whoow! You mean those…things, right? Or…do you actually mean the Balm trees?" he breathed drunkenly.

"Yes, I mean those things, Ben!" she replied, amused by his reaction to alcohol.

Ben called the others over in a less-than-sober manner.

Suze watched Nina and Max totter over to join them.

"What's up with…Oh my God, what the frigging hell...?" Nina gasped, tutted, "Ooowa…shit!" She almost tripped over the discarded tea towel Bailey had dropped. "Are they **actual** Palm trees? I've heard they once grew in reallllly warm places!" She stumbled forward, pointing to the majestic trees, their leaves hanging like flags on a mast.

"Annnnd Cornwall!" Ben slurred; a grin emerged on his face.

Nina frowned at him questioningly.

Suze rolled her eyes again.

Max hadn't even noticed the Palm trees; he was now concentrating on walking slowly over, carefully placing one foot in front of the other.

"Seeds? Floating in the breeze?" he offered at last.

"There's hardly a breeze, Max, not in that denseness of woodland, surely," Suze told him with her fists on her hips, then added, "It's thick with trees!"

"Seeds?" questioned Ben quietly, his eyes narrowing, unmoving from the tree line.

Suze whispered, "I've never seen seeds flying in different directions like that before. Am I really **that** wasted?"

"You're not the only one that's wasted," Max replied, eyeing Ben.

Nina giggled, "Oh right, not the Palm trees then…Oh Wow. What the hell are **they**? Never seen seeds shine like a light bulb before!" Her mouth hung open.

"Fireflies?" Suze suggested.

"A fly on fire!" Ben laughed painfully loudly at himself.

Tiny luminous entities floated gracefully through the trees, creating an ethereal display of beauty. They were not like anything they'd seen before and were almost like tiny stars, each one emitting a soft glow that radiated an otherworldly presence. They danced and twirled in intricate patterns, weaving through the branches and undergrowth like little celestial dancers performing an enchanting ballet.

Max tutted, "I'm sure Fireflies disappeared ages ago, didn't they? But then, they might still be real?" he said, feeling stupid. They nodded; everyone felt a bit stupid at that point, mumbling amongst themselves, except for Ben, who was still giggling loudly.

"Did fireflies have those long, wispy-like tails?"

questioned Nina.

"Mmm maybe, and weren't they usually a yellowy-greenish kinda colour?"

"Yeah...I think so Suze, but I've only heard the stories."

Max started to step backwards slowly. "Then, why are these an incredible, violet colour?"

"Palms trees, Aloe vera, flowers and bluey-ish 'fireflies'...Green stuff, sun and no sleet?" offered Suze, dumbfounded.

"And wine! I know, right? Are we all in the same damn dream?" Ben smiled broadly.

"Yeahhhh!" Nina agreed with a similar stupid grin.

"Oh nice...that's a **huge** Aloe! I'm liking this dream," she added, glancing around the garden area.

"And...we are all totally pissed in our dream too — at the **same time!**" Ben laughed, hugging his sides. This statement made them all laugh out loud.

Bailey had returned and was now beside his alpha again, resting his chin up the length of Suze's thigh and gazing up at her with his two big brown eyes and button nose. He leant heavily on her leg, covered in dirt, and green bits and was wet through. He had found water. He was like a water magnet; be it a lake, pond or puddle, he'd find it. He sat there panting, his tongue lulled to the left limply, like a lone piece of ham.

They all laughed at the sight of him.

But their joyousness didn't last long. Bailey darted straight towards the swarm of little lights in the forest, barking, scooting, and jumping in different directions. The lights flitted about back and forth, dancing around

his flapping ears.
Everyone sobered up in an instant.
"Oh shit! Mind the trees, they…" Nina started in alarm.
"…Aren't real…and WILL EAT YOU DOGGO!" Ben finished in a theatrical voice. Nina thumped him hard on the arm.
"Ouch, I was only messing you, goddam mad woman!"
"You're a bloody arse, Ben! Why don't you go and find a way out, alone? Leave us in peace, for crying out loud!" Nina stared at him hard.
"I might just do that Nina!" he retorted viciously.
"Oh, stop it, you two!" Suze insisted.
Max said, "But Nina does have a point, based on her bizarre experience with the new trees 'closing in' then…why aren't they doing the same to the dog?"
Max was right, Suze felt a little helpless and worried for the dog, so she called him in.
He didn't come.
"I really don't give a shit if none of you believe me, you saw the marks on me…"
"We believe you Nina. It's just hard to imagine that's all," replied Max.
Suze smiled.
Ben burped.
They watched the dog continue to spring from the forest floor, leaping to reach the lights. He still hadn't come to his recall; it wasn't unusual.
"What's he trying to do, eat them?" asked Ben.
"He does that to the rats. He's just playing; he's never hurt or caught a thing in his life." Suze told him, biting her lip, "Of course, there's always a first time."
Finally, the dog decided to return to his command, albeit five minutes late; he settled at Suze's feet, panting. His ear was partially lifted and askew.

They stared at him.

He shook his head fiercely, and a vibrant blue light flicked out and landed on the grass; everyone recoiled in horror.

They stared at it.

The densest part of the light was the brightest and the size of a Ping-Pong ball; it lay there as if stunned, sparkling and twitching. But within seconds, it drifted up and hovered directly in front of Suze's face, from it emanated smaller particles of dust that shimmered and rotated its outer edge.

She dared not move.

Bailey watched it intently; he promptly flopped on the grass and rolled on his back. There was a lot of feet shuffling from Ben, muttering from Max, and Nina took an audible sharp breath. Then they froze too, presumably in dread, as a thin tendril of vapour-like substance slowly twirled out from the body of light and touched Suze on the forehead.

Suze had the most bizarre moment — it was like she was having a full-blown migraine with absolutely no headache or nausea, just a magnificent visual display of lights. Blues, reds, greens, silver, and white shapes pulsated and twirled in patterns like a kaleidoscope. She briefly wondered if she was dying; her whole life story wasn't flashing before her very eyes, but she suddenly remembered her nan, her cuddles, kisses, hugs, and smiles.

This moment soon ended.

Max swore loudly, whipped off his hoodie and flacked the thing to the floor in an instant, he raised his arm, ready to swing and thrash it again. But Suze lifted her hand to protect the little light.

"What did you do that for?" she chastised him, crouching to her knees; the rest bent over the ultraviolet light flickering on the grass and watched it inquisitively. Bailey sniffed it, whined, and looked at Suze.

"It was attacking you!" Max yelled at her.

"I've never known a 'firefly' do that before!" said Nina disconcerted.

"That's because it's probably not a **firefly Nina**!" Max hollered, stating what was obvious to him. "My heart was in my mouth, I thought it was going to suck your brains out or sum-mut! Come on, let's go in!"

"But it wasn't attacking me, Max!" she insisted, not willing to follow Max's instruction.

"What was it doing then Suze, giving you an Indian head massage?" Ben scoffed.

Suze ignored them all, simply because she couldn't explain what it was doing. She extended her finger and gingerly began to place it into the little light; the other three gasped and grumbled in unison.

"Don't do that Suze!" muttered Max impatiently.

Suze recoiled.

It was pulsating quickly, like a recovering heartbeat after exertion. The little ball of light rose, hovered momentarily near Suze, and abruptly whisked its way back to the forest in a swirling spiral motion. She shuddered, and as she watched it disappear, the hairs on her arms and the nape of her neck stood to attention.

With the sunlight now diminishing, they quickly made their way back to the house after noticing a group of 'fireflies,' for want of a better description, gathering at the edge of the tree line.

They'd also noted while on the decking that the whole building was made of wood, like a huge log cabin, apart from the roof, which was thatched, and the windows looked like thinly cut crystal sheets; small imperfections slithered through the clouded patches, some areas totally clear to perfection.

After a lengthy discussion on the 'firefly' incident, their guard was up, nerves a little ragged and anxiety heightened. So, they decided to spend some time investigating the house in search of weapons, should they be needed. 'A hoodie and a hardback just aren't going to cut it,' Nina had said.

They met back in the kitchen a short while later.

"Didn't find a single useful thing at all," said Ben, appearing from the hallway, followed soon after by the dog.

Suze said, "Me neither. I'd have expected to find something, something the abductors had hidden away."

"Yeah, like ropes, drugs and axes!" Ben proposed. "Or my rifle!" he added.

"Knives, there are knives in the kitchen drawers over there. I didn't find my bar either." Nina pointed, then lifted her top enough to get to a grubby bum bag, unzipped it, and dipped it to reveal a small kitchen knife.

Everyone glared at her cynically.

"…Anyway, there's electricity here, must be generated from those solar panels on the front side of the roof…" Max said positively, "…and a few modern appliances, like the loos and showers in the rooms."

"Yeah, beats pissing on a train track," scoffed Ben.

"And washing in a puddle!" Nina added.

"You washed?" Ben asked, his face screwed up as he lifted his arm to smell his own armpit.

Nina wrinkled her nose. "Yeah. You obviously didn't."

Suze turned to Max, "…There's a kettle, cooking facilities, there's a steady supply of water too…"

Ben noted, "...these abductors — they must be living off the grid?"

Baffled, Nina said, "I wonder when they are coming for us?" She tapped her top lip. "I found some clothes in the wardrobes. It's not the usual type of stuff we're used to."

"Mmmm, what's that all about?" Max had seen them too.

Then Ben asked, "Ok, so if you lot aren't the abductors..." He looked at them intently, waiting for some kind of reaction. There wasn't one, so he continued, "...should we just venture into the new trees tonight, in the cover of darkness, and find a way outta here?"

"We are not the blasted abductors, Ben, Christ! It was obvious to me after we all sat at the table, if not before!" Nina waved her arms about; he really inflamed her temper. "You don't get plastered with people you don't trust!"

Suze smiled at her.

Max then said, "It's getting late, Ben. We don't know when the kidnappers are coming back, where we are, or what dangers are in that forest... I think we should rest in one room tonight; someone can be on guard. We could swap every two hours or so. What do you think?"

Max seemed to be a man who could be trusted; he always said the right thing.

"I agree with you Max," Suze stated, looking at the rest for confirmation.

"Agreed," Ben huffed.

Nina said, "Yes, agreed. I'll do the first watch."

Chapter Four

The Nü Gui

The First Night

Nina stood at the window of room number four, watching a mass of fireflies as they weaved in and out of the trees; number four was the only room that had not witnessed a random person appear from nowhere.

She couldn't get her head around the fact that there were trees, healthy trees, and lots of them. Where on earth were they? It wasn't just the one or two broken, burnt, leafless and lifeless trees she'd been used to; how did this happen? She couldn't think of one single place on earth where they might be.

The notion had completely mystified them all, and now that she was quietly alone while the rest slept, it played on her mind.

She found herself scanning the surroundings with mixed feelings of curiosity and uncertainty. She pondered those unfamiliar sights, sounds, and smells that had enveloped them all during the day — a moment to gather her own thoughts in the stillness.

The window she was looking through was a clouded crystal, like all the others in the building; the same darker veins crept throughout, distorting the view a little in places. She found it odd that she couldn't see any stars in the sky, not that this was too unusual with the war invading the sky day and night, smoke and dust marring all views. Now, though, the shimmering cloud had turned a dark silvery shade in the night, but she didn't think about it for long. After all, the new trees were a bigger wonder, along with the whereabouts of the abductors.

Periodically, she moved to the door and pressed her ear firmly against it, listening for the softest of footsteps creeping up on them; in the silence, her tinnitus was playing havoc with her hearing.

She tried to remember what she was doing in Westminster before she'd woke up here, but all that came to her was the brutal attack she had witnessed from the end of a street — she also remembered shouting to a soldier who was running in her direction, to alert him of it; she knew he wouldn't respond so she'd run the other way. Aircraft were in the night sky, thundering overhead and then all the lights too. She vaguely recalled attempting to hunker down in a dark car park near a burnt-out building

Her two-hour stint was nearly up. All was still, and she could hear nothing apart from Ben snoring and the dog noisily dreaming under the bed, his tail thumping on the wooden floor now and then. They had pulled two more beds into the room so three could sleep comfortably, while one was always on watch.

Nina studied them sleeping. She was able to relax her hard girl act for a short while, though she wasn't too sure how long she could keep it up — then she wondered if she'd needed to in the first place.

She'd nearly killed Max that morning when she'd wrapped her hands around his neck. His heart had beaten so fast, the blood surged through his veins under her palms — her nails dug into his skin, she'd wanted him to suffer so badly but felt awful about it now; he seemed like a good guy. She may just apologise one day.

Suze looked like an angel with her clear skin, long blonde, slightly tangled hair and little pink nose. Her slim arms rested above her head on the pillow; she twitched now and then. Nina envied her beauty, inside and out.

She knew now that Suze was a good person too, but the terrible fact was, she'd been willing to kill her as well.

Nina glanced at Ben, she disliked him with a vengeance, but somehow, she could see herself in him — why, she didn't know, but she knew she'd find out at some point. He was probably just as scared as she was — as they all were.

His face was partially covered with scraggy hair, his curls had fallen, covering his eyes and cheeks. One rested on his mouth, and with every snore, the single curl lifted and fell back down; she briefly wondered if he'd choke on it as he sucked it in. She shook the thought from her head and turned back to the window.

Movement caught her eye, she leant forward and squinted out to the inky gloom; her heart wrenched, chastising herself for not paying better attention. Nina's eyes shot up as a sudden, dazzling, blue haze shone through the canopy from above to the forest floor, illuminating the entire area and scattering the fireflies in all directions. She averted her eyes, then shielded them with her hand in order to look back. Her first thought was that the rebels and gangs were back, and the shooting would begin at any moment. The whole area was becoming filled with blue light.

Through parted fingers, she saw a group of tall, dark grey figures appear deep within the new forest. Her breath caught in her throat again; they were coming, and most probably with weapons. But as she continued to watch it became clear that this was not the rebels. The whole woodland was moving oddly, and uneasiness struck her body.

Then from the canopy fell three large golden balls. She almost fell back in shock but steadied herself; she placed her fingertips on the crystal pane.

The balls stopped abruptly amid the dark figures,

illuminating them somewhat; they didn't appear human because they had no form at all. The little fireflies scooted around in the shadows, circling the larger balls. In all her twenty-nine years of haggard life, she had never felt so completely terrified as she did at this moment. Fear of the unknown and the mere idea of what she was now witnessing was completely incomprehensible to her.

She was about to turn and alert the others when...

"Jesus!" Nina almost choked on her own spit; she swung around.

"Steady on, are you Ok?" Max flinched, having tapped her lightly on the shoulder — still wary of her temper. "It's my turn to watch. Anything happened?"

Nina pointed at the window, unable to speak.

"Oh shit! Who's that? Are they coming for us?"

Clearing her throat, she whispered, "I don't know. We'd better wake the others."

It was still dark; none of them knew exactly what time it was because no one had a watch.

They stood in the conservatory adjacent to the kitchen, looking through the crystal-like windows and roof. Fear filled the space; even the dog seemed worried. He whined, stood behind Suze, and began nudging the backs of her knees.

A very low-frequency hum started to irritate their ears and chest, like a muffled vibration from a deep bassline. The fireflies were accumulating in their hundreds if not thousands, and like hawks hunting for prey, they hovered, leaving a clear space between themselves and the dark grey, wispy forms. Then, they took turns rapidly swooping down in groups to touch the shadows before shooting back to their positions. It looked just like a feeding frenzy!

The huge gold balls hovered too, suspended in what seemed like a formation, all spread equally around the dark shapes in a triangle.

"We should hide, we can be seen…" whispered Nina.

"They're finally coming for me…I mean us!" Ben barked.

But no one moved, not even the dog.

Dark grey shapes milled about in the forest, like upright shadows having lost their person. The light from above was getting brighter, and the whole conservatory was illuminated in blue.

As the hum became more intense, steadily the shadows seemed to dissolve, diffuse — their edges became softer, like smoke rising from a doused fire. They started to shrink, change shape and colour, morphing into small round balls of ultraviolet blue light, like the other fireflies.

One dark mass did not disperse as quickly as the others had and seemed to split into pieces before vanishing completely.

There were small gasps as every little moment occurred. Then, the illumination from above blinked out, and they were left in pitch black once again.

The group watched as hundreds of firefly lights swiftly dispersed together, scattering every which way into the forest, soon followed by the gold balls, which ascended rapidly and disappeared in mid-air.

Collectively, they were aware that these might not be fireflies after all.

"We need to move you lot! But I can't!" Nina whispered again, her lips were tight and tense.

Unable to move his neck, Max's eyes bulged from the sockets as he tried to look down, willing his arms to lift and his legs to move. "I can't either!" he grimaced.

"Me neither," Ben grumbled, blinking quickly. He held his breath and grunted as he tried to move.

Suze managed to say, "I can't, I can't move." She was not only awe-struck but unnerved and alarmed.

Nina was trying to turn but couldn't. "What **are** those black things? **What are they?**" she yelled.

Suze began to sob, "What's happening? I want to go…please, let's try to get out of here! To hell with the killer trees, let's bloody well get straight out!"

"We can't, we can't move!" Ben managed.

"Calm down a bit, everyone!" said Max, his tone was less than calm itself. "They didn't come for us, did they? They stayed in the trees…"

"Not yet!" bellowed Nina impatiently.

Suze was beside herself, "They **will** come for us Max. What do we do? What do we do?"

"I still can't move!" gritted Ben. Spittle dripped from the corner of his mouth.

As if they weren't panic-stricken enough, the sound of a door quietly opened and closed from way back in the house. Light footsteps approached.

"This is it; they're coming, they know we're here, we're going to die!" cringed Ben roughly.

Instantaneously, they were able to move again. They clutched their ears and chests and looked at each other in disbelief. Immediately, they scrambled in a bunch for the conservatory door to escape this mad place; deadly trees or not, they weren't staying another minute.

Suze fumbled with the door handle, frantically twisting it and breathing heavily. Nina watched the dark woodland for approaching lights or moving trees. Max watched their backs for the ever-nearing danger inside the house.

Ben wandered about aimlessly with his hands on his head, repeating, "I should've found my rifle!"

Suze stammered, "The door's bloody stuck! Where's Bailey?"

Nina spun around. "Shit! I dunno." She began searching under the cane chairs.

"Sod the dog! Someone's coming, hurry up Suze!" Ben grabbed his face and dragged his hands down it.

"Shut up Ben, you idiot!" Max whispered hoarsely; Suze continued to fumble with the door.

"Ben, you're an imbecile — he's not here Suze!" Nina announced; she swiftly rushed over to help her with the door.

"Err, you lot?" stammered Max, pointing his trembling finger.

Everyone spun around.

Bailey came trotting in from the hallway, sat in the kitchen and looked back over his left shoulder; the soft, uneven footsteps were getting closer.

Suze patted her knees to encourage the dog to come.

He didn't.

They waited anxiously.

Bailey whined.

From the hallway, something terrifying hobbled in. Its brown hair lay lank and straggly at the shoulder, its face was dirty, and it gazed at them with red, bloodshot eyes.

"Dear God, it's like the Nü Gui! It's in the **HOUSE!**" stuttered Ben in terror. "No! I don't wanna run again! I'm not doing it, I'm not coming!" He grabbed Suze's arm like a vice, his fingers began to tighten, and his left leg shook — if Suze hadn't been so focused on the thing in front of them, she would have probably decked him.

Nina was wheezing hard.

They all stood staring at Nü Gui. The tension in the air rose, spiking them with electric fingers.

Max swallowed so hard that everyone heard it.

Suze feebly commanded her dog to come, but he didn't, and she could not move to retrieve him either. Her feet were heavy with fear, and her trainers stuck to the floor.

There was a long pause while everyone thought of their next move, eyes flitting questioningly to one another.

No one had a next move. It was a standoff.

Ben broke the silence with high-pitched yelling, "**Our father who art in heaven hallowed be thy n**..." He stopped sharply, holding his breath tightly in his chest because Nü Gui laughed so loudly until its shrillness receded into silence.

They backed up like a herd of sheep, chased by a zombie collie, choosing to press themselves against the conservatory windows.

"Please don't kill me! Don't take me! I won't do it!" pleaded Ben selfishly.

Nina shot him a glance.

"Nor any of us…just let us go!" Max said for the rest of them.

Suze croaked, "What do you want with us?"

"What the bloody hell is Noo Goo?" Nina managed breathlessly. Nü Gui laughed, its voice scratchy and harsh.

It limped forward.

They cowered; whimpers escaped through numb lips.

"Arhhh, we're doomed!" squealed Ben. He snapped around and shoved Nina and Suze from his path to get to the door behind them. The rest copied, turned, and watched him struggle with the doorknob, briskly jumping

up and down, hoping it would speed things up. But opening a door in haste had become a huge and impossible task.
Ben turned back, defeated. "Arrhhhh g…go away, we won't come with you!" he stuttered.
The rest swung around too. Shock covered their faces. Nü Gui had moved even closer. The dog was still in the kitchen, on his back, licking his front paws.
Suze whispered with bated breath, "Ben, what's a Noo Goo? Answer Nina, for crying out loud!"
"Chinese demon, long black hair, takes your soul!" His ear-piercing voice had just about reached its highest level.
Nina was back. She swore loudly and rushed forward, arms outstretched, fingers spread wide, ready to wring its neck on contact. But the demon held out its hand, commanding Nina to stop in her tracks.
"STOP!" it shouted angrily. Nina abruptly came to a halt, almost toppling forward.
"No! You stop right there, I order you!" insisted Max in a determined tone. He took a few steps towards it.
"You can call me Noo Goo, if you want to!" it said frankly, flicking lank, dark hair to the left.
"It's speaking like a human…" announced Nina, somewhat confused.
"Yes, that's because I am human, Nina," the Nü Gui said.
"It knows your name!" Ben squeaked. His face was red and screwed up. "It is not human! It's playing games with us, you fools! Look at it! It's changing, contorting!" The demon twisted its jaw, stretched its back out and turned its head from side to side with an audible click.
Suze recoiled when Nü Gui's mouth opened inhumanly wide and groaned.

"I'm not Chinese…!" the Nü Gui creature hollered loudly, its eyebrows raised.

They all flinched again.

Ben cowered; "Try the bloody door Suze!"

She tried the doorknob, but it was still stuck.

"Oh, shut up Ben, she's just a girl for Christ's sake! Can't you see? She's yawning, not contorting." Nina chastised him.

Max and Suze weren't so sure…

The girl stood there, waiting for the commotion to stop. She was dressed in a long brown trench coat fastened to the neck, thick black leggings, and a pair of bright red ankle Wellingtons. And when she noticed they were not settling, and as panicky as baby chicks in a fried chicken restaurant, she repeated a little quieter…

"I'm not Chinese…and I'm not a ghost or demon. My name is Becky." She rubbed her arms as if cold.

"See! What did I tell ya?" Nina's arms fell to her side.

"Who are you working for?"

Suze let go of the doorknob, defeated and turned, then asked, "Working for? Have you gone insane Ben? Shouldn't you be demanding to know if this girl is one of the abductors and what she intends to do with us?"

Ben shuddered beside her mumbling, "It's what I meant! I wished I'd found my gun!"

Max then asked, "Did you and your people abduct us, Becky?" he said, puffing out his chest, trying to look hard and fearless, "You better let us go; our families will be after you!"

"No. I didn't. Did you abduct me?" Becky returned the question with a scowl and tilted her head to the side. "And, you don't have any family, I heard you talking at the table yesterday, nor do I, for that matter."

They stood mystified for a moment.

"You heard us?" Nina asked, frowning.

"Yeah," said Becky, "I was the first here, I think. Ben was the last, wasn't he?"

"You were?" asked Nina, dazed. "I thought Max was the first..." She stuck her thumb back at him.

Becky explained to her questioning audience how she'd woken up in room number four the day before yesterday, snuck out during the day, and found no one else and no way out either. Well, not that she could see. She also noticed that the trees — moved.

"What did I tell ya? Didn't I tell you that?" interrupted Nina, perfectly satisfied with that statement; she flung her arms straight up and down, and her hands landed hard on her hips.

Becky continued, "...there wasn't a safe way out of the forest, so then I came back to the house, and after stealing an apple, went back to the room. I must have fallen asleep, I was cold... Then I heard arguing and banging about."

"Yeah, that's probably when Nina tried to kill me!" Max told her.

"Yes, I did, but...hang on...we were in room number four just now, and you weren't there at all girly! These were sleeping, and I was on watch." Nina's hands were now restless and fidgeting.

"I've been hiding under the bed since I heard shouting. I didn't know what else to do...I would have come out from under the bed before..." She continued to explain how scared she'd been. Bailey had kept her warm and hidden during the night.

Becky stretched her shoulders out with another click, yawned again widely, and then babbled, "I heard you'd seen the things outside in the forest, and you all left. Then, I tried to get out, but we both got stuck under the bed; we couldn't move." She gestured to the dog, "Then we could. So here I am." Becky took a deep breath and started crying quietly, "I'm so sorry I scared you all."

There was a resounding sigh of relief.

"It's ok, Becky, don't worry," soothed Max.

Ben tutted, and Nina flumped on a cane chair, blowing up her lank fringe with a puff from her lower lip.

Suze walked straight to Becky and hugged her.

"Not going to die yet then!" gawked Ben.

Chapter Five

Observations

Deep within the confines of the forest, it watched. It moved through the trees like the wind, slowly yet meticulously unseen and unheard, a slight breeze in the stillness.

They talked amongst themselves, reviewing the plans, reiterating the process, and discussing the characters of the new ones.

The orbs rotated above them, ready to intervene should they be required; it would take only a simple command, that is all.

Again, they could see where darkness could infiltrate, how the dark could take over — how negativity could consume effortlessly.

Their shapes shifted; they stood facing each other.

"They think they will die!" laughed an entity.

"There is nothing funny about death!" replied another.

The first entity withdrew to become silent.

"You petrified them well," someone said.

"Thank you, it was a team effort, but a decision I took upon myself at the time."

"Negativity can fall on those who let it. We may need to be quick if we are to succeed."

"Indeed, it may be problematic at this stage," came a reply.

The silenced one asked, "They can still be fooled by

their own darkness, can they not?"

"Yes indeed," replied the other.

"I was very close, and no one knew I was there! The one with pale hair is empathic, is she not?" asked the silenced one. *"I was concerned she may notice my presence."*

"You are correct, but she won't know a great deal right now," was the reply.

"They do not have the intelligence in their form to understand," stated one.

"No, but they will! All too soon."

"Will they comply?" asked someone. *"One appears easily overcome."*

"I will make sure of it!"

With that, they left.

Chapter Six

Run!

Day 2

After the introductions, they stayed in the conservatory and talked; they were too hyped up to return to sleep. Instead, they watched the morning light appear as the sun steadily rose somewhere to bring in their second day together; it cast a strange pinky-orange hue that filtered softly through the crystalline windows. The fireflies flitted about here and there, never breaking the boundary of the tree line; everything looked less threatening in the emerging daylight, they'd agreed. Ben kept marching up and down the room, much to Max's irritation.

Becky, they found out, was also a homeless young girl with no family and would have been last seen in an alley in London two nights ago.

They were safe for now, it seemed.

Max stretched and yawned. "Oh wow, it's 7:45 in the morning!"

"What?" Nina asked him, tapping her bare wrist in mockery. "No one's got a watch."

Max pointed, "It says so on the clock behind you and Becky...Jesus Ben, will you stop bloody moving!"

Nina twisted to look and nodded.

Suze shifted in the cane chair; it creaked loudly. "Let's go out there again today, keep our eyes peeled for danger, see what's outside. Try to find a way out?"

There was yet another silence.

"We could at least see if there's a way out," Max agreed.

Becky didn't look hopeful and shrugged. Nor did Nina, for that matter, but both agreed there must be a way out through these new trees somewhere.

"There's only been one danger so far, and that's the trees, no humans anywhere yet, no gangs, no Army — and even that firefly thingy didn't suck my brains out," Suze added.

Ben stopped pacing, side-glanced Suze, then said, "What about those dark things in the woods last night and the big round balls? We all seem to have forgotten about those things!"

"No one's forgotten them, Ben!" Nina told him.

"Perhaps they only come out at night. The fireflies didn't hurt us, like Suze said," Max offered. "Becky, did you see any dark figures and the round floating balls before we arrived?"

"Yeah," Becky nodded, "The night before you came." She shivered.

"Ok, well, why don't we find food to keep us going, then go out...I've seen a stash of eggs in there." He thumbed the kitchen. "Anyone fancy scrambled eggs?"

"Sounds good," They all agreed, getting up from the chairs. There was Max's leadership again; thank goodness someone was making sense.

"Whatever...I can't believe you're all so blasé about this." Ben pouted at last, shoving his hands in his pockets; he reminded them of a small child.

"I'm not sure we are blasé Ben, but I'm starving. Let's go fuel up, then find a way out, Ok? We seem to be safer in the daylight." Suze said, following Max.

Ben marched after them.

Nina spun around and mockingly said, "Blasé...Oooh, now there's a word I didn't think you'd even know Ben. I do wonder whose food we are eating, though..."

The food was eaten, and now they were ready for their escape. Now standing on the lawned area of the gardens, they bickered between themselves.

"I'm not going in first!" Nina told them, "Why don't you Ben?" She shoved him towards the tree line.

Ben belched loudly in her face.

"You're disgusting Ben!" she shouted in revulsion.

He just grinned widely at her.

"For crying out loud, you two!" Max was uptight. He looked around nervously.

Suze noticed the dog. "Look, Bailey's in there again. The trees aren't attacking Nina. Let's go that way, shall we?" She glanced at them all, waiting for replies.

"What's he doing?" Ben squinted.

"Digging."

Suze didn't wait for the others to respond; slowly and carefully, she started to walk towards the forest edge. She watched her dog — he was having such fun and didn't seem to be spooked at all. Clumps of dirt shot out behind him; he made Suze giggle, and she unwittingly stepped further into the forest. The rest were shouting behind her, but she was undeterred and didn't turn.

Bailey looked up and barked, and Suze giggled again when she saw a firm black circle of mud on his snout; he must have found a rabbit hole. By this time, Suze was within the forest by at least six steps, amid grasses, branches, and bracken. She had never, in her life, been surrounded by such lusciousness and inhaled deeply; the new smells made her feel good.

Small fireflies began to flit around her; she was mesmerised by their beauty as they danced through the air in swirls and sparkles. The bark on the trees appeared to quiver in the blue light as fireflies landed on them. The forest floor shimmered, and small blueish lights floated close to the ground, weaving in and out of foliage — diving in, then stopping, as if peeking back at her from the ferns. It was just like being in a dream, an enchanted forest, full of small magical beings.

She could hear the distant chatter.

"Suze? Suze, get outta there!" Becky called.

"What the hell is she doing?" Ben grumbled.

Nina muttered. "Who's going in to get her?"

Suze happily turned around to wave at the rest.

But then she felt a cool breeze; it touched her face, pressed on her lips and whispered in her ears. She shivered from the very base of her spine, right up to her neck; it was like little icy fingers slowly walking up her back.

Bailey came and sat at her side, covered in dirt and leaves, a stick in his mouth and a firefly stuck in his jib. He opened his mouth — the little light flew around his muzzle and landed on his head before whizzing off. He was so gentle, funny and goofy, she laughed so loud the others must have thought she'd gone mad.

"Suze? Are you coming back now?"

When Suze had composed herself, she looked up at them, wiping the laughter tears from her eyes and cheeks.

"Not yet, Max." She shivered again but ignored it. The rest stood teetering on the edge, concern covering their faces.

"Just get out, quick!" Nina blurted in a fluster.

The smile on Suze's face left and curiosity entered her. "Why am I not being attacked?" she whispered to herself.

Her dreamy gaze wandered above to the canopy. In the dense thickness, tree limbs swayed, the sunshine filtered through, and small fireflies hung around like little radiant leaves.

With slight trepidation, she dared to place her hand on the nearest tree trunk. It was warm to the touch. Her fingertips felt a small vibration; it emanated through her hand and started to make its way up her arm, filling her with the strangest sensation. Suze closed her eyes and allowed the feeling to continue; she could hear yelling in the distance, but took no notice.

Something touched the back of her hand, but she didn't choose to look.

To the utter terror of the others, Max had decided to walk into the forest to retrieve her and the dog. She seemed to be in some kind of trance. The thought of fleeing was not in his conscious mind at the time, only a caring emotion to get his new friend back to the safety of the house.

Max had reached the tree line.

"You ok, Suze? Suze?" His eyes scanned the foliage, looking for any strange movement, of which there was plenty, but he felt no threat as such. He took another step in, another and another. It came to him that the forest, apart from the little blue fireflies everywhere, probably looked like what it was supposed to look like. The smell of fresh greenery and healthy damp soil, the slight breeze moving the branches and leaves, was all new to him, but it made him feel good — with that thought, he moved slowly further towards Suze. Then he realised he needed to get to her quicker. The tree branch she was near was close to her hand.

In the meantime, back on the lawn, Ben had an overwhelming desire to escape again; it had encased him. Today, it seemed to him that the new trees weren't attacking; he decided to take a chance. Without hesitation and without a word to the girls, he ran straight for the trees, not to save anyone, but to purely save himself. He grunted and puffed, his feet thumping hard on the ground as he pushed on, gasping for air. He picked up the pace. He was not going to fail; he was going to escape today.

Max spun round at the commotion to see Ben hurtling into the tree line off to his right, with Nina and Becky shouting after him.

"Ben!" Becky shouted.

"Leave him, he's an idiot!" Nina bellowed.

Ben yelled from five feet in. "I'm getting outta here! Nothing's happening to me!" He waved his arms about and jumped up and down. "Nice knowing ya, but I ain't going back to them!"

"What's he talking about? Has he gone mad?" Becky wondered aloud.

Nina thought for a moment, "Mmm, who knows…"

"Ben! Calm down!" Max shouted, but Ben kept going. He watched him as he turned and headed further in.

From the depths of the forest, a bright golden-yellow glow approached, floating in the air, illuminating the trees with an iridescence that shocked them.

"Oh shit! Ben, calm down, something's coming!" bellowed Max.

Max had now reached Suze and stood there briefly; his eyes were wide with terror; she was definitely in a trance. The branch that had been touching her hand lifted and swung up, back to its original position, and Suze seemed oblivious to it all.

Every signal firefly had vanished.

Max looked behind him as a huge gold ball meandered further towards Ben. He held firmly to Suze's elbow and pulled her from the tree trunk. Dazed and unnerved, she allowed him to guide her away.

Max made sure his attention was on the trees. "Shh, stay calm!" he told her. "Slowly, stay calm."

Suze, although breathing heavily, followed his

instructions to the T.

Everything in Max's body wanted to sprint back to the tree line and out as he watched Ben slowly being encased and mauled by the new trees.

He gathered Suze under his arm. "Walk slow, stay calm, keep your head down, and don't attract attention. We are going back to the house," he whispered firmly.

"But...what is happening to Ben?" she muttered; her voice felt thick and muffled, her mind still fuzzy from the tree vibrations.

"He tried to escape; he ran. I saw him do it; he even announced it!" Max responded, then turned to the dog, "We weren't. ...Bailey, come on!" He patted his thigh and hoped the dog would follow.

"We weren't what?" she managed. Max didn't answer. He was too distracted.

Cries of help echoed from the forest as Max and Suze slowly made their way to the lawn, with the dog in tow — he'd come to his recall this time, clutching a stick between his jaws!

Ben had clawed his way back to the edge of the garden too, and was crawling out, followed closely by the glowing ball. He stumbled and fell while making his way back to the group. Blood ran freely from his face, arms, and hands.

"Run!" Ben screamed and ran, hell-for-leather straight past everyone and back to the house, not waiting for anyone.

"Back to the house!" Becky shouted, following him, waving to the others with an overarm swing.

Nina waited for Max and Suze to catch up, who'd finally started to run. They tripped over the dog; he'd run between their legs, which made them all bump into Nina; all three fell to the ground in a heap. Meanwhile, Bailey thought it a game and jumped all over them with his stick

— they fumbled frantically on the grass trying to get to their feet, and the dog off; he didn't seem to have a care in the world.

By now, the gold ball was above them, hovering, and a low hum rumbled in their chests. The dog jumped away and sat looking up at it. They didn't have time to get to their feet and run, so they rolled over on their backs.

"What the bloody hell **is that**?" squeaked Nina in utter fear, crawling backwards on her bum.

"I dunno, but there's another one coming, look!" cried Max.

Suze couldn't speak; shock had restricted her vocal cords.

Another huge flying ball joined the first, and then another one arrived! Within seconds, all three darted upward and stopped above them, about twenty feet in the air, then proceeded to circle while also descending.

Ben and Becky watched the scenario from the decking.

"We can't leave them out there, Ben!" Becky spat, "We need to help them!"

"You can get stuffed...!" he snapped. But Becky didn't listen; she was now halfway there, her ankle hollering for her to stop — she froze abruptly.

Panic ensued, followed by silence.

Chapter Seven

Awake Again

Day 4

They woke in their rooms. Max, Nina, and Becky had wandered out and met in the conservatory; next were Suze and the dog; she found them looking out into the trees. Max was scratching his head while Nina and Becky chatted quietly. Suze startled them when she spoke.
"Where's Ben? Did anyone check on him?"
They shook their heads. She glanced at the clock; it said 8.45 in the morning. The time didn't occur to her, or anyone.
"We just got up Suze," Nina told her.
The atmosphere was highly unsettled. The mere thought of him, not waking up like the rest of them, was disconcerting, to say the least. They briefly argued as to who would go check his room, but decided they should all go together.
In the hall, outside Ben's room, they hesitated, wondering what might greet them on the other side. Max gently twisted the doorknob and slowly pushed it wide open.
"What the hell just happened!?" Ben was already sitting on the end of the bed in his dirty combats, examining his hands and shaking them vigorously. His entire torso, neck, face, and arms were covered in angry red scratches, some of which had surprisingly already scabbed over — some still open and raw. "They attacked me…!"
"I told you so!" grunted Nina. "Didn't I tell you so?"

He groaned and flung himself back on the bed.

After some time, they managed to usher Ben to the kitchen, where they tended to his wounds. All they could find were soft cloths folded neatly in a drawer and so, decided to use those with water from the tap to clean the areas. But Suze had another idea; they watched her disappear into the conservatory and vanish out the door.

Slowly and carefully, she crept outside, scanning the skies and forest for golden glows. She approached the huge Aloe vera, nestled amid the herbs. Suze stood looking at it for a moment. Leaning forward, she placed her fingertips on the plant, ready to take a bit, but an overwhelming need to ask permission for a teeny piece of it encased her.

Feeling daft, she whispered. "Erm, may I have a little bit? It's for Ben…he's hurt." There was no audible reply, of course. So, she picked just a tip from one of the succulent leaves. "Thank you." She smiled and returned to the house while squeezing the Aloe gel between her thumb and finger.

After special treatment from Suze and Becky, Ben finally got up, with a muttered 'thank you,' and walked to the conservatory without saying another word; they left him in peace to get over his trauma.

"Tell me this? How the hell did we get back to our rooms, eh? Do you remember that? Do you remember going back to our beds?" Nina frowned and circled on the spot.

"I thought Ben was a goner!" offered Becky, seeing him at the window — he was looking at his hands again, then shoved them deep into his pockets.

"Well, I did warn him about the bloody trees!" spouted Nina. "And what the hell were those balls?"

"This place is getting a bit freaky; they looked like U.A.P.s to me!" said Suze, rubbing her eyes.

Bailey stood rigidly before stretching out his back legs.

"What's U.A.P's?" asked Max.

"Unidentified Arial Phenomenon or U.A.P.", Suze informed him.

"What happened to good old U.F.O.?" he asked.

"They changed that abbreviation nearly three hundred and fifty years ago, Max!" Nina told him. "And then decided to come up with U.S.O. too."

"What?" he asked, his face creasing.

"It stands for Unidentified Submerged Object or, plain and simple, an object submerged in water," she replied.

"Where the hell are we then?" asked Becky quietly.

Max shrugged; he'd never been interested in UFOs, nor did he believe in them, so he changed the subject.

"Is anyone else injured? Anyone violated in any way?" he asked, checking Bailey over for wounds, who lay quickly on the floor for fusses. "He's good." The dog got up and stretched again.

"I don't think so. I'm hungry, I feel like I haven't eaten for ages!" Suze noted, patting her clothes down. The dog was now quietly panting at her feet. So, she grabbed his water bowl and filled it to the brim with water, then scooped a generous portion of food into the other.

No one noticed that he never touched it.

Nina then had a feel for the knife; it was still in her bum bag. "No, I'm ok," she announced.

Becky agreed. "All good here." Her stomach grumbled loudly — embarrassed, she clutched it to stifle the noise.

Ben was still very quiet. He'd hardly spoken since

they'd found him in bed and patched him up. He was still at the window, silently studying outside.

"What happened to your allergy, Max? You haven't spluttered and sneezed over us for hours!" Nina wondered, tapping her nose.

"Good question! I must be getting used to the dog." He shrugged, then said, "I'm a bit hungry too Suze, I'm so surprised after that massive plate of eggs just over an hour ago!"

"Yeah!" She huffed. Then Suze noticed Ben's demeanour and approached him. Resting a hand on his shoulder, she whispered, "You ok, Ben? The Aloe gel will help your wounds, I learnt about a few plants from my nanna..." She trailed off.

He didn't turn, but said solemnly, his voice breaking, "This place isn't our home, is it?" he paused, then looked Suze dead in the eyes. "Are we dreaming Suze?" She could feel his body trembling under her hand, his eyelids were wet and red from sobbing.

"It's OK, Ben, we will get out of this mess. Who knows, maybe we are all dreaming." She tried to soothe him, even though she was uncertain herself.

"I don't think so." Ben shook his head, smiled thinly, and lifted his face to the sky. Suze followed his gaze.

They fell silent.

Chapter Eight

Beauty Beyond

She materialised softly by the water's edge that morning. Harmony emanated from her being. She crouched to dip the tips of her long, pale fingers into the water. Dozens of small ultraviolet lights began to surround her and flit dizzily, making soft humming sounds in their excitement. She held out her hand and closed her eyes, sending a thought to the forest. Within an instant, an entity appeared and settled in her palm. Opening her eyes, she smiled, nodded and lifted her arm. The entity gave a burst of energy, flew up, circled her, and dashed back to the forest, leaving a trail of glittery specs glinting in the air like diamonds.

Entities from under the water came to the surface to greet her, illuminating the pond, whizzing around, causing ripples, bubbles and little wakes. Her smile grew wider. They jumped from the water, twirled, and splashed back under in a dramatic fashion, only to resurface quickly.

She greeted them, clasping her hands together. *"Precious awakenings to you, too! You look so wonderful, how bright you shine for me, thank you one and all, I wish you a magnificent Wakentide."*

A sphere descended from the treetops; it greeted her with the utmost respect.

"Phoenix." The sphere dimmed in submission.

"Orb-2? Progress report?" she questioned.

"They are being observed very closely. Sol has also ordered the unmasking, though not entirely," he replied.

She dipped her head; her exquisite elegance was

astounding.

"Yes, upon my wish. They will be on the move again soon, I suspect. I did not expect the escape so soon, and we may have to intervene once more."

"They have noticed this change," O-2 informed her.

"And what of their initial reactions?" Phoenix asked.

"They appear nonplussed and presumably concerned at present." His colour dimmed as if bowing before brightening again to his full ability. "May I ask, will the others join you this Wakentide?"

"No. We will gather here as usual unless the circumstances change. I came only to check on these." She waved her arm and continued, "There was an injury sustained when the group was introduced."

"Yes, so I heard. How does it fare?"

"This individual is well enough now and was just stunned — it was a mistake taken by the human; he will learn."

"Was it kin?" O-2 asked quietly.

"It was. Perhaps it was excitement that made her approach; she should have known better." Phoenix sighed.

"What action do you wish me to take with the E.V. now?"

"Nothing at all! She is not to be punished; do you hear?"

O-2 agreed with a dip, "Of course, and what of the male's actions?"

"Nothing. I am here, and I can feel them. I will call upon you if needed."

With this, O-2 dimmed his light and left respectfully.

Chapter Nine

Back in the conservatory, the other three steadily joined Ben and Suze at the window; they stared upwards vacantly, unable to make sense of what they were looking at.

All five wandered outside to the decking and stood frowning, mouths hanging loosely open, eyes blinking rapidly and utterly speechless.

After a while, Nina stammered, "What's…happened to it?"

No one said anything until,

"…Errr…" Max couldn't take his eyes off it; he scrubbed his chin.

"What **has** happened to it?" Suze muttered, glancing at Nina.

There was another long silence; they squinted, trying to justify what they were looking at. It was way past the wispy clouds.

Becky said, "Was there a nuclear blast last night? Was that even there yesterday?" Tears welled in her eyes.

"Wouldn't we have heard it, though?" questioned Suze.

"Nuclear blast? On the moon?" Nina blurted loudly.

Becky repeated. "But it wasn't there yesterday, was it?"

Their stomachs jumped into their throats as hysterical laughter punctured their thoughts. It was Ben.

"I **must** be dreaming!" he declared, unable to stop laughing. He bent over, clutching his belly, trying to breathe at the same time. "Ohhh dear, I get it now." He finished his bout of laughter and abruptly turned to walk back inside; he grasped his waist, trying to comfort the cramp that had started before a full-blown stitch gripped it.

Nina chased after him. "What's so goddam funny?"

"Where are you going?" Suze hollered after them.

"Back to bed, until I wake up again!" he mumbled.

Nina stood in front of him, blocking his path.

"Move Nina! I'm tired — this is a big bad dream!"

Nina moved quickly, pinched him hard on the cheek and twisted her fingers, reopening a small wound. Ben screwed his face. He screeched and slapped her hand away, then touched his bleeding skin.

Now he was mad.

He was about to plant her one, but she quickly stepped back and shouted, "You felt that, didn't you, Bonehead?" She stood waiting for his answer.

A series of three "ouches" erupted nearby, as Suze pinched Max, Max pinched Becky, and Becky pinched Suze.

"I guess so," he said, dipping his head low; the anger rapidly slipped away — to be replaced with a surreal reality.

"We aren't dreaming Ben. Looks like there's been an attack on the moon!" she told him. "It explains that silver in the sky must be the radiation falling!"

Ben crumbled and sat on the deck, shaking his head; Nina joined him. They watched the other three standing like statues on the grass, looking up.

"Sorry, I just needed you to see. This, whatever this is…it's bloody real, Ben." Nina was hesitant but slipped her arm around his shoulders and pulled him to her and said, "We have to stick together; not fight like a bunch of morons."

"But the **haze** was there yesterday, Nina!" Max called over.

The others backed up to join them and turned at the

last minute to sit alongside them on the decking, all staring upwards.

"It **is** the moon, isn't it? Why's it that colour?" Suze asked warily.

"What the hell else would it be? It'll be the radiation from the nuclear blast!"

"But is it gonna hit us, do you think, Nina?"

"Maybe Suze."

Max sat with his elbows on his knees, nonplussed. "Don't look like it's falling…"

Bailey shot across the lawn chasing a firefly.

"But there wasn't a moon **at all** yesterday, Max!" Becky repeated yet again, wiping fresh tears from her cheeks. She was being ignored, presumably out of their complete confusion.

"It's not coming down to earth, there'd be loads of fire…and noise. Besides, we've been watching it for at least half an hour…if it were falling, we'd be dead by now surely!" Max thought aloud.

Nina nodded, "True that Max! But what about the radiation? That's deadly!"

Bailey rolled on the grass, legs in the air.

Max watched the dog. "OK, so if this is really real, and we are not dreaming," he started, "let's consider this: if the moon has been under attack. Why? What's the point?"

Ben was still shaking his head. "Are you not listening? Beck's right! That's just appeared outta thin air!"

"No…we just never noticed it, Ben, with all the fireflies and stuff!" reckoned Nina.

Max stood up, ignoring Ben's comment, and circled, then said, "OK then, suppose this is the situation…it has been attacked, but by who? It doesn't make sense!"

Suze was mystified. "I'm confused." She looked at Becky worryingly. "I think you are right Beck. I never noticed it before!"

"It's crazy. We've been attacked by glowing, flying circles…attacked by the new trees and the moon up there that don't look like the moon anymore."

Becky huffed. "Nina, that's because it's blue!" She slapped her own forehead. "And it **was not there yesterday**!"

Nina sat gawping at Max, wandering back and forth, waiting for him to shed his thoughts. Then he looked outside and watched as the dog bounded and bounced like a mad thing into the wooded area again.

Suze felt utterly muddled up. "Ok, so here's what you're saying then Max…there's been a nuclear attack on the moon that we never noticed before, or that's **just appeared**…and, or, we've been kidnapped at the same time?"

Max looked surprised, "Yes, No… I dunno. I just don't know. It doesn't make sense at all; look at the dog! He's acting like he hasn't a care in the world, and the trees aren't moving at all!"

Suze sat in deep thought, chewing her lip.

Nina screwed her nose, "Listen, I can't explain why that happened to me, nor Ben, it just did!" Then she asked, "What are you thinking Max? Because I'm as confused as hell here!"

"It's like the dog doesn't see any danger, or this whole thing just doesn't seem weird to him." Max watched as Bailey sprang into the air, barked, and dashed off further into the forest. "Maybe, there is no danger, Nina."

"No Danger?" Nina lifted her leggings to reveal her wounds. "Er, I did have marks…they've just about gone!"

"Unreal! And you reckon we aren't all dreaming?" smirked Ben, picking the 'very real' scab on his arm.

Nina rubbed her face.

Becky got up and murmured under her breath. "The moon wasn't **there** yesterday!" She went out to the decking, paused, then started walking around the garden, occasionally looking up to study the 'new moon'. They watched her momentarily, then,

"Oh My God!" Suze shot up suddenly and scrunched her scalp.

Nina jumped up in panic, "What? What now?"

"Nothing, I'm just confused and pissed off, that's all!" she replied.

There was a lot more bickering after that, including finger-pointing, harsh words and the odd tear.

Suze then spun round and clutched Max's arm, and he winced. "Hang on, I think I have it!" she announced.

He studied her curiously, peeling her fingers off him. She turned so that she was standing in front of them all. "Don't you see?"

"No!" Nina spoke for them all.

Suze pivoted sharply to face Nina, "Simple, look at my dog in the forest!" She pointed to Bailey. "…I was fine when I went in. Max, you were fine when you came to fetch me; perhaps we just have to go in with the dog?"

"He's hardly a demon protector Suze, he's a Golden, let's face it! Besides, Ben wasn't alright, was he? Look at the state of him!" Max pointed out. They all winced sympathetically at Ben. Then he added, "And a branch was touching your hand when I got to you!"

"Yeah! And…you've not shed any light on the blasted moon either!" Ben scowled.

Suze shrugged; she was in utter shock at Max's comment, and tears welled. She vaguely remembered something had touched her.

"Whatever, never mind…" Suze managed, quietly perturbed, "I thought I had it, Max, you said something else to me in the trees, and I can't remember what it was now, it doesn't matter."

Despite his joyous behaviour, Bailey acting like a goof wasn't the first thing they noticed when silence fell on them. It was Becky. She was now running and skipping in a figure of eight.

"My ankle's fixed!" she shouted happily. They'd noticed her limp on her arrival but had said nothing.

Nina took a moment and thought about what Becky and Ben had said about the moon not being there yesterday. She cast her mind back to the night before when she was keeping watch at the window. She soon realised they were, in fact, right, and made sure Max and Suze knew it too.

A surreal lull in the reality of their existence washed over them, like an ocean dragging the sand away to its depths, taking with it the very air they breathed; a calm, tranquil moment overcame them.

Becky had explained about her ankle. Her father had shoved her one morning; she fell against the rubble and appeared to be knocked out for a few seconds, but her parents had abused her, beaten her, and neglected her from the day she was born. They'd bruised her, broken her fingers, cut and burnt her skin.

They didn't deserve her; they'd agreed.

She went on to explain that her parents had taken her to the medical tents some weeks afterwards, telling them she had fallen on some derelict steps and hit her head, blacked out, and when she'd woken, her ankle and foot were blue and swollen.

"Jeese, Becky, that's terrible, and that's why you ended up on the streets?" Nina asked.

She nodded. "I ran away when I was fourteen, I hid in the streets; no one ever came to look for me, I don't think."

Ben huffed, changing the subject, "Very sad but has everyone forgotten what's just happened here?" he asked in disbelief at the sudden bonding moment. He was being ignored again. "Let's all act like we have all the time in the world, except we don't." Irony seeped from his pores like little angry insects.

"How old are you?" Suze asked her curiously.

"Nineteen."

"Me too," she replied. Suze then poured her own heart out. "My mum died when I was twelve — never knew my dad. I stayed with my nanna for a few years in a rundown basement. We were nearly always safe. She died when I was fifteen. I just up and ran."

"Sorry to hear that, Suze," offered Max, briefly placing a kind hand on her shoulder.

"I then met Nathen soon after. He was a year older, we were on the streets hiding, surviving together for two years, and then he died too." She felt her eyes starting to sting as they filled with the memory, but she carried on.

"He was caught up in a shooting. I had to decide to leave him and run or stay and die as well." She looked at Max and smiled, thankful for his comforting gesture.

Bailey came to her side.

"Where did you get him then?" asked Nina, leaning over to scuff his ears.

"He was Nan's pup; she found him poorly under a truck and made him better. I just took him with me." She bent down and kissed his snout; he melted into a furry heap on the floor.

"Well then, since we are having 'a moment,' here's my story…" Max placed his clenched hands between his knees. "…I had a place, in Manchester; an old shack in someone's back yard, all abandoned like. I had a girl. We were doing ok, me and Isla, or so I thought. But she started to go out a lot 'n' staying away for days on end, I worried about her. She'd met some people, done the wrong thing — got into that new drug… I told her, I kept saying, 'You gotta get off the stuff. We can't go on like this,' She…" Max went silent; he stiffened, trying hard to stifle his sorrow.

At that moment, everyone felt so bad for him, then he continued, "…she was pregnant, with my kid, it was early days, I think." He smiled mournfully, wiping a solitary tear that had escaped down his cheek. He couldn't speak. His mouth twitched. "She lost the baby one day…" he mushed his face in both hands, "…blood everywhere, we made a grave..." Max sobbed heavily. "Then she left, and I never saw her again."

Nina wriggled restlessly in her seat. "…never came back?" She put a hand on her face.

Max shook his head.

They waited patiently. They watched him wordlessly.

Becky sniffed back her runny nose.

Nina and Suze side-glanced at each other.

Ben fidgeted.

Max continued, "I left 'n' headed for London, I had to. I couldn't get over losing the baby or wait for Isla to come back, so I went fully on the streets, my choice. I blamed her. Anyways, I was twenty-one at the time."

"Awww," Becky whispered with empathy; all three girls nodded.

They looked at Ben.

Ben shuffled in his seat. "Nothing that dramatic for me. I just like being alone, end of."

They practically disregarded his flippant remark and his lack of feelings and turned to Nina.

Nina was already slowly shaking her head, "Nearly all

my life on the open streets and…no, I don't…I really don't want to talk about it, but thank you for sharing your stories." She got up, stood for a moment, made a gesture that she did not want to be followed and walked outside. None of them had had a great life, full of trauma, sadness, pain, and loss. They were silent.

Max got up and went after her; the rest stayed behind like he'd asked them to.

"Nina, you don't have to talk about anything you don't want to." Nina didn't turn.

Suze had excused herself and gone back to the room where she'd woken. She needed a moment alone.

Sitting on the bed, she thought about the moon. Could it have been there yesterday? Did they all really miss it? Had it been cloudy, and they couldn't see it? She didn't think so.

She lifted her arm, sniffing the pit. She felt, smelt, and looked nasty and was sure it was safe enough to shower and change quickly into something fresher.

Just then, the dog walked in.

"Won't be long, Bay." With clearly no fusses to be had there, he turned around and went back out. Suze closed the door behind him and headed for the bathroom.

Moments later, she'd finished. With her hair screwed up in one towel and another wrapped around her body, she wiped the misted mirror with her hand. She'd forgotten what she looked like — gently touching her cheek, she moved closer to her reflection and looked deeply into her brown eyes. It had been a long time since she had washed properly, never mind a full shower — emerging feeling clean and warm. A small smile formed;

she enjoyed the flowery, fresh smell emanating from her skin; she felt happy for a moment, like things were possibly better.

Why was it that she felt comfortable in this place?

Was it because no one had come to kill them? Was it because of the immediate things surrounding her, the things she had never experienced in her entire life — creating a moderate feeling of safety? Or the new people she had met? Or was this all a trick, just a simple dream?

She left the bathroom and headed for the bedroom area, having brushed aside her conflicting emotions and opened the wardrobe door. Suze stared at its contents, counting just two hangers, each with a garment hanging on them, both in a dark grey colour. She touched the material with her fingertips; it was lightweight and smooth, yet warm and cool at the same time. It made her shiver.

She pulled out a hanger. On it was a long all-in-one suit; she held it up, frowning. There were no buttons, zips, and nothing to undo or do up. Suze shuddered again. The arms and legs dangled; it looked like someone had been skinned and then placed on a hanger to dry out — she dropped it frantically, wiping her hands on the towel wrapped around her body. Suze tentatively peered down the gaping black neck hole; it was like the mouth of a corpse. She half expected to see dried blood, bones, and gross bits — oddments of skin and hair pulled out from the roots, but no.

After taking a deep breath, she bent down, ready to pick it up. She squeaked, startled, as the towel on her head unravelled and dropped directly on top of the grisly material. Suze kicked it out of the way and stood looking at the garment lying there lifeless. And after scrubbing her fingers through her damp hair and flicking it backwards, she picked it up again.

She smelt it, nothing, no odour at all.

Suze dropped the towel from her body and prepared to squeeze into the garment. It was at least clean; she could wear it while she found somewhere to wash her own clothes.

She slowly backed onto the bed to sit, and since there were no other holes, other than the ones for hands and feet, she slid her legs through the neck, straight down; it was surprisingly easy to get into. Two feet emerged at the other end. She slipped her arms in until her hands were free.

Suze stood up, wriggling, stretching her legs to either side, from the hips. It felt like a second skin, though it wasn't completely skin-tight. She smoothed her hands down her body, then walked back to the wardrobe and took another garment out. It was a three-quarter-length jacket — again, same material, same colouring, except there was a hood hanging loosely on the back. Suze slipped it on, feeling for some buttons or some kind of fastening.

Nothing.

While she was examining the material, looking for seams and stitches, and wondering how the jacket closed, something very disconcerting happened.

The front moulded together unexpectedly.

She stared at it in disbelief, then frantically pulled at the front, trying to part it where she knew the zip or buttons should be, but it wouldn't. She panicked — the notion that the whole thing would start constricting like a snake devouring a deer engulfed her, and then worse, she'd pop from the holes of the suit in a huge, bloody mess.

"SHIT! No, this can't be happening! Gotta get it open! Please open..." she begged breathlessly, fumbling with the material. She didn't want to make too much noise and panic the others. They would only come running in and see her blood and guts spread all over the floor — after all, at that point, it was only her own panic restricting her; her ribs hadn't snapped one by one, yet.

Just as this thought crossed her mind, the jacket parted. Suze took a breath and held it in her chest; she fell back, landing on her rear. Had the jacket just opened on her command? No, surely not!

She clumsily whipped it off and threw it on the floor, then jumped away, half expecting it to scurry back and eat her alive; she stood with her toes curled in a moment of disgust.

It lay there, unmoving. She watched it closely.

"I'm gonna pick you up, don't kill me!" she told it, she shook her head at her own, ridiculous comment. With a trembling hand, she swiped it up and looked at it, only to drop it again as Nina's voice echoed from the hall.

"Who are you talking to Suze?" she asked with a harsh tap on the door.

Suze thought quickly, "Myself!"

"Righty O." She could hear Nina's footsteps walking back down the hall. Suze stared at the jacket by her feet; she picked it up and put it back on.

She stood rigid, neck bent, "Jacket, close up!" And to her utter astonishment, the front slowly moulded together, not constricting her ribcage at all, although she pulled at the front just in case.

She waited a moment and said, "Thank you." She shook her head, another daft comment. Suze had no idea why she'd said that; perhaps because her Nan had brought her up with manners. She briefly wondered how she would get it off again, but as soon as she'd thought it, it parted just like that.

"Wow, that's so awesome!" she gasped and promptly reached for the footwear sitting neatly at the bottom of the wardrobe. She took them back to the bed and sat looking at them. They almost reminded her of a pair of pumps that her nan had acquired for her once, nothing too different to her normal pair of trainers except the sole was thicker, the tread deeper, and the top seemed to flap about like a shoe-sock.

This time, she didn't panic; she slipped the shoes fully on her feet, and as she did, they visibly moulded to a perfect fit.

Now, how on earth would she explain this to the rest?

There was a roar of hysterical laughter as Suze stepped into the conservatory where all were gathered. She stood there, arms folded, waiting for them to stop.

Max placed his glass of water on the cane table and put his hands to his mouth. Bailey sniffed her legs, circled, and promptly flopped to the floor for another sleep.

"Have you all finished?" Suze questioned; a smirk crossed her face. "I didn't think I looked too bad?" She twirled around and struck a pose, which resulted in yet more laughter.

Nina walked over and looked her up and down. She touched the fabric on the shoulder and said, "I'm going to get changed too." She smiled and was about to turn and leave when Suze spoke.

"Wait, before you do, there's just one thing you might want to know…follow me." She made her way to the rest in the conservatory and stood in front of them, feeling a bit like an idiot and a lot like a new attraction at a circus from the old days. Nina followed.

"You gotta get in it from the neck hole. There's no

other way to get it on; you slip it on and up…" she told them, with the help of a few arm gestures.

"Is it comfy, Suze?" Max asked. "It looks comfy."

Suze nodded. "It is Max. Now listen…and watch."

With that, she held her arms away from her body, took a breath and passed a thought asking the jacket to open.

It did.

"What the hell…No hands!" Ben was so startled that he fell back in the chair, kicking the table and knocking the glasses of water on the floor. Which in turn spooked the others, and they stood up and backed off.

Nina was visibly disturbed, as was Max.

Ben stayed seated on the floor; the chair was still tangled around his legs.

"Suze?" Becky whispered.

"Explain this quickly!" ordered Nina. Suze could see the old Nina from the first day creeping back.

By late afternoon, all had washed and changed into their silvery attire and decided they were, in fact, much comfier than the clothes they'd come in. Apart from Ben, who spent an hour or two pulling the material around his armpits and crotch, he soon relaxed and settled. Much to their surprise, his scratches and scrapes had healed rapidly during the day. Nina's marks had just about gone on her legs, and Max had stopped sneezing altogether!

Becky sat for ages talking to her jacket, watching the front open and close on request, while Nina, Max and Suze tried to figure out what the material was made of.

They never did.

Chapter Ten

Phoenix had finished her examination, and although she was satisfied all was well in Sector 4, something wasn't quite right. Her only concern was the Stygian; she could feel it near, and although it was possibly still light years away, she knew this fierce darkness was roaming.

She had not mentioned it to the others yet, and no one had approached her, but surely, they knew her thoughts; surely, they knew light was always accompanied by the dark, somehow — somewhere; **she** knew, of course, for her age was now timeless. Could the darkness of the Stygian fool her into believing she was weak, that it could penetrate her? Could it be that the darkness **had** already fooled her and was nearer than she expected?

She drifted upward, leaving a trail of light particles behind her and headed for the Mother Illumination.

Silently entering, she saw Sol; he was studying a monitor. She veiled her emotional energy.

"Thank you for ordering the partial unmask," she said, approaching her companion.

"They were petrified for approximately twenty-five clock hours. It was a wise choice to introduce their surroundings in the meantime," replied Sol. He turned to her. *"Is everything well in this sector, Phoenix? You are well? You were out at Wakentide."*

She watched him closely before saying, *"Yes, the EV in question will recover completely."*

Sol nodded and paused, eyeing her carefully. He'd recognised the fact that she answered only one of his questions.

He said, *"There were a few Essence finding it hard to adjust...but are now showing signs of minor balance. If they haven't fully adjusted soon, I could order further analysis. Although I suspect it is the usual reaction."* He walked smoothly to the curved windows and looked out.

"Yes, of course, you may proceed, if necessary." Phoenix replied, then said wistfully, *"Indeed, they sometimes don't have time amid their confusion to make sense of their choices."*

"This is true." He took her by the hands and kissed them tenderly; she smiled at this entity's purity. *"All will be well, Phoenix. In a few more days, we can address them. They appear to be a good assortment; we have chosen well."*

She was taken aback by his comment; he appeared to be reassuring her. She nodded at his remark.

"They are becoming acquainted with their surroundings as we speak now that we have activated a partial unmask — in their superficial minds it will all seem like a dream, they will either wait for themselves to wake — do some figuring out, or try to escape once again, and we cannot allow the latter, we must not allow injury."

"So be it, Phoenix. They are all different." He turned away briefly to shut down the monitor he'd been observing.

"Yes, give it time for their circumstances to become known; one of them has cleansed and suited up, and of course, the rest copied."

"So I heard. Good, it is human nature to cleanse." Sol smiled.

"They are still unaware of their conditions — we need to keep them controlled until the tenth day arrives."

"Of course!" He turned fully to her, *"If you will excuse me, I must depart, have a gathering with River and Sage, while you stay informed with the Orbs here, if I may, we are to discuss the larger influx of Essence in*

Sector 2." He bowed slightly. *"I will keep you updated; Amber is nearby. I will try to **travel quietly**!"* With that, he left Phoenix gazing out on the treetops and rugged rock line below.

She studied the gentle movements of life, their auras shimmering, bright and beautiful. It must stay this way; the light must stay.

She then headed for the stones.

Chapter Eleven

New Discoveries

Day 5

They had kept a low profile by staying indoors for the best part of a whole week. Things had been quiet. No moments of sudden waking in their beds or being flushed out by floating golden balls, and even though they were spotted from time to time, they never really seemed to be threatening and never came near the house.

There were no signs of radiation poisoning from the nuclear blast on the moon's surface either. Fireflies still darted about the forest and had even approached the house on a few occasions during the daylight hours, hovering outside windows as if peering in.

Nina had stood staring at one from the kitchen window for quite some time, taking in its movements and curious colouring, its iridescent shimmery tail, as it slowly moved left to right. She was partly fascinated, mystified, but also concerned as to what they were and why they were so close.

Then, Ben had approached her from behind, purposely scaring it off with a holler and vigorous waving of his arms. He'd had enough of the shocks; he'd woken that very morning, pulled the curtains open in his room and found one hovering outside his window.

After growling 'Go away' loudly, the little blue firefly burst its colour outwards as if in fright and then flit away in the blink of an eye.

Suze, Max, and Becky had encountered a group resting on the conservatory's crystal roof. They looked comical, shuffling along and placing themselves directly above their heads. After about five minutes, they lifted and spun away like dandelion fluff caught in the wind. These little fireflies were becoming more amusing and intriguing by the day and were clearly harmless.

Of course, Ben would not have agreed to that.

Anyway, during this time, they had only ventured as far as the garden and made sure they were inside when it started to get dark. No one dared go back out, instead deciding to sit in the conservatory, talking about their next move while gazing at the broken blue moon, which was visible both day and night now, all realising that they had not missed it at all; it had appeared from nowhere.

Those Dark shadows arrived each night, with the same scenario — bright blue lights, low hum and the synchronised movements of the fireflies, all staying within the confines of the forest. With only one difference, the group was never again frozen to the spot like the first night. And still, there was no sign of the kidnappers.

Max stood at the conservatory window that morning, tapping his forehead, then spun round and said cautiously,

"I think we should explore the outside a bit better today. What do you all think?"

"And go where exactly? We've been around the roses more times than I can count!" Ben huffed; the rest stopped what they were doing and shuffled on the spot.

"Well, perhaps just further round the garden, that's all, on the other side, that way." He waved his arm, indicating to the right. "Stand on the edge of the forest, have a look for a path or something. Don't you think we've been waiting here long enough? No one's coming...we can't stay here forever!" he finished.

"Yeah, we haven't ventured that side," Suze noted.

"I did! Remember?" Nina exclaimed, gesturing to her shins. "And there's no pathways there either!"

"Max, we have been safe inside. Nothing bad has happened! Do we need to go out?" Ben sounded like a toddler.

Becky sat, chewing her nails. "Yeah, the food supply is good. We don't need to go anywhere!"

"But how are we going to replace it when it's gone, Beck?" Suze wondered.

Becky shrugged, "Mmm, good point."

Nina started biting her fingernails too but agreed. "Yep, I'm in. Let's go, there has to be a way out to somewhere."

Ben knew they were right and reluctantly nodded.

Donned in their new silver suits, all five left the house together and walked with vigilance across the lawned area. They stood looking at the trees for a few minutes.

"For crying out loud, I'm so glad no one else can see me in this blasted outfit!" Ben shuddered.

"Oh, shut up, you big girl!" Nina poked him, only to see a tiny burst of light at the tip of her finger.

"Jesus, Nina! Do you mind? Your finger's shocking!" he bawled. Brushing his arm, he wandered off.

Nina closely examined the end of her finger, squeezed the tip, flicked her hand about, paused, shrugged, and then caught up with the others as they disappeared around the house.

They silently passed the patioed area, where they stopped to explore a bit, found nothing of interest, mumbled amongst themselves, and then moved on.

Max led the way, making a sharp left which brought them out to the right curve of the forest, on the other side of the house.

Nina's heart caught in her throat briefly. She thought she'd seen a gold ball, floating far back in the denseness amongst the fireflies, but decided to say nothing to the others.

Blue lights flit back and forth, the group gazed at them with wonder as they skimmed through the leaves and grasses. Bailey didn't have a care in the world and was running rings around the group, swinging a stick and growling for attention, goading his friends to join in. This brought smiles and a huge sense of peace among them. Suze chased him; she skipped and played with him while the rest giggled.

The smell of pine, grasses and blooming flowers filled their nostrils; it was like paradise. However, Nina soon knew they were letting their guard down a bit.

"Can we all please pay more attention to **where we are** and what **might happen**?" she told them with a firmness that made them stop abruptly; disquiet and understanding crept across their features.

"Nina's right, be careful, come on, let's go straight on," Max agreed. With that thought neatly planted in their minds, they moved forward.

Nina then noticed that the tree line stretched far ahead of them; it almost seemed bigger than before.

"This is odd, it's not like...like it was." Right now, she couldn't even see the curve which joined the other side of the forest.

"Why?" Ben asked.

"Because I couldn't get out of this bit! It was all

closed in, curved to the other side, the garden was treelined…it's like it's grown outwards." She was disorientated. "And now there's a hill! Of course there is!!" she added, bemused. Nothing was normal here.

They moved on despite their uneasy feelings.

The ground started to slope upwards; they trudged up slowly. The dog had already completely vanished over the rise.

When they finally arrived at the top, the left side of the curved tree line came into view and swooped round to their right and out of sight because now, the right-hand side of the forest had also swooped to their right, creating a corner that no one could see beyond.

Without saying a word to one another, the group descended to the other side, a soft and easy decline. The dog was rolling in the grass at the bottom; he flipped up like a spring lamb and sat waiting for them.

They continued following on to the right and around the corner, where, once on flatter ground, they came upon a wide path; it was covered in small, round, crystal-like stones. Ahead of them, the trees opened even more.

As they slowly walked forward, breathy gasps of shock and astonishment followed; five jaws hung loose. A moment of silence encased them; all sound, senses, and physical awareness had momentarily blanked out, caused simply by the gargantuan sight before them.

They observed quietly.

In a large clearing was a stone circle, unlike anything any of them had seen or heard of before; it was huge. Five colossal oval-shaped, pure white stones stood perfectly upright — like silent guards waiting for their purposeful command in the morning light.

No one moved because their sheer size gave great unease to everyone.

Except for the dog.

Suze watched him; he ran straight up to one of the stones and stood for a moment.

Had he just cocked his leg?

He'd possibly peed — possibly sniffed it and also, possibly licked it too; she wasn't too sure.

He ran back to his pack, stopping with Ben for a quick face fuss before he went off exploring once again. Suze turned her nose up and wiped her mouth subconsciously at the sight.

"Wow!" Ben muttered. "Aww, thanks, Bailey, me old mate." He nodded and smiled at Suze, who was wiping her hand on her leg. "He loves me after all," he added with a grin.

"What in the **bloody hell is this**?" choked Nina.

The five explorers approached the stones slowly, craning their necks to see the tops, then stopped in unison.

Suze detected a vibration rising from the ground and glanced at her silver shoes. She looked up at the others — they were still gawping at the stones. Back at her feet, she was shocked to see very tiny glittery specks emanating from the underside of the soles. She stamped her left foot hard on the ground; the specks dispersed in a puff and vanished.

"They look like crystal!" Becky whispered in awe.

Max ventured closer while running his eyes down the length of one of them and stood by it.

"It's elevated from the ground!" he said in amazement. "How is that possible?"

The others joined him inquisitively. Nina bent at the waist to view the two-foot gap, only to see the forest edge far beyond the stone's bases.

"How the hell are they not dropping?" she gagged; she didn't expect a reply. "Better step back a bit!"

No one did.

Suze approached, "They must be at least twenty-five meters high!" She looked back to where she'd been standing before for any sign of the glittery footprints from her shoes.

None.

Max lifted his hand ready to place it on the surface; Nina noticed in time while straightening up, and advised he 'really shouldn't do that'. He took his hand away with a snap, resting it on his chest for a moment and continued gawping.

Ben was almost speechless. "Wow!" he muttered again, approaching a stone on the furthest side; he stood staring at it. Suze followed him but wavered off to his left. The stones were set apart from each other by approximately forty feet.

Becky noticed a shimmer coming from the stone on her left, next to the one Suze was looking at. She blinked it away and headed for it.

A sudden, horrific murmur of voices filled their heads. A spasmodic, jabbering, vocal interruption that none could understand or stop hearing.

"What in the hell is this?" Nina thought to herself; she'd wandered to Max's right and stood in front of a stone totally drawn.

"Who said that?" thought Suze.

"What?" asked Ben.

"Oh my god, what is…" Nina said to herself.

"What?" shouted Max aloud, then added, "What did you say, Nina?" Bailey came to sit beside him briefly, then darted across to Suze.

"I'm scared," thought someone.

"I never said a word. Who's scared?" Nina tutted; she was entranced by the shimmering smoothness of the stone's appearance.

"Yes, you did Nina!" Max told her.

"I wonder who's scared?" said someone.
"What's he bloody talking about...?" Nina thought.
"What did you say just then?" Suze demanded aloud, turned, and glared at Nina.
"Me, I'm a tad scared, but also mildly fascinated!" replied Becky.
"Where's Bailey?" pondered Suze.
Nina stood stunned. *"How did she hear me..."*
"I dunno how, but we all heard you..." thought Becky, now turning to the centre.
"Oh, there's Bailey... The dog is here!" shouted Ben.
"Yes, I heard you the first time...I think, Ben?" Suze remarked, highly unsettled.
"Hello...?"
"Are we talking with..."
"Yeah, think so..."
"Hello, Ben." Becky giggled.
"What is going on...?" Nina spun round to face the rest.
"I dunno, I..." Suze started but lost her words. She then thought to herself, *"What the hell is happening... Oh, here he comes ...*Oh yes I see him..."
"Suze?" asked Nina.
Suze stood staring at the dog.
"This just can't be real, it..." Max thought, *"I'm going to touch it, stuff what Nina says."* And extended his finger to the stone. It felt like a force dragging him forward, like a string tied to the end of his index finger, pulling gently.
"What the hell, Max!" Nina exclaimed.
"Me too Max!" Becky answered aloud.
Max nodded in agreement. *"Come on then!"* But he frowned, realising he'd replied to someone who'd just replied to his own thought!
"Don't...be stupid..." Nina was clinging to her hair in

desperation.
"Let's do it!"
"Let's."
"What did you two just say?" Nina's eyebrows arched high on her quivering forehead.

Max gaped, "I didn't say anything out loud, did I? Shhhhh! Listen. What the... What's that...?"

They all staggered round to face Max in a circle, totally bewildered, just as a sudden whooshing sound came from overhead, scaring them witless.

"OK. Let's go, now! RUN!" Max shouted.

Along with the fact they knew they were partly conversing without their mouths — and then the sudden whooshing noise from overhead scaring them almost to death, understandably, a sheer alarm had set in. They'd run straight back to the safety of the house without stopping or looking back.

In quiet bewilderment, Nina poured five generous glasses of wine and spread them out on the table.

Suze lay on the floor, flat on her back with the dog; her neck craned over her chest, tapping her toes together, half expecting to see flourishes of sparkles.

Becky sat at the table, staring at Max as he paced the kitchen. Ben stood by the telescope, not even thinking to look through it, but as soon as he heard glass clink on wood, he came straight in, took the nearest glass, and swigged the contents back in one swallow and gagged. He waved his empty glass at Nina, who then poured him another. He gagged again, almost unable to swallow it.

It was a strange feeling, once their prison, an unfamiliar area surrounded by uncertainty just a few days ago, now appeared to be their haven. Locking the outside out and the inside in.

Nobody had spoken a word as they'd run back to the kitchen, mainly because they couldn't, concentrating only on the forward motion of their legs while breathing heavily, had been a far better option. Like robots, they filed inside quickly and silently, locking the door behind them.

No one dared to **think** at all. Just in case it was heard by another. Perhaps they were all going crazy.

Max now counted the freckles on his hand.

Becky sat quietly with her eyes closed.

Ben silently swirled the wine in his glass, wondering why he couldn't stomach it.

Suze now twiddled the dog's right ear.

While Nina watched them all.

Max finally broke the silence. "I didn't use to believe in that mind-talk stuff!" He walked slowly to the table and sat next to Becky. Nina dragged the chair and sat too.

"You mean telepathy Max?" asked Becky.

Max stared at Becky and replied with thought to test the water, *"Yes Becky, I mean telepathy."*

"Max? Are you ok? Do you mean telepathy?" she pushed.

"Yes, I mean that." He sounded relieved, thankful it had all stopped now.

"It's not happening now, at least I don't think it is," Suze announced; she lifted herself from the floor to join them.

"How do you know that?" asked Ben, finally pushing the glass of wine away to the middle of the table.

"Because I think Bailey peed on one of the stones, but I can't be sure, and I just this minute thought *'I wonder if any of them saw it'*. When nobody replied to my thought, I had another thought."

"What was that?"

"That I wish I had told you, I think he might have 'possibly' licked his own pee just before licking your face, Ben." She bit her lip and then said, "But it shows no one can hear our thoughts right now. And I'm not sure he actually **did** pee sooo....!"

Ben slowly got up and went to the sink, turned the tap on full and stuck his head under it. They waited for him to dry his hair and face with a tea towel, with suppressed chuckles.

Their chortling became louder as Ben smiled grimly at the dog because he was now in front of him, wagging his tail furiously. He patted his head and then wiped his hand on his silver suit.

"So, it only happened at the stones then?" Nina composed herself.

Max cleared his throat. "The pee? Or the mind-talk?" By now, they were all howling — except for Ben; he stood with his arms folded, waiting, tea towel dangling at his side. After a moment, Becky spoke,

"We have to go back, you know," she announced seriously.

"Not on your goddamn life!" Ben proclaimed, chucking the damp tea towel on the floor.

"Yes, altogether, we have to do it all together, don't we?" she added, looking at the others for confirmation.

"And do bloody what Becky? Have a conversation in our heads? Do you know how crazy that sounds?"

Suze butted in, "She's right Ben, we must go back, there's a reason for all this. Us being here...there's a process of some sort happening. I don't understand it yet, none of us do, but there's a reason... And we have to find out what it is!"

"Right. OK, what do you suggest then Suze?" Max asked her calmly. She began to open her mouth, but he answered himself, "We go back, we need to touch the stones again, I felt something."

"Me too, I felt it too." Becky acknowledged.

"Yep." Nina and Suze agreed in unison.

"Really? You're all bloody well crazy!" Ben shot at them before swiftly pushing himself away from the sink and storming off — then turned on his heels and huffed. He stood there with his hands on his hips, tapping his toe on the wooden floor, and gathered himself.

They waited patiently.

"Ok, look, here's what I think, we seem to be safer here than in the cities, the hunger, thirst, homelessness, gangs, guns, attacks, not knowing which way to turn to save our lives. And we know there are **things**…out there that aren't normal, but I somehow feel a bit safer…just different dangers I suppose…fear of the unknown…" He paused shuffling on his feet. "You're all right. We **do** have to go back, and soon!" he finally admitted.

Chapter Twelve

A Timely Judgement

Day 5

Amber stood with Phoenix by the water's edge, playing and talking with the little entities; she loved to spend time with them. They lifted her fine hair; it twitched softly as they played and twirled within it. A few scooted away into the water with a splash. She swung herself round to face Phoenix.

"They have discovered the gate without us, all by themselves! Their energy must be settling Phoenix, quicker than anticipated too," she smiled.

"Indeed, they have surprised even myself, though I feel it is only their curiosity that willed them to explore," Phoenix whispered.

"I was discreetly observing them. Orb-2 accompanied me. I instructed the forest; I hope this was a reasonable judgment on my part without consulting you?"

"Yes, I believe you passed a timely judgment." She looked at Amber then continued, *"This group is very special I believe, but we will see."*

"Is something ailing you, Phoenix?"

"It is nothing, Amber." She flicked her hand.

Amber dropped to her knees, lay flat on her front, dipped her fingers into the water and wriggled them. A flurry circled just under the surface.

River joined them swiftly and without sound. *"Perhaps, dear Phoenix, but our hopes are high,"* he added to their conversation.

Amber twisted her neck and kicked her feet up behind

her, *"Good Waken River."*

He nodded his greeting. She then turned away to carry on playing with the entities in the water.

"River, it's a joy to see you. Good Waken, is all well within Sector 2, you visited last Waken with Sol and Sage did you not?"

He lowered himself to sit beside her, *"Yes, we did, all is well, Phoenix, they had some 'choice' compilations at the last minute, therefore the influx was higher than expected."* He winked, a turquoise iris disappeared behind a lid briefly, then reappeared with a twinkle. *"There are only two main choices to be made, but I suspect it can be hard to choose."*

"Indeed. Where is Sol?" she inquired, tilting her head.

"Overlooking our arrivals as we speak, he wanted to take over from Amber just before the gateway was reached. We may have to unveil and show ourselves before the usual time?"

"Maybe I will speak with Sol regarding this," she told him.

Amber rolled over to her back, spreading her arms wide on the warm grass and smiled at her friends; in a dreamy voice she said, *"Yes, Sol commended me for my forward thinking, I could feel the energy stronger than ever before, O-2 was a great help, advised and guided me,"* then quickly added, *"though you have been the greatest mentor for us, Phoenix."* She nodded and rolled back to her front, letting her hair float on the water's surface.

Phoenix giggled at Amber's quickness in not wishing to upset her.

"And Sage? Where is she this waken?" Phoenix lifted her chin towards River.

"I have just left her in the medical bay — we have Essence boarding; she was visited by Aqua earlier, with

regards to a choice issue they have. Aqua is leaving here shortly for Marinas, it is likely that our arrivals will notice."

Amber whipped around, eager to please, *"Shall I monitor them, Phoenix?"*

Phoenix studied her and said, *"That won't be necessary, but I thank you."*

In the centre room of their huge Mother Illumination vessel, Sage's light form undulated in mellow shades of green, while tiny glints of silver flickered about her — she was observing Essence as they embarked from one of the transporter light crafts; the huge crystal windows gave good light. White walls and ceilings curved around and over, like the inside of an empty eggshell, giving a panoramic view of the whole room with no obstacles.

The dark masses panicked as they came through the portal to the first-care unit. Some floated straight to the ceiling like a dead goldfish, coming to rest on an unseen surface, unmoving. While others simply held their position wherever they ended up, others writhed in panic, squirming and curling.

She materialised, placing her flat palm on the crystal pane. Black tendrils of twirling emotion filled with dark fear emanated from every Essence; they engulfed and flooded the space. The window soon became blackened with an undulating fog of terror, confusion, and helplessness; a room of utter despair.

Sol arrived quietly behind her.

"You need to turn off Sage. Why do you bring yourself open?"

She snapped her hand in, it dispersed in an instant. *"It*

is only right to share their pain. I don't always open, just sometimes. Are these earth or water Sol?"

"Earth, a few waters also, but nothing large," he replied, his fresh golden-yellow glow mingled with her colour as he neared, creating a haze of blue.

She then turned away from the blackness and drifted to the other side of the room to another window, where she tapped a panel to the left. A screen hiding the space beyond dissolved, revealing the subdued lighting of a smaller area. Her fingers deftly accessed a series of buttons, where all monitors in the controlled-temperature unit blinked to life; she ran her eyes over them all. Happy that they were stable, she then turned her attention to the see-through cases suspended there.

"Marinas has another huge influx of water this eventide," he interrupted her.

"Yes indeed, though they are well experienced and will manage," she replied.

The door opened silently behind them, closing with a soft hum; it was Phoenix, shimmering in ultraviolet and glints of silver.

"Sol? Sage? This delivery...it has been successful, yes?" she asked, approaching them, then added, *"We may have to start initiation early this eventide — they are heading back to the gate very soon."* Her starlit eyes rested on the cases in the smaller room.

Sage engaged the screen once again, and the room vanished from sight.

"Are they? How interesting! These are an inquisitive bunch," noted Sol.

"There is a chance they will notice Aqua's departure, Phoenix," Sage realised.

"Indeed, I am aware of this. It is obvious to them that things aren't normal." She materialised, walked across to the first care unit, and initiated the high tranquillity

setting on the side panel. All Essence became still, a mass of blackness, suspended in time and space.

Sage nodded. *"I will notify the others of our intentions."* Then, she also took her shape, soon followed by Sol.

"Let's be on our way!" motioned Phoenix. *"We must fully unmask."*

With that, they left the vessel.

Chapter Thirteen

Back to the Stones

The Afternoon of Day 5

The five had only just passed the house and turned left to follow the path of trees back to the stones when a low rumbling, followed by a soft hum, filled their senses. It came from the sky.

They stopped abruptly, looking upward just in time to see a silver streak shoot at unimaginable speed overhead.

Everyone scattered, running towards the forest for cover, only to double back to the pathway at the last minute and freeze, unknowing of which way to turn for the best. They stood like bent statues and waited, except Becky, who fell to the floor and lay in a fetal position.

"Again? What the **hell** is that, Max?" Nina probed.

"Who knows? Let's keep moving; it's gone now!" he reassured her.

After a short while, they regained their composure and carried on in silence, unease and apprehension eating at their core. Suze was walking the slowest, in front of her were Becky and Ben, then Nina, and Max was way up front. Bailey was nowhere to be seen — but now and then made an appearance, darting from the forest, checking his pack was still in sight, soaking wet and covered in bits, before shooting off again.

From time to time, Max would turn around to make sure everyone was there and not too far behind. He had now reached the brow of the hill and lay in warm grass on his side, waiting for everyone else to catch up. He sat thinking to himself. His thoughts ran rampant, scattering through his mind — not knowing **where** they were and **how** they got there. It was such a strange place, but it was certainly a lot nicer most of the time than London. He truly believed that if they all stuck together, they would be OK.

He breathed deeply, filled his chest with clean air and let out a long, heavy sigh. Oddly, he saw his own breath — plunging forward in hefty plumes like it used to on a cold day. Except this was a little different; it was as if he'd expelled glitter from his lungs, he watched as the tiny bits glistened, fell, and vanished in mid-air…

"…What the…" He coughed loudly.

The rest soon caught up and joined him on the grassy hilltop.

Nina asked, "Alright Max?"

Max nodded and wiped his mouth with the back of his hand, deciding to keep his 'glitter breath' to himself.

They sat in a group, each contemplating the moment they'd start hearing each other's thoughts.

"We can't be close enough yet," huffed Becky; she felt drained.

"No, otherwise you'd have heard me use **very** unpleasant words back there! Now tell me, what the hell was that shooting overhead?" Ben crossed his legs and messed with the grass. "We **totally** crapped ourselves!"

"I've seen those before, in London." Becky told them, "It looked like a shooting star."

"Well, it probably was then." Max rationalised.

Ben said firmly, "Max, has it not occurred to you yet that it's not out of the realm of possibility…that you are not in London anymore?!" His voice was getting louder, "After all you've seen so, bloody, **FAR**?"

At that moment, they were all startled again as another horrendous noise emanated from above. The trees shook and started swaying, dancing in a chaotic frenzy. Their leaves rustled, and branches swung and trembled, and thrashed about like wild beasts. And then, without warning, a gust of wind descended upon the group, forcefully rolling them all from their rears, leaving them sprawled on the ground, staring up at the heavens.

The ground juddered under their bodies.

Thunderous clouds rolled and tumbled inwards in huge, violent waves. The silvery aurora borealis twisted, flickered and erupted, causing angry streaks of lightning that spanned the entire sky. Light beams tried to fight through the clouds in flashes of gold. Fiery reds and oranges writhed in the turbulence as the vaporous explosion thundered towards them like a collapsing vortex. All they could do was watch helplessly as the mighty wind flooded down while the forest lurched and rocked brutally.

Then everything became still.

Slowly, the pressure eased, and the mistiness vanished. The air was finally finding its way back into their lungs; they gasped and gulped. With trembling hands, they poked and prodded a clear film that had settled on their body suits.

"Holy shit!"

Everyone turned to Max's outburst. His head was tilted far back on his shoulders. They looked up.

All they could see now was another moon suspended far, far away, but this one was different to the first moon; it had multiple shades of pale green, odd blobs of blue and a lot of white.

No one moved from their positions as they watched the silvery haze calmly take back its place overhead.

Becky declared, "See! That one just appeared outta thin air!"

"Now I **know** where we're not in London!" Max panicked, getting up quickly.

The rest began to shift on their rears, looking from one moon to the other in disbelief. Bailey came running around the corner barking.

"So that's not **our** moon after all?" Becky questioned.

"We gotta get outta here!" Nina yelled frantically.

"But where the goddam, hell, are we?!" shouted Ben. "And go bloody where?" His chest was heaving wildly.

Suze reminded them. "But what about the stones?"

"Sod the stones…" Ben started…

Then, from all around them, it seemed…a voice.

"I can help you with that question, but first, you must calm down. Get up and follow your intended path to find the answers."

Max spun around in a daze. The rest stayed seated, frantically twisting their necks this way and that. There was no one there.

"Ok, who said that?" Suze asked quickly.

Their eyes were flitting to all angles of the area, all warily watching each other; this was enough to tell Suze that none of them had said or thought anything.

"Did someone think it and not realise?" Max quizzed.

Nina got up, "We aren't close enough to those stones for that, Max, surely," then thought… *"You dumb Dingbat."* No reply from him. She was right!

"It said 'follow your intended path', didn't it?" Becky said, shakily getting to her feet.

"Yes, but **who the bloody hell said it**!? Shall we get back to the house?" Nina questioned.

Suze then bounced up quickly, "Dunno. No, let's keep moving. It could just be a case of group hallucinations."

They all agreed to disagree with Suze's hallucination idea, but agreed they should continue carefully to the stones. After all, they knew they needed to go back — but not without standing silently for another ten minutes, to look at the new moon hanging far above them.

They found the dog sitting in the centre of the stone circle, devouring a stick. He was still soaking wet and covered in dirt. They approached with caution.

"*Can you all hear me?*" Becky asked.

Nina said, "*Yeah.*"

Max said, "*I can.*"

Suze said, "*Yep.*"

"*Yes, for crying out loud! Do we have to speak like this? It's not normal.*"

"*Nothing here is normal Ben,*" Max told him with a glance.

The crystal stones shimmered as they got nearer, and soon, they were standing in the noisy centre with the dog.

It was hard enough to focus on their own thoughts, let alone the thoughts of the others milling about — their brains were battered: five confused, babbling minds and a barking dog.

Ben knelt in discomfort, his features contorting on his reddening face. He tried covering his ears with the palms of his hands, but it didn't work at all. Max, Suze, and Nina ran from the circle to rid themselves of the chatter and panic, leaving Ben and Becky behind; chatter followed them, no matter where they fled.

Becky started to follow but tripped. She struggled to stand, but having not gone far from the stone, she reached out and placed her hand on it for support. Peace took hold in an instant, and silence filled her mind. She breathed a sigh of relief. It took a moment for her to refocus, propping her shoulder against the warm surface.

"Come back!" she shouted, trying to catch her breath. "We just have to touch the stones!" No one came back. "Please…trust me!" she begged.

Their need for silence was desperate. They'd all just about heard Becky's instruction filtering through the constant moaning and groaning and stumbled back, each choosing the stone they had stood by earlier. Ben crawled on his knees to the last stone left, falling near it. He sat up and pressed his back firmly against it.

Silence.

He clutched his forehead, his eyes watered behind firmly shut lids.

"Jesus," he said, breathing deeply, "I'm never coming here again. I can't cope with that!" As he opened his eyes and looked around the circle, each one of his new friends had copied him; all were sitting with their backs to the stones, heads tilted back and resting just like him. It made him feel good. The dog was standing beside him, he landed a heavy paw on his thigh.

Ben eyed him breathlessly, "Ok, but no kissing mate!"

They talked, projecting their voices loud and clear across the stones for over an hour, not daring to move, wondering how the bloody hell they would manage to get back to the hill without being talked to death. Someone suggested that they all thought of one word until they reached the safe zone, someone else suggested they 'just make a run for it', and then someone said to 'take it in turns to run and then meet on the hill.' But the truth was, their experience had drained the lot of them.

Someone had to come up with a plan soon because nighttime wasn't far away.

"My arse is numb," Nina announced, "I need to get up, let the blood back in…" She did this easily enough, by always maintaining contact with the stone, sliding her back straight up; she was now standing leaning against it. Everyone else did it the same way; she hoped none of the stones would topple on them; after all, they weren't even securely bedded in the ground!

Ben's legs were shaky; he couldn't maintain the strength he needed to haul himself up. He landed on his side.

"Shit, get up!" Max yelled over; Ben didn't move, he just lay there motionless. So, Max pushed himself away from the quiet safety of his stone to help and stopped abruptly.

Ben lifted his head. "I hear nothing!"

"Me neither!" he replied.

They all ducked in panic as someone spoke.

"All is well, now that you have connected with your stones." The tone was androgynous: *"Be upstanding."*

All five eyed each other, waiting to understand which one had spoken. Max purposefully made eye contact with everybody, raising his eyebrows questioningly. A series of slow headshakes followed.

"What does it mean 'connected' with the stones?" Suze questioned.

"Is that the same voice from the hill?" wondered Nina.

"Be upstanding," repeated the voice.

Only through fear and not obedience did the group stand, spinning around searching for the owner of the voice.

"Where are you? Show yourself, you bloody coward!"

"Nina, please don't, you'll antagonise it!" pleaded Becky.

"What the hell do you want with us?" Max yelled into the open air.

"A good first question, Max Adamson. A kind man and a fine leader, a loyal friend with good intentions. Welcome," the voice said.

Max's eyes were wide, flitting back and forth. He gulped. "Ok, here's another. **Where are we**?"

"*All questions will be answered in good time.*"

"Jesus Max, shut up!" Suze panicked.

"Now's the good time! Answer the damn question! What do you want with us?" It was Ben. The five had never seen him quite so demanding before; they stared at him.

"*Ah, Sergeant Ben Rudd, at last, you show your true self. A good man, a man who knows wrong from right, a soul full of true objective — no need to hide that any longer, welcome.*"

This statement shocked the others.

"I'll explain another time," he assured them, waving it off.

"*Suze Higgins, Becky Flatwood. Your empathic natures, kind hearts, psychic and healing abilities did not go unnoticed. Welcome,*" the voice greeted. They looked at each other weakly.

Nina bit her lower lip, she knew it was coming and shivered.

"*Welcome, Private Nina O'Donnell. A woman strong of heart and fearless, with a determined character; one who connects and loves deeply.*"

"What?!

"Later Max," she told him, rolling her eyes. She glanced at Ben; he was gaping at her.

"*Turn to face your stones. I have information for you; some questions will be answered, and you may sit if you wish,*" the voice commanded.

"Now why would w…" Nina started.

"*Face the stones!*" the voice echoed through every cell in their bodies. They all sat immediately, apart from Ben and Max, who stood firm facing the stones.

The stones flickered with small white lights. This was

then accompanied by flashes of bright blues and violets. Streaks of pale greens and silver danced in circles around the entire breadth, spiralling up and down the length at the same time. The tension was high; each one of them looked at another's stone, realising they were all doing the exact same thing.

And then, it began.

A picture story was projected from within the stone itself and settled on its surface; it began with bursts of colour that flared with flamboyance and extravagance. Particles of matter and gas forming shapes, finding their rightful places, swirling like an epic film playing at high speed. Oceans, woodlands, rainforests, deserts, snow, and ice, developed in all corners of the curves and bends.

The mysterious voice spoke again, straight into their minds.

"Billions of years ago, she was assigned a supreme mission. She willingly gave rise to her challenge and vowed that life would have everything it ever needed.

She gave a promise to Creation. She designed herself with the use of gravity, rotating around her star and gathering nothing but dust and gases to form her core and skin.

In time, she became a beautiful creation.

And in time, she became strong, while her beauty blossomed.

She prepared to accommodate and nurture, to protect and love, to share her skin, her space. To deliver the unlimited gifts that she alone could produce to nourish, sustain, and heal.

She kept her atmosphere relatively safe, clean, and breathable. She made sure all plant life released a never-ending supply of oxygen into her atmosphere, and in return for this, landwalking and aquatic life would give back carbon dioxide, which the plants and trees could absorb, ensuring a truly giving cycle for life.

The far-off light shone, warming her skin, and giving light and nutrients. Her nighttime Luna neighbour kept her oceans moving; while some life forms used its magnetic force to navigate and migrate from one area of her body to another.

Certain areas of her entirety required different weather systems, which she commanded and maintained to the best of her ability. She experienced natural climate changes, only to find that life pulled through somehow and continued to evolve.

Her balance worked for millions of years."

The group was filled with awe. Emotions rose at the sight of the vast magnificence of her.

"Why do we have to watch this, though…?" whispered Nina, glancing around. Suze and Becky were completely captivated, their faces tilting upwards. Max was scrubbing his chin, and Ben stood with his arms folded in front of the stone. Nina shrugged and turned back round to watch the show.

"Her beauty remained, on, above and within her skin.

Life promised to love her, pledged to keep her safe, watch over her and respect her. Life loved her, and she loved life.

For many more millions of years, she gave without hesitation; she gave everything and anything that she was able to offer.

As the millennia came and went, a race of life evolved, making good use of her gifts for their promised survival. Whenever life took from her, it lovingly, attentively and ceremoniously thanked her; her selfless response was to produce more of what was taken, simply to maintain life.

Never did she waver from her promise to safeguard and defend, ensuring life always had the things it needed to remain safe, to be healthy and to thrive, even in times of disconcertment. She watched on, with the adoration of a new mother, gazing upon her children as life came and went, changed, and evolved quickly.

Hardly ever did life witness disease or illness; they used only natural remedies, finding the vitamins and minerals she produced from the surface of her skin; this alone was enough to restore health and harmony. Light, along with a balanced diet and a clean atmosphere, healed one and all, keeping life in an overall harmonious state."

"Is it Earth before the wars? I don't get it!"
"Wow, yes Nina, how beautiful!" Becky gasped.
"Oh, it's so amazing!" Suze added.

"But then...that race evolved further. And darkness set in. Nothing that good lasts forever."

At this point, the stones went dark. All five turned round with questioning eyes. Little did they know they would soon be filled with the worst feeling of despair and grief that they had ever encountered.

The stones flickered to life once again.
"Oh nooo!" Becky pleaded.

"She had started screaming. Screaming to be saved for thousands of years, it had become harder to keep her promise to protect life. Her beauty was vanishing. She had been violated, poisoned, wounded, and ruined; she was now weak and dying.

She wept day and night as her abusers tore through her skin with appalling intentions. Pain from their broken *promises and so-called life's progression consumed her for aeons to come, scarring, defacing and damaging her deeply.*

No one listened. No one seemed to hear her cries for help; she was faced with ignorance, indifference, and bitterness; life was now selfishly cruel and unforgiving."

"The Noise!" Becky realised.

"Oh no please...!" whispered Suze, her chest heaving uncontrollably, as the sadness ebbed its way to her soul; realisation was taking hold.

"It was The Noise!" Becky's brow furrowed, and her tears ran freely.

"Oh, dear God! Yes, I heard that too, all the time!" Nina cried, lowering her head into her hands. "But why do we have to see this? I still don't understand!"

"Then over time, as life forms progressed, some tried to claim their dominance with the use of corruption, terror, greed, and blackmail. Others worked hard in undesirable workplaces to find what little money they could to pay their way, raise their young and live the best way they could in this sorrowful existence. Many others became reliant on unnatural substances to help them through their minutes, hours, and days. This was a place filled with nightmares, negativity, darkness and death; it lingered around every corner and through every door, whether open or closed.

Her atmospheric conditions had started deteriorating long ago, and her pollution levels were alarming. Her safety layers had weakened, becoming incredibly compromised; she could not protect life any longer — copious amounts of harmful gases had thwarted her air. Her star shone with such sorrow that it could not stop its deadly ultraviolet radiation from penetrating her,

poisoning everything that she had given life to.
Frozen areas of her skin had melted once again, but this time it was due to life's creations, not hers. It resulted in the extinction of creatures that had evolved, ones that had walked upon her for millions of years.
Her oceans had not only risen, causing flooding but were also polluted with unnatural substances, which killed and choked her aquatic life. Natural habitats of land-living life forms were all but gone due to the deforestation of unimaginably large areas.
Earthquakes rocked her, and wildfires raced, stripping her every curve, forever rushing to engulf anything they could devour. Severe, uncontrollable weather systems, droughts, famines, and other indescribable, unnatural disasters had stricken her regularly. She was finally giving up and could only watch her beloved vow wither away. She had no way to save the life forms she had nurtured any longer.
To her utter despair, life was at war across her vastness, fighting one another and blaming each other. The negativity was all-consuming and contagious."

An audible gasp of awareness filled the stone circle because each one was wrapped in their cloak of anguish; they covered their faces as the tears continued to fall.

"The assault kept coming decade after decade, and innocent life forms died for no reason at all. Many extraterrestrial entities had visited her from far away to try and help, yet it seemed to no avail; they had been gunned down and destroyed. She dreaded the one weapon that would destroy everything in an instant, yet no governing body had been able to release one single nuclear bomb; all nuclear stations across her entire surface had been instantly unarmed overnight — and

there was nothing that any life form could do to reinstate them; it had dumbfounded them for many years to come.

She knew something outside of her atmosphere had helped somehow, but who, she did not know.

Negativity had taken a terrible hold on the universe.

And since her cries for help were overlooked, she mustered all the strength that was left inside her. She would have to die a terrible death along with all her beautiful life forms and hope that, in some way, peace would blossom once again.

For all the harm they had done to her and themselves, she still loved them deeply."

The voice spoke one last time, giving the group instructions, before the crystals went dark once more.

Chapter Fourteen

On Reflection

Five saddened faces stared blankly at the floor in the conservatory. The story of planet Earth had been a miracle, a beautifully astonishing creation — but then so very disturbing, cruel, and unforgiving.

The wondrous universe and all that lived there, for all the astounding knowledge it held, for all the life it had given birth to in its vastness, could not stop the Earth from dying. The thought of what mankind had done was inconceivable.

The picture show told of the effects of industrial pollution in her atmosphere and on her ozone layer, it showed her oceans full of rubbish — artificial substances and the painful deaths of aquatic life. It showed war and killing, hate, prejudice, greed, and corruption. Weapons of mass destruction. Excavation for fossil fuels and precious metals, deforestation, and many other disturbing scenarios, simply for greed and 'progress'. It was brutal.

They were all safe in their knowledge that none of them had contributed to the devastation; they had just been trying to do the right thing, trying to live as best they could in their ruined world. None of them had seen the earth so beautiful as at the beginning of this story; how they wished they had! They were disgusted, unable to rid their minds of the dreadful images they had been forced to watch.

No one spoke.

Not only were they thinking about the desperation of the planet Earth, but also Private Nina and Corporal Ben and after asking the questions, they now understood why

Ben and Nina had not wanted to talk about why they'd ended up on the open streets. Both were soldiers and deserters, leaving their posts to hide among the people and ruins of London.

Nina explained that she was ordered at gunpoint one day, at the tender age of sixteen, to serve the country; she had no choice, like many others. She was given a weapon and told what to do with it. Her division had been ordered to 'round up' the elderly and take them to a warehouse on the outskirts for their own safety. This went on for eight years. The numerous squads did as they were told time and time again, not only gathering the elderly, but others too. Some covered their faces, and soldiers didn't know what age they were — only to learn years later that innocent lives were being ended, not saved. At the age of twenty-five, Nina absconded.

Ben's story was much the same; he too was given a gun and promised a high rank when in the south of England, 'to save the world'. This continued for five years. But in the end, he realised he was passing devastating orders to the lower ranks; the truthful information about the mission was kept by many and kept away from many more. Neither could live with the knowledge of what they were doing.

The 'Armed Forces' was not the Army after all. Instead, a huge group of rebels derived from long-existing gangs over the last seventy-five years or so; they were to be feared for good reason. They seemed to have been cleansing the country of those who had no hope and were ready to mount a revolution.

"So, do you two know each other then?" Becky asked.

"I've never seen Nina before now," Ben muttered, keeping his head low, not wanting to look the rest in the eyes; his guilt was overwhelming.

"No, not seen him before now either. Sorry guys, I

feel so numb about it all. You must hate us right now."

Suze got up and knelt in front of Nina, "But you both ran when you knew you did the right thing in the end, and that makes you good people, ok?" She patted Nina on the knee before turning to face Ben. "Ok? Good people!"

Max then said, "Yeah, and you managed to survive too. It does make me wonder if they got Isla…"

After that uncomfortable moment, there was an unexpected group hug. Each one of them vowed this subject would never surface again.

They had bonded at last.

"We'd better get ready; the voice told us we gotta meet back at the stones in 'late Darkentide' — I presume that's nighttime…tonight," Ben informed.

"Yes, but where on earth are we, and what about those black things?" asked Becky.

No one answered her.

Chapter Fifteen

As Darkentide drew near, deep in the heart of the forest, where light struggled to penetrate through the thick canopy, a very different darkness was emerging, crawling in shadows, biding its time, keeping low, and remaining quiet.

Drawing ever closer, like moths to a flame, its hunger grew, waiting for a chance to begin the feast. Though it seemed a struggle to pick up momentum, as if weighed down by the heaviness of its own presence; a thick and oppressive air, trying to cast shadows on its vibrant and lively surroundings.

As the negativity meandered sluggishly through the forest, it lingered lazily. And despite its efforts, it remained partially stagnant, unable to break free from the confines of the forest for now. It was trapped in a cycle of its own making, not only unable to escape but unable to spread its influence beyond the trees.

The forest stood hard as a barrier, holding back the tide of negativity and preserving a glimmer of hope amidst the foliage.

Entities dithered, whispering to one another, telling tales and watching closely. The grass rustled. The trees hung their branches low, feeling for the danger in hiding.

A ripple of unease began to spread.

Chapter Sixteen

Of Astounding Beauty

Evening of Day 5

Obeying the order given by the mysterious voice, they purposefully headed back to the stones and stood in the centre, waiting.

It was almost dark, and dread had started to creep in; all were concerned about the shadows reappearing. It would be the first night that they'd left the safety of the house — they kept well away from the trees. Suze thought it wise to leave the dog asleep on her bed, locked in — with his track record, he'd be running about in the dark, causing them to panic for his safety.

Stars began appearing in the diminishing light, so far away in their remote blackness. The moon-type structures held their positions amongst them.

"Look!" Nina pointed towards the forest. A wave of fireflies was floating in their direction, illuminating the forest in a haze of ultraviolet blue; it only became brighter as their numbers grew.

"What? They are gathering already!" Ben told them steadily. "We know what that means…"

They watched with agitation, scouring the depths of the forest for the creepy shadows. More little lights gathered until the entire edge of the forest was completely encircled by thousands upon thousands of them, so much so that they could no longer see through their light.

A confused feeling engulfed the group — anxiety and marvel. There were no words to describe the magical beauty of the lights; they sparkled and flickered while gently pulsating. They were then jolted back to reality by another unexpected vocal.

"These are the Elan Vital; they are all very happy you are here."

Nina twisted her neck from left to right, wanting to ask anyone what an 'Elan' was. But she couldn't make her voice work.

Based on the last disembodied voices, no one was expecting anyone or anything to be there in the circle with them. Therefore, they didn't turn to this one.

"Where are you?" Max said in a loud voice.

"Good Darkentide, I am behind you," the voice greeted them.

The group spun around, arms flailing outward.

A lustrous, oval-shaped ultraviolet light hovered there.

Unable to move or speak, they watched as a humanoid being of the utmost beauty softly materialised through the radiance until it stood fully formed and smiling in front of them; the edges glimmered with a delicate purple aura — she allowed them time to observe her.

She was tall, at least eight feet, with slim arms and long fingers. Her fine, white hair was softly streaked with iridescent purples, all shimmering with different shades in the glow of the Elan. The length floated behind her as if gravity no longer existed, an unusual yet beautiful contrast against her pale skin. Wide, upward-slanted eyes somehow twinkled in the darkness as she blinked, her metallic silver irises glimmering with life, and long dark lashes fluttered like delicate butterflies on her cheeks with every blink.

She was dressed in intricate, finely woven material, long and flowing, drifting effortlessly about her like a sheet of white silk flowing in unseen waters. It was tied loosely at the waist with an equally ornate purple belt.

When she spoke again, no one uttered a word. Her small mouth formed only a smile, no words; her delicate chin and jawline stayed firmly still.

"My name is Phoenix. I am the Overseer. I'm in joint command. Guardian, healer, and advisor for all."

Still, no one could manage one single word. They gazed in awe at her grandeur and demanding elegance.

Phoenix continued, *"I welcome you one and all."* She observed them closely, feeling their emotions, full of wonderment at her appearance, their uneasiness, their utter terror, and fear. *"Do not fear me,"* she told them.

Becky fell limply to the ground.

Suze rushed to her. Crouching, she stroked Becky's forehead and spoke softly to her, patting her cheeks and trying to bring her around.

"Easy for you to say!" Nina told the entity. "What have you done to her?"

"Nothing," Phoenix said calmly; she started to walk over to Becky and Suze.

"Stop right there, leave her!" Suze quivered.

"Very well. She has faded; it is to be expected. All will be well in a moment."

"Faded?" yelled Nina.

Phoenix ignored her.

"Just where the hell are we?" Ben approached the being, somewhat perturbed. He stood directly in front of her. His wide eyes glided steadily over her.

"What — are — you!?" Max exclaimed from behind. His tone was a mixture of alarm and quiet wonder.

Becky started to twitch on the grass, muttering. Suze sat her up and supported Beck's back with her own body, offering comforting words.

"All in good time, you have nothing to fear." She replied, waving her hand gracefully, then said, *"But first, I will acquaint you with the others."*

"Others?" Ben scoffed, stepping back.

Phoenix nodded. *"I introduce Sol, River, Sage, and Amber. We are the Elites."*

Nina was frightened, frustrated, and angry. This creature's calm demeanour was making her want to yell and shout at it, but her tongue had unwittingly frozen.

Five dumbfounded faces watched intently as four more shining ovals gradually emerged from behind the crystal stones, in an ever-changing tapestry of light and colour.

As they joined the first entity, their radiant auras illuminated the space with each movement they made; the air vibrated with energy. And as they greeted each other with what seemed like gentle merges of colour, a rainbow appeared, emanating from their forms in a display of dots and glittery particles. The colours danced and swirled around them, leaving the group mesmerised.

Then they began to change, morphing into humanoid forms.

Suze and Becky — Nina and Max closed together in a huddle, nervously backing up at the same time. While Ben stood closely in front, safety in numbers and all that!

The beings looked alike in shape and height, all similarly dressed in long flowing garments, except for some colour differences. They then presented themselves individually.

An entity stepped forward to greet them, making the group cower.

"Greetings, my name is Sol. I am in joint command; I am also advisor and healer to one and all." Sol's voice was the same tone as Phoenix's. He was tall too, and just as graceful, with the same long fingers and limbs. His white hair was tied up at the front, letting the rest fall its full length down his back; it danced in slow drifts. Yellow-orange and gold strands shone with the intensity

of a sunset, marred only by the light of the Elan.

His skin was so pale, and his wide slanted eyes blinked slowly, the irises soft, yet disturbingly yellow. He nodded, stepped back, and turned to his companion.

Another walked forward, his voice almost the same.

"Welcome. I am known as River. I am the Head of Security. Joint guardian, carer and advisor." His pale blue hair was tied back in a loose bun at the nape of his neck; wavy strands of white, silver, and paler electric blues had escaped and were drifting about his fine features. His turquoise-blue irises flickered in waves like reflections in crystalline waters — he watched the group with unnaturally slow, blinking lashes. He also nodded and took a step back, then turned to the entity on his right.

"Welcome, my name is Sage. I am a Mentor for our areas, I am a Master empath, Clairvoyant and Clairaudient, and healer to all." Her hair was gathered to the side; a myriad of soft curls fell over her left shoulder to the waist. Amid the pure white waves, ringlets in many shades of green and silver bounced as she spoke in her colourful tone. She smiled, turned away, then nodded to her right.

The last being took two steps towards the group, her light, nondescript voice drifting outward.

"Good Darkentide, I am Amber. Second Empath for Essencia, and general security assistant to all areas here. I must inform you once again that you are safe." Amber's dark, saffron-coloured eyes flickered like a fire in shadows; she quietly watched the group. Her hair, also long and white, was streaked with dark crimson and vivid gold. She flicked it with her slender hand, bringing it round to sit on the left side of her face.

Total silence followed from both groups.

The Elites waited patiently, hands crossed loosely at

the front of their forms.

The five friends waited, each one carefully watching the beings for sudden movements. Becky slowly got up to stand with Suze, and they linked arms.

"I'm Becky," she told them in a quiet, shaky voice.

"I'm Suze."

The Elites smiled simultaneously.

"Max."

"Nina."

"Ben…although I don't feel safe! Two of us have already been attacked by trees!"

"Yes, our sincerest apologies. You have healed quickly, yes?" It was Sol — his mouth still; how it was so obvious it was Sol speaking, no one knew, they just knew!

Ben tutted.

"What about those big gold balls on the lawn? They did something to us!" Nina said in a less-than-quiet voice.

River then spoke, and their eyes turned to him. *"By my command, our Security Orbs 2, 3 and 4 — they rested you, we were simply protecting you from yourselves and further injury, that is all."* He bowed his head.

"Rested?" questioned Ben impatiently.

The five jumped out of their wits as River raised his arms and lifted his chin, and his eyes fluttered shut. The group gathered even closer together, suspecting something else was afoot. Then, from above and literally out of nowhere, descended the three security orbs, bringing with them a low-frequency hum. They came to rest, hovering behind the Elites.

Sage stepped forward and gently approached Suze, who stepped back, dragging Becky by the shoulders until she was behind her.

"Your canine, Bailey..." Sage began…

"Don't hurt him…" Suze stammered; she held her

eyes so wide open with terror that she felt the strain building in her lids; they welled and flitted to Sol as he spoke.

"*No one is here to be intentionally harmed,*" he said as he glanced at Phoenix. She did not return his gaze.

Suze tried to steady her breathing, unsure of why her dog was mentioned.

Sage told her. "*He's a kind, obedient soul. But he is fearful, he is locked in by your command; he wonders where you are and won't leave unless prompted.*" Suze began to sob; how she wished she had brought him with them.

"He's locked in! He can't leave!" shouted Max.

"He's safe inside! Isn't he?" Suze sputtered.

Nina walked steadily over to the girls, standing between them and the entity. She faced the creature, looked it in the eye, jutting her chin towards it and then turned cautiously to the girls.

She smiled, leaned forward, and whispered in Suze's ear, "Don't worry, I will go get him, bring him to us now, they can't stop me!" She spun round with anger firmly fused in her face.

"*There will be no need for that Nina, he is joyous now!*"

"Max rushed forward. "What have you done to him?

"*Please stop!*" River commanded and raised an arm towards him; Max stopped instantly; it felt like he'd hit an invisible wall. The three orbs moved rapidly, coming to rest above River.

"Ok, ok, no need for that..." he stuttered, his hands up, attempting to placate.

River waved his security away.

Suze broke down, crumbling to the ground in a flood of despair. The group quietly bit back the sadness, trying to hide their sorrow, staying strong for Suze's sake. This had to be war now; how could they kill a defenceless dog like Bailey? What harm could a Golden Retriever be?

Grief flooded their hearts. Ben wiped his face slowly with one hand, Max was staring into space, and Becky stood with limp arms. Nina was standing by Suze, who was, by now, slouched against her left leg, sobbing deeply.

"You misunderstand us," offered Amber, tilting her head to the side.

"Oh, we understand you all right!" spat Nina.

*"**No. You do not.**"* It was like all the Elites had spoken at once, each vocal tone resonating in pitch-perfect harmony.

"Look." It was Phoenix, her arm swung high and back, gesturing for them to look behind her.

Everyone except Suze saw him, a creamy flash in the night, bounding round the corner like a clumsy racehorse. His ears stuck close to his head with his blundering speed while his tongue flapped about his face. He was followed closely by a horde of Elan, as they appeared rounding the same corner as if chasing after him.

In his eagerness to join his pack, he stumbled and rolled, but recovered, lying on his stomach for a second. The Elan stopped and danced above him before he jumped up and thundered the rest of the way to the centre of the stones.

Bailey hurtled straight through the Elites as if they were ghosts or puffs of smoke.

Ben was about to comment — but didn't even start; he couldn't put the words together to ask what he had just witnessed!

The dog came to a skidding halt on Suze's lap; she hadn't seen his haste, but she could feel him now. She buried her wet face in his soft fur, crying with joy and relief. He smelt warm and fluffy…and of damp grass and soil. The five crowded around and greeted their crazy, furry friend.

"*Love and kindness,*" whispered Sage, moving nearer. She leant forward to touch the soft fur. And no one stopped her. "*He was fearful, I asked the Elan Vital to escort him so he may join us. He wanted to come but did not want to disobey you, Suze… The Elan told him you'd agreed to the release.*"

"How did he get out? The bloody door was locked!" Nina scowled.

Not one of the Elites answered.

Suze lifted her face from the fur. "Thank you." She hardly cared how he'd got out.

"*He knows only harmony Suze.*" Sage touched the dog's forehead, and Suze let her. "*You are his world, and he loves you desperately. There is no need to leave him anywhere alone here anymore. Have no fear when he plays with the Elan in the forest; he resonates with them now, and they love him.*" With the other hand, she gently touched Suze on the top of her head and said, "*Close your eyes. Do you see? Do you feel him?*"

Suze did as she was told; her chest juddered with leftover sobs. She knew her dog loved her, but the feelings she was having told her just how much, far more than she had ever realised. Behind her closed lids, in flashes of light, she saw and felt him; glittery dots flew in and out of his creamy fur. His big brown eyes showed only love.

She felt how he'd felt when he had been alone, frightened, and anxious, and compared them to the euphoria he was giving off now. His devotion for Suze poured from his soul in the purest form she had ever known.

Phoenix then spoke, "*You are not here to be intentionally harmed, nor are you here to be intentionally* taken advantage of. You are not here to serve us, nor are you here to fight and struggle — you will see."

"Oh yeah...? That'll be why the trees attacked us then. Because we're bloody safe!" Ben supposed sarcastically.

River spoke. *"Indeed, this happens. I'm afraid they were overzealous, far too enthusiastic upon your arrival, they sensed you were trying to escape — to leave them."*

"That's because we were trying to bloody well escape!" Nina enlightened him. "How did the dog get out?" She questioned again.

"You can't leave. This sector is vast; you will have time to explore." Phoenix told them, then turned to Nina. *"All in good time, Nina."*

Nina huffed and folded her arms across her chest.

"What are you talking about?" quizzed Ben. "What 'sector' is that?"

"Where are we? Can you tell us that?" asked Becky politely.

Suze got up, leaving Bailey loyally sitting at her feet.

"What's **Essencia**? She pointed to Amber, "That this one here mentioned?"

*"You are **on** Essencia."* Phoenix dipped her head.

They took the words in.

Essencia.

'On' Essencia.

No one had heard of it, so no one tried to understand it; the word sailed up and away. However, Nina **nearly** managed to ask where in the world 'Essencia' was, but Max started talking.

"**You** kidnapped us. Why?" he asked them.

"No, we did not. We escorted you safely here," offered Amber.

"What the hell for?" Ben asked, shaking his head.

"Because not only have your characters the utmost good intentions...you all chose to attend," Sol told him.

"What the **hell** are you talking about? I didn't decide to come here. None of us knows how we got here!"

"*All in good time,*" he replied.

"*Where you are now, will become clear to you this Darkentide while you sleep. Please be at peace in the knowledge that you are safe.*" Sage said as she rejoined the other Elites.

"*Tomorrow, we will meet here at the circle. We have more to show you, but we have other things to attend to, and you are not ready to witness them yet. River will send the Security Orbs to escort you nearer tomorrow's Darken.*" Phoenix informed them. "*In the meantime, I suggest you make use of the tools we have left for you. It is imperative to educate yourselves; information can be understood better this way.*"

"*We bid you Good Eventide.*" With that, the entities started to flicker; their forms undulated.

"Hang on a minute!" Ben cried after them.

Max shouted too. "What are all those firefly-Elan things?"

The collective, harmonious voices of five Elites spoke one last time, before dissolving back into the light forms they'd arrived in.

"*All in good time.*" They floated upward, flying away at high speed in an iridescent rainbow mass — rapidly followed by the security orbs.

The fireflies, or Elan Vital as they now knew them to be, swirled away in droves — back to the confines of the forest. Whatever they were, was still a mystery.

Now left alone in the sudden darkness, they stood quietly together.

"Are you sure we aren't all dreaming?" asked Suze.

"Dunno, but let's get back inside before the shadows start roaming the forest, and things turn into a nightmare!" Ben advised.

Back in the house, the conservatory clock told them it was nearly midnight; the evening had been exhausting. The Elites had told them they were 'on Essencia.' They'd discussed it for a long while, wondering where on Earth Essencia was.

Was it an island just off Great Britain?
Could it be a secret, new continent?
And that the word 'Elan' left them utterly confused.

After offering every tangible idea they could think of, they all sat in silence. They'd been quietly staring at each other for over half an hour and decided it was time to rest — so they all went to their rooms.

Unbeknownst to the others, each one had stood by their windows alone, watching the dark shadows as they milled in the forest. It made everyone's blood run cold.

After the shadows had dispersed, they got into bed and waited for sleep to take them...

Chapter Seventeen

A Night Full of Dreams

In vivid splendour, a flash of brightness dawns.
Feeling light and airy, a resonating tingling sensation accumulates in the air, soon to spread. It touches their fingers, arms, and legs, and finds its way to their core, up their neck and illuminates their heads. They begin to evaporate into plumes of white beads that sparkle like a million diamonds.
Distant notions of knowledge cloak them.
Emblazoned in light, their senses are heightened. The beings hang suspended in a dark night sky, though not for long.
At the speed of their own light, they vanish, travelling upwards so fast that long radiant streaks appear to escort them at their sides until they come to a steady halt, poised and still. Beneath them, in the dark void, is a solitary planet, covered with an expanse of greenery and areas of fresh blue water, distinctly separated into four quarters by a lengthy golden light that runs horizontally and vertically around.
In the distance, something materialises, buoyant in the blackness, alone and grandiose; again, a faint gold hue separates four quarters. They head for it; light particles dance around them all the way. Onward, further and further.
As they descend towards it, a slivery haze gradually parts for them, and the picture becomes real. Another world covered with water, dotted with areas of green and white land. Islands, large and small.
Getting nearer still, the body of blue, fresh, clear

water undulates and surges below; it rises, it falls, waves curl, releasing white foam at the peaks as they break, it ever pushes forward — giving way to wash softly on a shore somewhere.

It is teeming with life forms. Shadows under the surface, moving shapes twist and turn smoothly. Creatures push through the water, up and out, before arcing, gracefully diving back in; they appear to play joyfully.

Meanwhile, other enormous beasts join the fun; some surface, expel air, and create huge sprays of watery mist. Others breach in glorious waves and dancing water droplets before plummeting back into the depths and some lobtail, beating the surface with their flukes.

A swarm of colourful, iridescent life forms sparkle as they float aimlessly, blooming in transparent shimmers. Dark, pointed shapes rapidly surge through the surface, careering forward, flitting this way and that. The beings of light dart through the sky high above, dipping and rising.

Warm air from below drifts upwards, which leaves a saltiness on their senses. The clean air rushes and takes their breath away — they squeal with exuberance. The feelings of zest and vitality captivate their very souls. Things join them while they fly, swooping, zipping back and forth, under and over them.

Until a downdraft hits them.

They are free-falling instantly. Plummeting towards the ocean at high velocity, none have time to recover before they enter its surface.

They are submerged in an instant.

The sunlight filters through the clear waters, and a multitude of bright, glittering shafts of light waver, penetrating down to the depths. The troughs overhead are filled with frothy channels forming the waves above,

which then rise and crest.
They are not alone. Sleek, fast, and streamlined specimens bring sensations of intelligence, empathy, and affection, swim circles around them, through them, over and under them, in swirls of bubbles, clicks, and whistles.
Soon to accompany them, are beasts immense in size, who gently swim near them, hulking closer and closer. One of which eyes the light beings with a big, beady eye, before it calmly turns and moves away.
Fierce-looking individuals skitter around the perimeter of the fun-filled water dwellers, all different in species and sizes; they agilely cruise in wide circles. Other organisms flicker in multi-coloured lights; their tendrils float in a slow, lethargic manner like phantoms as they capture the undercurrents.
Lifeforms plunder above; their long, front, scaly legs flap in the water, dipping their heads as if to greet before they continue by. Below them is an array of life.
Beautiful plants hug together below in all colours, reds, blues, oranges, and yellows, while brightly adorned creatures with patterns over their bodies meander within.
But all too soon, they are being dragged, pulled; the water around them pushes them upwards.

Then another, sudden, glaring light.

In an instant, they find themselves looking down on what seems like a never-ending carpet of dazzling white. Huge structures jut from the oceans below.
More creatures swim in the coldness, while dark shapes flop into the water to join them; others lie sprawled at the edges, like they have nothing else better to do there.
Further on still, frosted white trees stand in rows upon rows, furry four-legged animals dart in and out of the

white forest. Creatures with huge sculptures mounted on their heads gallop, trot, and jump. Further ahead, large white bundles of fur play with smaller creatures who look the same, frolicking and sliding on the whiteness.

And darkness engulfs them…
Plunged into dazzling light again…
Lifting in brightness, once more…
Feeling light and airy, the tingling sensation in the air soon reaches their fingers, arms, and legs, finding its way to their core, up their necks, and to their heads. Before long, they become plumes of white beads, sparkling like a million diamonds, with feelings of euphoria and distant notions.

They hang suspended in a dark space, and then at the speed of light, they vanish again, coming to a steady halt.

They wait.

Then it begins to materialise.

Another enormous green world with smaller flashes of white and blue, buoyant in the blackness, the four golden quarters visible.

Once again, they descend further and further, through the silvery haze that parts; below, a world covered in a flush of green stretches as far as the eye can see. Trillions upon trillions of leaves proudly hang on their trees, rippling in a breeze, as if waving.

As they near the canopy, a flock flies up to join them. They continue together as a group. Huge airborne creatures soar by and eye them, their wings majestically keeping their bodies up while letting out high-pitched whistling sounds, before they grandly dive downward.

In a surprising moment, the sky is full of these creatures of every description. A murmuration dances to an orchestra in feathered silence.

The light beings approach a large body of water; this time, the water is still. They glide to a stop. Below is yet another sight to behold. Colourful winged creatures grace the water's edge. Wildlife swim attentively on the surface, accompanied by others amid the green oasis. Smaller life forms flutter about, flashing their unique colourations while they go about their business.

The beings of light shoot onward swiftly, only to find they are gazing down upon another endless white carpet. Large, dark blue patches in the whiteness scatter further ahead, with those huge white, pale blue structures protruding from the water. Creatures they've seen before line the shores; some play happily in the cold waters, and some fly in flocks over the coolness, while others sail the waves in droves.

Then a blaze of light engulfs them…
Then Darkness.

Chapter Eighteen

Nightmares

Day 6

It was now the sixth day. The clock on the wall told Ben, Max, and Becky, that they had woken early that morning. Suze and Nina were still in bed; they left them to sleep in; it was only 5:25.

"I had the weirdest dream last night. It wasn't a nightmare exactly, but it was a bit strange and felt quite real." Becky took a bite of the apple in her hand, and then looked at it — she frowned; she could see small dots of colour in the grooves where her teeth had bitten in. She rolled her top lip, then set the apple to one side.

Ben nodded, "I did too. I was flying to different places."

"And me. Did we all have the same dreams?" Max asked, surprised.

"Sounds like it." Becky replied, then added, "They looked like beautiful places in my dream, like the crystal picture show — it reminded me of how Earth once was."

"And me," Ben assured her.

"Anyway…what confuses me is, the Elites did say to 'make use of the tools' we have…I was awake for ages trying to figure that one out."

Ben tapped his chin in hope. "And did you figure it out, Max? Where those tools, are?"

He shook his head.

Becky pushed the apple about on the surface it lay on; the colours had vanished, then asked, "Where are we, though?"

"Essencia? Like they said. I really don't know what tools they are talking about either." Max shrugged.
"Yes, but where **is** Essencia?" Ben pressed.

Suze stirred. She tapped her thighs; for a moment, she thought they were made up of diamonds. She tried to turn over but felt paralysed.

Glancing down towards her toes, she saw the hefty weight stopping her movement. The dog was lying on his back, sprawled across her legs, snoring, his mouth wide open and his tongue hanging out. She slowly dragged her feet from under him, silently turned to her left side and promptly fell back into a light sleep.

She is running hard. She must get to safety, running, running for her life amid lights, and people...she is heading for the bridge. People are shouting and screaming. She stumbles and falls on the dead bodies. She's covered with their blood...or is it her blood? It's hard to get to her feet...the dog is at her side, he sniffs her, she is pushing herself up, it hurts but she continues to run.

*She is bleeding; it **is** her blood after all!*

Smoke, dust, and fumes are engulfing her; it stings her eyes and fills her throat. The lights are shining down on her, blinding her path.

She can see the bridge, it's so close. The dog is far ahead, bounding over broken things. She is trying so hard to catch up with him.

An onslaught of gunshots.

Someone falls in front of her...she is falling too and hits the ground hard.

Amid the darkness and dim pain, her hearing is dulled and muted, her ears feel thick and fuzzy...she can feel soft wetness on her chin, and soft fur on her cheeks.

Someone is whispering to her now, but it is too quiet for her to hear...soft lips, move slowly, forming silent words; she tries to reply, but can't.

Suze woke with a start; her hair had stuck to her face, and she was breathing loudly. She looked down at her chest, then twisted her arm to touch her shoulder blade with the back of her hand, expecting to see blood.

None. Just a dream, although this knowledge didn't stop her heart from racing.

Bailey watched her from the end of the bed, then came right up and sat under her chin, for a hug.

Nina was still dreaming too; she'd been tossing and turning, unaware she was tangled in the bed sheets; her legs thrashed, and her arms swung out; her pillows were wet from panic.

She began muttering and grinding her teeth.

She's shouting; she can just make them out, her vision is blurred in a thick red haze, her head is pounding, her legs are burning, and her arm feels numb. Three or four down-and-outs are gathering around her and closing in. She shouts at them again; they are rushing at her for the third time, with those long bars. She fumbles for hers and cannot find it. She is crying out as something strikes her shoulder from behind, then another blow to her thigh; the pain surges. She is confused, frightened and angry.

She is being hit again; her eye feels like it's about to

pop. Her head is swimming, she's rocking...her legs fill with weakness, and she is falling to her knees... she can see blotches dancing behind her lids — but...the gang have stopped, they are now standing still — staring at her; they've dropped their weapons and are quickly retreating into the shadows.

Nina's eyes snapped open; she lay staring at the ceiling, panting hard.

She swung her body from the mass of covers and sat on the edge of the bed, gagging profusely; her fingertips gently touched her left eye, she looked at them, no blood, felt no swelling — just a nightmare. She stretched her arms, rolling them on the shoulders, got up and made for the door.

Two doors were opened at the same time, Bailey rushed out from behind one. Nina and Suze stared at each other in the hall; their hair was knotty and tousled, their cheeks flushed and sweaty.

"You ok?" Nina asked her with a chuckle.

"Yeah, you?"

"Kinda...I think I just had a nightmare..." Nina replied, wiping her forehead.

"Me too, I think I died in it!"

Nina's eyebrows rose. She poked Suze on the cheek, smiled and said, "Nope, you're still here! Not dead, all's good!"

They quietly left the hall to join the others in the conservatory. Becky was walking towards them.

"Morning." Nina and Suze spoke together.

Becky giggled at the sight of them. "Too early for me. I'm going back to bed for a bit."

Becky headed for room number four and quickly got into bed and snuggled down; she was soon asleep.

She is in the alley.
The snow is falling heavily. She sees movement above and to the left and lifts her hand to touch it. It's a leaf in the wall, trying hard to survive just like her; she feels mesmerised and brushes the thin layer of snow from it.
Her toes are numb.
She is looking to her right. Old Tom is stirring, she doesn't want to talk, she feels frozen, so tucks her shoulders under the rags.
The moon is so bright, she's smiling at it. She is shivering and tired; her eyes are closing, but she wants to watch the moon. She sees her breath plunge in front of her, it freezes in a dense mist and is now drifting away like a big white ghost. Her nose is running; she sniffs.
She falls asleep, dozing and frozen, her eyes just won't stay open any longer, but...someone is calling her name. Her spent eyes open slowly, no one is there; she must have been dreaming.
She is now breathing into her cold, cupped hands.
Someone is running frantically, passing her by, she is happy she hasn't been seen.
From the corner of her perishing vision, she sees a streak of light in the sky; she is making a wish.
The shooting star tells her a story, soft and quiet, but she is too sleepy and too cold to listen.
Finally, she is sleeping in the bleak darkness.

Becky woke, pulling the covers around her; she was shivering. The chill in her bones throbbed, her fingers and toes looked white with cold; she lay there begging for the blood to circulate. She was sure she could still see her breath as she exhaled. With the back of her hand, she wiped her runny nose.

After just a few minutes she was starting to warm a little; she snatched a blanket from the end of her bed and wrapped it loosely on her shoulders, then got up.

She shuffled down the hall and stood in the kitchen unnoticed for a moment; she sneezed.

Ben spun around. "Couldn't you get back to sleep?"

"Yes, I slept. I had another dream."

Max was surprised she was back so soon. "Never! You've only just walked off Beck!"

Nina and Suze sat quietly looking at each other.

"This time, it was a nightmare. I froze in it."

"In what, Becky?"

"In my dream Suze, I froze in it; it was different from the first one I had."

"The first one?" Nina enquired.

"Yeah, I flew to beautiful places. Max and Ben did too."

"Places?" It was Suze; she was confused as hell and still trying to get over her own nightmare. She had said nothing to the others yet, only Nina. "Yes…the places…" A memory was surfacing.

Just then, a golden orb approached the house. It moved slowly and low to the ground, its bright golden glow mixed with the grass underneath and created a bluish-greeny-yellow colour. The group in the conservatory stood quickly, watching as it came closer to hover outside the windows.

"Good Waken," The orb greeted them in a deep, penetrating tone.

Max swallowed hard and told the golden ball, "It's early, it's not time yet, surely!"

"Indeed, it is early still. I will arrive later to accompany you to the stones, but first, I must obtain an answer from you all."

"To what?" Nina asked in a brisk tone.
"Did you dream last Darken?"
"Why?" Ben asked.
"Maybe," Suze replied.
"You each should have received two very different dreams, is this so?"
"I did..." said Becky, swinging around to see what the rest would say.
"What's that got to do with anything?" Nina probed.

With that, the group shuffled, fidgeted and glanced at one another, then took turns telling how many dreams they'd had; everyone bar two had dreamt twice.

"I insist you return to sleep Max and Ben; the Elites wish to offer information while you are safe. Please, sit down now."

Nina was annoyed. "What information?"
"I'm not tired though!" Ben sat reluctantly.
"Me neither!" Max sat.
"Then I must assist you."

With that, the boys slumped back in their chairs like rag dolls and were out for the count. Becky watched the orb as it headed back to the forest.

Nina slapped Ben across the face a few times, while Suze shook Max's shoulders. No matter what they did, they could not wake them.

He enters a derelict building and looks for food and water, he's standing in the broken doorway, he feels so hungry, so cold. People are running by; he shrinks back unseen and hitches his rifle to his chest.

Drops of dirty water are landing on his hair and shoulder, he lifts his face to allow the rank droplets to enter his mouth; it is trickling down his chin and neck; he wipes it, and the taste of damp concrete slides down his throat.

He can smell urine, excrement, and marijuana. He turns to see a woman slouched against the inner wall. She is covered in dirt and blood; she offers him a puff of her joint, but he shakes his head. He briefly wonders if he should make a run for it, and get back to the underground where it's safe, but he's searching for food. He recoils as rats scatter in all directions. He is considering catching one, to ease his chattering belly, but gags at the thought — and decides against it.

Through the dilapidated roof, he can see lights; they shine through, blinding him. Now the woman is panicking, she's shouting, he tries to calm her to keep her quiet, but she carries on; he is panicking too.

They can hear the explosions, getting nearer and nearer, a deep rumbling as a building collapses, crumbling to its final resting place, then more commotion, people screaming in terror and pain...now others join them in the run-down building. There's a loud craft above them, floodlights move back and forth, the building is moving, shuddering...things are falling from above, flashes of light...darkness...someone is talking to him, he can't make out the words, the explosion has deafened him...he tries hard to reply but his face is not working.

Ben woke screaming, thrashing his arms and legs, clawing at his face and eyes, feeling for his left ear — the girls gathered around him and tried in vain to calm him.

Max, however, appeared to still be in the land of nod.

He is hurrying away, commotion is everywhere, and the smell of death hangs thickly in the air. It's so cold, he hunches his shoulders and pulls his hoodie over his head. A woman is running towards him, he is wondering if it's her, is it her? She is begging for his help; it's so hard to hear her words. Gunshots ring out behind them, along with screams and cries for help. She runs off before he can speak to her.

It wasn't her.

He is moving on, he is sticking close to the buildings, keeping in the shadows, he is trying to find a place to be safe, nowhere is safe, nowhere!

He has bumped into a girl, she drops her bag, and he speaks to her...he can't see her face; she isn't looking at him. She isn't listening to him either. He is telling her...about the dangers, he is going to leave her, but tells her once again, the girl is nodding; she hears him.

He is rounding the corner, he can feel the sting of sleet as the wind pushes into his face...he can hear the shouting, he tries to focus...there are a group of people thundering towards him, guns raised and ready to shoot.

They are shooting.

He can see the bullets leaving their weapons; they rush forward in slow motion, getting nearer...something is above him, he knows they will start to shoot from above soon too, lights flicker overhead, as hot pain strikes his chest.

He is falling. His head hits the ground, and the hood on his top flicks back to lay on his shoulder. A shaft of purest blue shines down on him...

Max woke up, shaking his head and sobbing quietly. Becky went to him and touched his arm for reassurance.

Ben had calmed down and was just glad to be awake.

They'd all by now remembered their first dreams; it was only the second one that caused anxiety.

"I died...I died in my dream..."

"It's ok, you're still here too Max," Nina told him calmly.

Chapter Nineteen

Birth of Light

Day 6

On that sixth evening, they all trudged back up the hill as the sun started to set somewhere, O-2 in front, O-3 and 4 coming up the rear. The dog roamed about, and despite Sage's words the other day, the group watched for his whereabouts and safety.

They constantly searched the forest with darting eyes, looking for the shadows; it was a bit early for their appearance yet, but it was the one thing they all were extremely worried about. They had managed to avoid them every night so far, yet tonight, they knew there might be a chance they might not make it back in time.

Everyone had been silent, glancing now and then at their golden escorts, but Ben couldn't keep quiet for much longer.

He demanded an answer. "What's gonna happen to us?" The orbs said nothing. "Answer my question!"

"All in good time." O-2 replied upfront.

"Jesus, they always say that! — *'All in good time.'*" Max mimicked as he trudged on.

"Listen, 'orb man'…we wanna be back before those black things start roaming about, you got that?" Ben ordered.

O-2 boomed, bringing everyone to a standstill.

"Ben, you will all follow. You will all watch and listen to our Elites. You have no authorisation whatsoever to pass orders to the Security Orbs, is this clear?"

It was clear.

Despite their reservations, they knew they had no choice but to continue. Filled with uncertainty and hoping that their choice to submit would be worth it, they continued without a word.

Just as they reached the brow of the hill, a heavy mist formed deep within the forest; it illuminated in flashes as the Elan Vital whizzed here and there. It steadily found its way to the outer trees and was now tumbling towards them, dispersing, while grey clouds rolled and started to gather overhead.

Bailey appeared at the tree line.

Max became disturbed and stopped. Something was wrong. He began patting his shoulders in panic. "Crap, what's going on?"

"Shit, what's this?" Ben stuttered; he clutched his upper body with crossed arms.

"Let us keep moving." O-3 encouraged them.

"This is a trap!" yelled Nina. She tried to run but fell instead because her suit started to restrict her movement too. "Something's crawling inside my suit!"

"Perhaps then, it is better to stand still." O-3 finally told them.

"So be it. Let us remain still." O-2 instructed.

Suze glanced at her dog; he sat watching the spectacle unfurl, in the cover of the branches.

A cry of alarm came from Becky as the hood on her jacket curled its way around her neck. They spun round to see her frantic hands clutching the material, pulling it away from her skin. Suze ran to help her but stopped mid-stride as her own hood squirmed, climbing up and up to the base of her head; in Suze's mind, all she could see

was the 'snake and deer' scenario.
O-2 made his way back to the group. *"Please be calmer."*
Max, Ben, and Nina pulled hard on their suits, yanking the 'silver skin' out and away from their bodies. Soon, all five were writhing on the floor, fighting with their invisible foes.
The hoods on their jackets had by now covered their heads and were closing in around their cheeks. Hands were soon enclosed in the silver material, and the soft sock area of the shoes was creeping slowly up their calves.
Everyone was shouting and crying out for help.
The dog ran over to them, he barked so fiercely that his front legs lifted from the ground. Yet the three golden orbs simply hovered above.
"Please calm down. Your garments are reacting to the conditions," informed Orb-2.
"Arhhhhhhhh…" yelled all. No one was listening to hovering balls!
"Be still!" Orb-3 ordered firmly.
"It is just The Flourishing," O-4 told them. *"You are safe."*
Slowly, they stopped rolling around and sat on the grass, as heavy drops of clear liquid fell on them, bouncing and splashing off the silver material.
"I believe you call this — rain." O-4 added.
"What?" breathed Max unsteadily.
"It's…raining…" Becky noted under her breath.
The others sat spread-eagled, wiping and flicking droplets from their suits as they landed, with their silvery-covered fingers.
"Yes. The Flourishing. Your garments are protecting you from becoming wet." O-2 said.
The group peeked out from under curved hoods; a lip

on the edge caught the rain and diverted it away from their faces.

Then it started hammering down.

All five were startled as out of nowhere, a clear visor slotted into place from the lip and came down over their faces, then sealed itself to the edges of the hood.

Ben grappled with it. Max pulled at his, Suze tapped hers, and Nina just huffed and glanced at Becky, who sat quietly waiting for something else crazy to happen.

O-2 added, *"Your garments will safeguard your light against weather systems and atmospheric conditions, for now."*

"Why, what's up with the rain?" Suze stopped abruptly, tapping her visor. "…Light? And what do you mean, 'for now'?" She glanced worryingly at the others.

"The suit is simply reacting to your surroundings and is keeping you dry. You will soon not need them." O-2 told them matter-of-factly. *"Stand, we must continue. The Darkentide is approaching, and you are to observe the arrival of the Essence."*

Max pressed him. "What do you mean we won't need them?"

"What's Essence?" Becky wondered quietly.

"Don't tell me…All in good time, eh?!" Max scowled.

They got up and trooped on.

Up ahead, they could see all five Elites gathered in the centre of the gigantic stone circle, glowing and shimmering like colourful flames. The group approached with caution, and as they did, the Elites turned to face them. Bailey ran straight in and sat next to Phoenix, waiting for the rest of his pack to arrive. Phoenix touched him gently; he melted at her feet.

As they got nearer an Elite spoke; her head tilted to the side as her smile widened.

"Good Darkentide friends," greeted Sage; the other four Elites nodded.

Nina glanced at Suze. "Friends?" she mumbled under her breath.

By now, the heavy rain had stopped and settled into a mere mist. Everyone flinched as the visor flicked up and out of sight, the hood crept away and lay back on their shoulder blades, and the sock bit of the shoes slowly retreated from their calves and shins. They watched in bemusement as their fingers gradually appeared from under the silver skin.

They'd reached the centre.

Sol spoke, *"Welcome. I see you have arrived without complications. You are just in time."*

"In time for what, exactly? You really could have warned us about the man-eating suits, too!" Nina exclaimed, disgruntled.

"Our apologies, you were in no danger, I trust the orbs updated you on The Flourishing process," Phoenix replied. She patted the dog again, and he got up and wandered off to sniff and explore.

"In time for what?" Nina repeated.

Sage stepped forward, *"In time to observe the arrival of our Essence, Nina, you may find this emotionally disturbing and tiring for now, particularly Suze and Becky, but you will learn to lift your shields and protect yourself. In the meantime, I will shield you, should you need it."*

All five were stricken. For now? Shield?

So, Ben spoke for all, "What **bloody** crap are you talking about?!" He looked at Sage.

Suze frowned, not only bothered by Ben's language,

but also the mention of her name, and went to stand near Becky and stated, "You said we weren't in danger here. You told us!"

"And you aren't in danger; that is not our intention," Amber told them, her head dipped slightly forward; her fine hair fell around her features.

"Not making much sense, are you!" retorted Nina, stepping back.

River drew closer; they didn't dare move a muscle.

"You are aware of the Essence in the forest during the Darkentide, are you not? The forms that appear. They become the Elan Vital. You will have noticed them by now," he said.

Amber giggled and added, *"It can be a commotion at times."* She pushed the hair back from her face.

Max frowned at her — just then, her mannerisms almost seemed human! Then he turned to River.

"Oh, you mean the black things?" He glanced at the others, who were by now all breathing a little heavier. "We want to be back inside before that mate!"

"Arh yes, you have seen them, I thought so," River replied, ignoring Max's last remark.

"What are the black things? Why do they change to the Firefl…Elan…things?" Nina corrected herself.

No Elite replied to this.

"Can you all speak properly? Not in our heads?" Ben shot at them.

In an unnerving moment, all five Elites turned to him and spoke as one.

"We cannot. We do not have the ability to speak other than with our minds, Ben."

He scratched his head, unable to comprehend their words.

Becky strode forward in defiance, demanding to get a reply she could understand. "Answer Nina…about the black things! Why do we have to be here anyway?" She shuffled on the spot, waiting. No one replied to her; they just watched her. Becky's stomach clenched tightly. Feeling awkward, she slowly backed off, putting her arm around Suze's waist, she added, "We don't want to see them, they're scary!" A tear welled in her eye; Suze hugged her closer.

"We understand they appear to be worrying, but in truth, they are not to be feared; they only want peace. It is what they were promised." Phoenix stepped forward to stand in front of the frightened group. *"Allow me to explain this."*

Confused eyes switched to Sage as she spoke instead, *"The Essence is full of anguish and sadness — they are frightened and in need of the light and are the birth of the Elan Vital."* She paused and moved close to the group.

"Welllll, that explains it all now!" scoffed Nina sarcastically, still none the wiser.

"It explains **nothing** at all!" Ben faced the Elites. "Explain!"

"Phoenix has already explained you must educate yourselves; you must look and listen — it is the only way to truly realise. Take the information offered — you already know the answers to your questions." Sage said patiently, adding, *"First, allow me to explain the Essence process."*

Slowly, she made her way to a stone and touched it with the flat of her hand.

The enormous crystal lit up like a beacon; the purest of silvery white glowed in the darkness, with flashes of soft ultraviolet lights that scattered up and down it.

The group ducked in reaction.

Moving to the next stone, she continued to speak.

"Tonight, you will observe the arrival of the Essence." She touched the second stone, it flashed to life. She

stopped and looked back at the silent group — they followed her with unsettled eyes, their bodies rigid, as she moved on to the third and touched it. Again, it illuminated.

"Here, from above, they will descend and accumulate within the circle centre." She turned again to the group. *"This crystal circle is a safe place for them during transfer, a place of light, birth and empowerment."*

Max turned slightly to Ben. "She's talking in riddles!" Ben was on high alert and wondered if the centre was the best place to be standing!

They watched as Sage touched the fourth stone. The illumination was now almost blinding; their human eyes were squinting, their hands shielding them.

"Once all the crystals are activated, they will connect, and the portal will open from above. The Essence will be transported here automatically, and quickly too." She moved to the last stone. *"Before I touch the fifth, please move behind your previously chosen stones on the outer edge of the circle — follow us."*

The group spun on the spot, bewildered; the Elites had started moving away.

Bailey appeared, then disappeared.

"Hang on a bloody minute!" Nina crowed.

"Go to your stones and stand behind them, please," Sol told them firmly.

"Calm yourselves, you need not be afraid. Suze, come with me at once." It was Phoenix; she deftly moved so she was positioned behind Suze's stone. Suze didn't hesitate to follow and scurried after her, only to find Bailey sitting quietly there already.

"Nina, follow me now, please," instructed Amber.

River told Ben to follow him as Sol nodded to Max. They followed.

Becky stood alone, frozen, and for a moment, frantic,

but she soon came to her senses — her stone was empty; she dashed behind it. Sage was already there, and after checking the circle was clear, she touched the fifth stone.

"Observe, everyone, be calm. You will now all be known as The Paragons." The Elites spoke in one, symphonic voice.

A low hum surrounded them. The crystal tops far above their heads produced a glow so intense the group were worried it could blind them; they turned away, only to be told *'all was well'* and to *'continue watching'*. The Paragons tried hard to keep their gaze upward, and surprisingly realised they could see everything without too much trouble.

The Elites positioned themselves directly behind them, placing both hands on their shoulders.

Bodies tensed as the nighttime darkness was suddenly illuminated in a flash. Five shards of pure white lightning shot from the tip of each stone and met in the middle with a crack. That burst of energy projected a blaze above, which rapidly spread back again to meet the stone tops; it was radiant gold, like a cloud caught in a shimmering sunset. No one could speak; whether it was through sheer awe or utter terror, the Paragons didn't know. All that could be heard from them was the occasional gasp, moan and whimper.

"Be calm. You are safe with me."

Each Paragon briefly wondered why the hell the Elites had spoken together again and said — *'me'* — all at the same time.

In another unexpected instant, the gold mist drifted quickly down the edges of the stones, filling the gaps next to each, along with the gaps at their bases, creating a big round barrier between the groups and the centre. Now, no one could get in, and more importantly to the Paragons, nothing could get out!

Then, through the golden, heavy mist, they fell — like a dense, ominous fog; they undulated, squirmed, and writhed. There was a unanimous and unquestionable inner hope that the barrier would hold.

"Holy shit! Why are you bringing them here?" questioned Nina, trying to back up. Amber was in her way, her hands firmly fixed on her shoulders. "What are they? Let go of me!" she pleaded forcefully, wriggling her upper body in an attempt to free herself.

Amber towered over her; she had to bend considerably in order to lean over her shoulder. Nina shrank away on hearing the whisper in her ear.

"Shhh Nina, be still, and watch."

The rest of the Paragons were moaning and struggling in the same manner, yet none could escape the grasp of the Elites behind them. All they could do was watch in alarm, their bodies shaking, perspiration breaking out on their skins, with heart rates that were tipping off the scale.

Suze and Becky were suffering the most, feeling unbelievable amounts of pain, sorrow and confusion. All they could do was clasp their heads with rigid, clawed fingers and cry out. The others cried too, though they didn't feel the same tormented agony as them.

Bailey whimpered at their discomfort.

"Allow me to assist all. Your light isn't fully developed. It is hard, I know, but trust me." With that, Sage extended her light-shield in the form of an arc to encase and soothe all five Paragons and their dog.

Soon after, harmonious sighs of relief rang out, shoulders relaxed, and their breathing became less panicked. Bailey sat, lay down and placed his chin neatly on his front paws. It was like taking pain medication; the peace they felt was unfathomable.

Becky saw something, "Who's that!?" she whispered, her face screwed up trying to find the answer.

Sage gently squeezed her shoulders.

Before their eyes, behind the golden misted space in the circle, was a huge, black, misshapen, vaporous mass that twisted and turned in silence — it was contained and trapped.

From their vantage point, it became clear the golden ceiling was changing colour. In waves that spanned from its centre, along the top, down the sides and between the enormous stones, the misty golden glow changed to a beautiful bluey-purple haze. The one hundred or more long, dark shadows now within the circle suddenly became still at once.

Suze and Nina had witnessed something very strange in the circle, something blurry but nevertheless, familiar. They didn't know Becky had seen it too.

Very slowly, and just a few at a time, the dark, unmoving masses softly lifted to where they'd first come from, floating back up to the new radiant ceiling, where all immediately vanished.

The haze at the sides and bases that had separated the groups from the shadows suddenly dispersed, leaving just a perfect round disc of light hanging atop the crystal stones. It spun steadily and ascended slowly — but in the blink of an eye, it accelerated straight up, coming to an abrupt halt high above those below. A low hum murmured in the Paragon's chests.

Now spinning faster, it moved towards the forest, where it stopped once again over the treetops. The Paragons and Elites held their positions and watched.

Gradually, everything became darker as the Elan Vital that had gathered at the forest edges swiftly followed the disc and scattered beneath the canopy.

The Elites took their hands from the Paragons.

"Bugger off!! You're **feeding** us to the dark thingies?" Max spun like a top, his face red with anger.

"No."

"We have to hide you lot!" blurted Ben, his arms spread wide, gathering them together like toddlers.

"Where? Where can we hide?!" Nina yelled.

"Ben, you must stay here. You do not need to hide. Max, you are not to be fed to them!" Sol informed, then added, *"Come with us; we will show you."* With that, the Elites moved as one to the forest and glided in; they did not turn back.

The group shot glances at one another, wondering who would make the first move forward — who would follow.

"Get stuffed! I saw something in that morbid mass!" protested Nina, and turned to go the other way, but stopped and folded her arms sternly.

Go where she wondered? She spun back around to the group, just in time to hear Suze.

"I'm following them…I'm not standing out here! Come on!" Suze's voice was high-pitched and shaky; she gently grabbed Bailey's scruff and pulled him along.

"Yes…let's get nearer to the **black things, shall we Suze?!**" jawed Nina from behind. She stood her ground, arms firmly folded, her stubborn mouth set.

"Come on, let's go! There's nowhere to escape to." It was Max; he marched with purpose after Suze. Ben nodded to Becky, then grabbed her elbow — she allowed him to take her.

Nina followed, eventually. She stood next to Becky and Suze and said, "I saw something hazy in there, something familiar. Did you see it?!"

Suze turned quickly to Nina and was about to speak, but Becky dipped her head to the girls and whispered,

"So did I — I don't know what it was..."

"Thank you for joining us, Nina." Phoenix turned to face them all. Directly above them, the disc had lowered itself so that it was directly above the canopy; the trees below became a shocking shade of ultraviolet in its light; it hovered there in silence, albeit with a low hum.

She then added, *"Please be silent, observe and try to stay calm; there is no need to exert energy. Terror is negative; you will learn, and soon you will have no negativity at all."*

Ben stepped forward, letting go of Becky's arm. "Now, what's that **supposed** to mean?"

Phoenix turned away. *"Observe."*

So, that's what they did.

Unexpectedly, swarms of Elan came out of hiding. They darted back and forth in streaks and flashes around the Paragons and Elites at the speed of light. Some stopped, hovered and carried on flitting here and there.

Suze lifted her arm, and several landed on her hand briefly, like butterflies in a blooming garden, before shooting off again. The edges of her lips curved involuntarily, forming a smile of awe; she gasped as more whizzed and whirled around them. It even made Nina smile, thinly.

Then, from above, the three security orbs assembled as the shadows fell: their darkness glitched like a flawed TV screen.

The Paragons froze, and smiles left their faces as they backed up.

But all in all, the process they were witnessing

happened so quickly that they didn't have time to run before they realised that they weren't in danger after all. Because within seconds, the shadows had fallen, soon to be encased in the little Elan lights. They soared to and fro, up and down, through the dark masses and out the other side, touching and...

"What's happening?" Becky muttered breathlessly as she watched the spectacle.

"Are they **feeding** on the shadows?" Nina pressed in disgust.

"No, Nina, it is much simpler than that. The Elan Vital are gifting their light." Sage answered. *"An act of kindness. To bring light to the Essence."*

After a few more seconds, the shadowy masses became calmer, wispy at the edges. And as the Elan continued to gift their light, the Essence soon became cloaked in peace; they shrank to tiny ball shapes and darted off with the other Elan deep into the forest.

It was over.

"Congratulations, dear Paragons, you have witnessed your first Essence Light-Gifting," Phoenix told them.

"First?" Max asked, his brow raised high over his wide eyes.

"Indeed, your first, you have much to learn yet," Sol told them, smiling.

"Now you realise the Essence and Elan are not to be feared?" River inquired.

"Why were we separated from them then, by the barrier?" Becky wondered; she folded her arms in defiance.

"Hang on, we still don't know why we are here! What's all this got to do with us?" Ben asked seriously.

"Or where we **are**…or how we **actually** got here! What is all this?" Suze added.

"All in good time…" Phoenix replied gently. Max

tutted, looked up and exhaled steadily. Phoenix gazed at them with love and kindness. Suze thought she saw sympathy too, but brushed it aside as she spoke again,

"*Becky, their energy is too negative when they first descend. The barrier is just a protection measure, and although they do not seek anything to prey upon, it would be unwise to be in the centre at the time of their falling.*"

Sol continued, "*All we will say for now is…you are the last five Paragons to join us on the planet Essencia — you are in Sector 4.*"

Mmmm, there was that word again. 'Essencia' and now it was accompanied by another one — 'planet'! They all stood perplexed, considering those two words.

"*You are in the EMA Galaxy, approximately two hundred and fifty million lightyears away from the galaxy holding planet Earth.*"

Mmmm, and now another two, EMA and Galaxy.

It was like an aphonic dream; all sounds were mute, and even the silence was silent. A thickness surrounded them like the air had been sucked from their lungs, their bodies numb; their brains unable to comprehend at all.

Nobody had anything to say.

Did anyone take **any** of that information in and process it into something they understood?

Nope.

They all stood staring vacantly at the Elites.

Were they just figments of their imaginations after all?

Ben spoke; everyone turned sluggishly towards him.

"How did we survive that?" He grabbed his forehead. With mouth agape, he ran his hands down his face until his fingertips caught and hung on his lower teeth.

"How…how did we get here?" Max stuttered, examining his hands. "H…How…come we're not all dead, or haven't **changed,** got older, or younger…melted, or…whatever!"

"**Two bloody hundred and fifty? Bloody million?**" Nina gagged loudly. "But…how long did that take? You must be making this all up! We are dreaming, aren't we?"

"You are not dreaming, Nina. None of you are dreaming," Sage replied.

"For crying out loud, stop talking in riddles! **Will you just explain?!**"

"We will explain Max, but this will happen on your tenth day. For now, you need to re-energise; we suggest you go and rest. Please find the tools we have left. It is imperative you learn at your own will, for the growth of sustained knowledge and understanding." Sage felt for these souls; they were completely dumbfounded as usual, but they all seemed to be coping better than some of the first Paragons of Essencia had in the other sectors.

Utterly confused and in silence, five new Paragons and one dog from Sector 4 made their way back to the house, got into their beds and fell asleep until mid-morning of the seventh day.

Chapter Twenty

A Tool

Day 7

Come 12:30 p.m., everyone was up and about. They milled around solemnly — glanced through windows — brushed down the cushions and sat quietly in the conservatory, biting nails and deep in thought.

Last night had brought forth a revelation that left everyone in a state of disbelief. The sight that had been unveiled was so unexpected and startling that it never actually sank in. They were gathering new information all the time, yet didn't quite know how to process it.

They discussed the Elan; it was clear to them, that the Essence changed — from dark masses of 'something or other' into teeny, little lights. As they understood it, the Elan 'gifted' their light to these dark shapes, and that's when the shapes 'changed'.

It's as far as they'd got, so far.

Max got up and wandered to the telescope standing on its tripod in the corner. It had been there for seven days, and no one had had the notion or taken the time to look at it or through it. Until now.

He tentatively placed his right eye against the eyepiece and tilted it to the direction of the open door and the forest beyond, nothing but very blurred nature and Elan light fuzzies; he refocused the lens and watched them for a moment, they were indeed quite comical, some whirling about in the air, others crawling up trees — while many simply floated here and there serenely; a far cry from the dark things they used to be in the circle.

Then he raised the end, trying to find the first moon they had noticed days before. He turned the eyepiece to focus.

He remained silent for a moment; his arm shook, making the view unsteady, so he grabbed the scope with two hands.

His heart slowed to a pace that took the breath from his lungs in an instant — involuntarily fast breathing took over, while his mind tried to figure out what he was looking at. It was a sight that defied his human eyes.

What he saw was as clear as day.

"Holy shit!" He recoiled from the telescope, stumbling straight down onto Suze, who was sitting behind him. He tumbled over her and rolled off; he sat on the floor, staring at nothing. Heads snapped in his direction, having been clawed away from their own deepest thoughts.

"WHAT THE HELL?" Suze managed, jumping up and reaching down to help haul him up.

"S…sorry, so sorry Suze, are you ok?" he stuttered, pulling himself up to stand.

Suze nodded, "Yes — are you?" she replied, frowning.

There was a lull in the air, a silence so loud it was becoming unbearable as they waited for the explanation for Max's outburst. But he pointed to the telescope; his finger was shaking.

The rest were becoming impatient and fidgety, worried glances made their rounds from one face to another.

Max was stupefied; his jaw moved up and down in silence, and finally, the words escaped, "It's the 'tool' — the **TOOL. Use the tool!**"

Uncertainty crept across their faces.

Nina got it first. She stepped towards the telescope; four pairs of eyes followed her. Her lashes touched the telescope; she nudged nearer, refocused. Her mouth opened slowly.

"Oh. My. Good god!" she hissed at last. With both hands, she grabbed the telescope and swung it round to the other moon on their right. It hit the crystal window with a crack, though it didn't shatter.

"NINA! What is it?" encouraged Ben loudly.

She said it again, slowly. "Oh, my god!" Then backed away, turning steadily to the rest.

The look on her face was indescribable.

"Nina!!?" Ben shot up and grabbed his hair with both hands, digging nails into his scalp, waiting for answers.

After a few seconds, which seemed much longer to the others, they got off the chairs and quickly bundled over to the telescope, and following a brief disagreement as to who would go next, Becky pushed through the bodies and took hold of the optical tube. She adjusted the scope finder and refocused.

Planets, not moons. Covered with ocean and green lands, snow and trees. Mountains, islands and flatlands.

The planets from their dreams.

Chapter Twenty-One

Another Tool

"So, we'd have found this out before now, had we used the blasted 'tool'?" Ben couldn't believe why no one had looked through it, even though he'd stood by it just a few days ago.

Becky had gone back to the scope. "I can't believe we were up there." She turned to the group.

"We weren't up there Becky!" Nina slapped her own forehead with her hand and added, "It was just a dream!"

"**I mean in the dreams**! How come we dreamt of them?" She pointed up.

Max tapped his chin, "The dreams...they must be one of the tools! But what are the other tools? They said 'tools' not 'tool'!"

"The telescope? It's outright sorcery, that's what it is, I'm not entirely sure they are as 'good' as they say they are!" Ben spouted.

"Who?"

"The bloody Elites Suze!" he replied recklessly.

Max was thoughtful, "Yes, there must be more tools because we still have a lot of unanswered questions..."

"Yeah, like, why am I not hungry anymore?"

Ben said sarcastically. "Perhaps it's our recent discoveries Nina? Put us off our food? It's messed with us all — don't you think?" He stomped into the kitchen and opened the cupboard doors. And closed them again.

In the last few days, no one had made food, drank water, or wine. Even the dog had not begged for anything.

"Must be something in the air!" He'd wandered back

in, not getting food after all. "Besides, there's hardly any food in there now!" he chided.

"Really?" Max went off to look for himself.

"It's funny, but my ankle hasn't hurt at all since a day or two after we got here," Becky mumbled, taking off her silver footwear and examining the area. She looped her foot one way, then the other.

They discussed the fact that Max'd stopped sneezing and that Nina's wounds from the trees had healed quickly, her tinnitus was silent, and in turn, her 'brain ache' hadn't been triggered.

Suze then remembered her teeth from the first day they had found each other in her room. Nina's nasty, snarling face with a few bad teeth still hanging on, nestled amid a few whiter ones. While Nina had been talking just now, Suze had noticed that her teeth were now, nearly, all perfect. She decided not to tell Nina. How would she start to explain that anyway? Nina must have noticed they were different, with hardly a sign of discolouration — so instead, she remained pensive.

Ben's deep scratches had also healed rather quickly from his 'tree attack' in the forest.

It was as if Nina had heard Suze's thoughts.

"Yeah, and have you seen my teeth?" To which everyone took a quick look, frowned and complimented her like it was normal.

Suze asked, "Are we healing? We have no illnesses, aches or pains. Perhaps we don't need the food like we used to — we must be getting healthier?" She circled her friends. "Plus, Nina and Ben both lost their weapons... they've gone, so perhaps we don't need them either." She tapped Bailey on the head and let him out into the garden area, he shot off to the trees to play with the Elan Vital, who gathered rapidly to greet him.

Suze stood for a moment watching them.

Max was still thinking, his eyes vacant and wide. "Why are we so far away? How the bloody hell did we get all those lightyears away from Earth? As far as I'm aware, that's quite an impossible task — unfathomable!"

Ben paced, then surprisingly spewed out a ton of information.

"Yeah, and as far as **I'm** aware…we can't and never have been able to travel at the speed we'd need to get **that** far away and have nothing happen to our bodies! We would never have reached this place alive! As a human race, we'd never have been able to reach that speed, **ever**! Then, the wars started, so we wouldn't have pursued space any further! I also know that if we'd travelled two hundred and fifty million lightyears, we would be **way off** our solar system — because if I remember right…with **just one lightyear** of travelling…**at light speed, by the way — which we can't do I might remind you again**…we would **still** be in the middle of our own solar system!"

Ben looked up to see four amazed faces and shrugged, then added, "It's surprising what you overhear in the underground!"

Suze then had a thought, so she quickly and quietly left the conservatory, heading for her room. She swung the door ajar, stepped in and stood staring at the dresser under the open window. Then she moved to sit on the bed next to it. With slight uneasiness, she leant forward and pulled the drawer open; it was right where she'd left it on the first day.

Suze picked the hardback up and touched it gently with her fingers, studying the title. **EARTH**. She marvelled at its captivating cover. The title was written in a floral greenery, foliage intertwining over and under the word **EARTH**. Delicate pink roses seemed to come alive as her fingertips brushed over them, all nestled prettily against the backdrop of a luscious, mystical forest. There was a tiny Elan amid the roses. She knew the book held a secret, perhaps many secrets, all waiting to be discovered.

Dare she open it?

Could this be yet another tool the Elites were talking about?

The dog came trotting in with a stick and proceeded to chew it to bits on the clean rug. Suze rolled her eyes.

She opened the book. Nina had been right about one thing on the day they'd met: it was thin. And no wonder it only had ten pages altogether; two with text and another eight, all completely blank. She lay back and started to read.

The future of Earth had been hanging in the balance for thousands upon thousands of years; the race of humanoids that evolved upon her surface had doomed themselves, and her; their entire existence was damned.

Suze snapped the book shut and puffed out loudly. Bailey stopped chewing his stick, looked at her and got up to lick the book.

She knew all this! This wasn't a tool after all! She sat up, tapping the cover, thinking. But with nothing better to do other than figure out what the tools might be, she wiped the dog's slobber from the cover with her sleeve and opened the book once again.

She continued to read…

During the planet's timeline of the mid-17th century, one entity alone made an existence-changing decision and invested itself in an operation that was unlike anything ever witnessed in the history of the universe before.

And so, colossal preparations began.

Between the Earth years of 1900 – 2243, and with the intention to safeguard and continue this planet's life in some form or another, operation EMA-G proceeded faultlessly.

Very important choices were given to just sixty human life forms during this period, and upon agreeing to these choices, they were transferred to the EMA Galaxy forthwith, whereby they were housed to continue life thereafter.

Suze stroked away a solitary tear that had crept down to her lips, blinked, then continued…

However, there were conditions that befell the candidates for the entire EMA galaxy, chosen specifically from five of Earth's continents.

Not all would be suitable for this existence.

-All personalities must fit a certain criterion.

-All had a small window to make the choice.

(Those chosen and struggling to understand amid their confusion would be assisted, based solely on their promising characteristic traits)

-All would agree to live in, and live with, the light.

-All parties were assured to be fed the knowledge slowly, through the usage of the given

tools, to self-educate, to ensure their light would grow in a positive environment.
-All life forms must agree to gift their light and use their light to heal and protect.
-All Paragons will agree to oversee and encourage other life forms thereafter.
-And all must understand they would survive forever.

Suze slammed the book shut and sat quickly; her eyes were wide with distant understanding.

Just then, Nina burst in. "Alright, Suze?"

Suze jumped out of her skin, then babbled, "You have a book? Have you read the book?"

Nina was puzzled, then glanced at Suze's hands grasping a book close to her chest.

"Oh, the hardback you were gonna chuck at me?" Nina laughed, "I've not been in your room since that day!" she laughed again.

"Go...look in your dresser drawer Nina! You will have one too!" It wasn't a polite request; it was an order.

Nina quit laughing and left immediately, heading for her room without question.

Suze opened the book once again and read the last paragraph.

By the Earth year 2243, the EMA Galaxy will be Paragon completed. After which thereafter, only the integration of other life forms in need and/or in threat of extinction shall continue to proceed entry.

Upon the tenth day, all Paragons will come to the knowledge of their choices, existence — their powers; their newfound abilities.

Suze blindly closed the book and stared blankly into space.

In the kitchen, everyone had their copy.

Each one read a line of the criteria set before them. And amid their confusion, they started to put the pieces of information together.

-**All parties were assured to be fed the knowledge slowly, through the usage of the given tools to self-educate;** they had been learning odd things here and there ever since they arrived. The dreams, the telescope with views to the planets...not moons. And now this book, which they all agreed, would have helped if they'd found it in the first place!

-**All personalities must fit a certain criterion;** the Elites had already spoken of such traits in each.

-The word '**Paragons**', as they would now be known, which in turn, according to the 'list', meant other expectations were coming.

-The '**gifting of light**' too. That was about it. The rest of the 'list' was somewhat bewildering.

"What's '**a small window to make a choice**' mean?" asked Ben, tapping the page.

"'**Live in, and Live with, the light**'?" questioned Max, turning the book back and forth, in the hopes of finding something he'd missed. "...And what's with the blank pages?"

"Mmm, it's the '**Live forever**' bit that I simply don't understand. How's that gonna happen?" Nina wondered, closing her book and flicking it over her shoulder to an empty chair.

"Dumb tools if you ask me!" snapped Ben, and swung the conservatory door open. Bailey pushed by him.

Becky stood inspecting her hands, "It says we have abilities just here, look!" She pointed to the last paragraph, "We have powers now? Like superpowers?"

"I highly doubt it, Beck," Ben answered, closing the door again.

Max was in the corner, looking down at his hands and huffing outward after Becky had said that. He remembered the glittering breath on the hill and wriggled his fingers, half expecting a myriad of magic sparkles to appear. Nothing happened, though he did notice that his nails weren't ragged and the skin on his palms was smoother, probably because he hadn't been scrabbling in and over rumble debris for a whole week.

Suze pondered the last paragraph over and over again. In a quiet voice, she said, '**After which thereafter, only the integration of other life forms in need and/or in threat of extinction shall continue to proceed entry**'.

She placed the book sharply on her lap and stared into space. "What does that mean?" she questioned herself quietly.

Nina was looking at the dog.

He was sitting in the middle of the lawn, watching an Elan; it was circling him. It rounded him three times and shot off behind a bush. Nina giggled inwardly when Bailey jumped up and followed it. They both soon burst from the undergrowth; this time, the Elan was chasing the dog. Nina noticed a group of Elan lights had gathered at the tree line. And as if both the dog and the playful light entities had been called to heel, they swiftly joined the group at the edge of the forest. The dog barked, pawed an Elan gently and vanished through the trees.

Nina turned and realised Suze had been watching too,

"He'll play with anything…he'll be back later," Suze said, otherwise in deep thought.

Nina smiled and shrugged.

And he was — sooner, rather than later.

This time, he had six Elan in tow. Bailey lay on the decking while six little ultraviolet lights nuzzled into his creamy fur and became still.

"Now that's cute!" Becky gushed, "Are they all sleeping together? Awwww." The others wandered to the big windows for a better view.

Ben sniggered. He tossed his copy of the book onto the table. And said, "He'll be inviting them in next!"

And he did.

Bailey got up, trotted to the door, and just stood there — all six Elan lights followed and danced casually around him.

Suze shoved the book under her arm and attempted to open the door.

"What are you doing?" snarled Ben, grabbing her wrist.

She snatched herself away. "What does it look like!?"

She opened the door so Bailey and the Elan could come through. Without hesitation, the dog 'walked' and lights 'floated' into the kitchen, continuing straight through the hall to Suze's bedroom. She started to follow them, but turned to Ben before entering the hall and said,

"What difference does it make that they're inside? When we went to the stones, the Elan got **in** somehow to let the dog **out!** — I'd locked him in, remember!"

After a bit of grumbling, Ben locked the door, and everyone followed Suze to her room. She stood in the doorway, transfixed. The rest bundled in behind, peering over her shoulder.

The dog was sound asleep on her bed, along with six little resting lights.

"Made some friends then!" sniggered Max. Nina and Ben eyed him. "Sorry, just trying to make *'light'* of all this. S'cuse the pun Suze..." he mumbled. Suze, on the other hand, never heard a word of it. She hadn't moved; her book was still tucked under her arm.

Becky pushed forward in front of them all, looked at the bed and then Suze, who never noticed her there; her mouth hung open. Becky was blinking hard as she turned her attention back to the bed. Tilting her chin up to the ceiling at the same angle as Suze's, she looked some more, then squeezed her eyes shut tight and rubbed them hard, opened them again and waited for the blur to fade. Indeed, just six little Elan snuggled in the dog's fur, all settled and still. But that's not what she thought she'd seen at first.

The room was silent, no movement, no more comments, only soft breathing could be heard, until...

"Greetings, dear Paragons," Phoenix materialised outside the bedroom window. The group was snapped from their trances in an instant.

Suze gave a sharp intake of breath. The book dropped on the floor and clattered loudly, after raising her hands to clamp over her mouth.

Becky clutched Max's arm, making him jump out of his skin, and Nina swore loudly.

"Jesus, Phoenix! Was that necessary?" Ben chuntered, slapping his hand on his chest.

"I am sorry to have created a worry. May I enter?"

"You as well?" quizzed Nina, getting ready to leave for the conservatory. "You might as well. Everyone else is in here! Wait, I'll go open the door, I think Ben locked it again."

"Too right! Why do you need to come in anyway? We can hear you perfectly well from here, with all that brain talk, remember?" he informed her.

"*As you wish, I understand.*" Phoenix dipped her dainty chin. "*But I wanted to be sure you were all coping well; I feel your light is coming forth. There is a trickle of tension also. Have you studied the tools?*"

"We may have looked at something!" muttered Suze. She glanced back at the bed — one dog and six Elan...

Becky quietly pointed at the dog fast asleep on the bed. Phoenix leant forward to see, though she did not touch the crystal pane.

"*This is wonderful, he is integrating with the light well.*" A smile formed on her small lips. She craned further to count the Elan.

Ben saw this. "Ohhh, for crying out loud, wait, I'll open the bloody door!" he told her. The others looked at him questioningly. "Yeah, I know, I know! Does it even matter? Nothing's normal here!"

"*Thank you, Ben, but there is no need to open the door. Please be calm, be still and observe.*"

With that, Phoenix lifted, moving away from the window, until she couldn't be seen. The Paragons waited, wondering what she was up to and where she'd gone. They moved a bit further into the room, away from the door, and towards the window to look for her. Bailey glanced up briefly, rolled on his back and promptly fell back to sleep. The Elan Vital repositioned themselves; four drifted under his fur, while two settled on his warm belly.

"Look. Look, there she is, she's coming towards the window fast. Get back quick." Suze announced, mystified. They did as they were told; Phoenix got closer and closer.

Her luminance was so bright, it shone like a flood light through the window and settled on the floor as she neared and to their utter terror, she was gathering speed too. She was just about to make contact, crash into the pane, and smash it into a thousand tiny shards, but just before entering, something surprising happened.

The flowery wallpaper around the window began to ripple like a crystal-clear vertical pond. Softly, quietly, the petals on the flowers quivered — blooming gradually with intense colour. The once flat design protruded its foliage as it grew away from the paper; the leaves surrounding the flowers fluttered and curved outward.

The Paragons stepped back further as tiny, bright particles started to pass gently through the window.

"Sorcery!" proposed Ben, but he was gallant and swiftly stepped in front of the group. Max stood beside him. The three girls bunched together closely behind them, although they didn't want to miss a thing and slowly edged forward until they all stood in a line.

Then the fragrance hit them, bringing a trail of elegance with the most beautifully fresh aroma. It seemed to emanate from the walls like little floral notes, singing happily in the room; it was sweet and intoxicating — evoking mild trust and tranquillity, but no one could relax completely!

In the silence, tiny purple, white and silver light dots slowly erupted through the closed window, colliding with a few overzealous floral throngs crawling onto the windowsill.

Gracefully, the little pieces of light and colour danced and intertwined, creating a thrilling display. They began gathering in the centre of the room, each one coming together in perfect harmony in the colours of Phoenix's light — fluid and synchronised.

Having taken their place, some waited patiently, while more smaller sparkles of light appeared to join up. The dots zipped straight in toward her from outside, revolved and pirouetted like a small, magically controlled tornado.

Of course, the resting Elan had noticed the commotion

and were now swirling around close to the ceiling above her. Bailey sat upright on Suze's bed, his eyes fixated and his snout turning in circles in time with the Elan's twirling motion.

As the light particles crowded together and became compact before the Paragon's eyes, Phoenix's form began to take shape. And as the last few particles joined her, the group could already see her smile shining through the glow.

The window behind her had by now become a flat crystal pane again. Duller and much less impressive after that show!

They stared at her beauty.

"We have a door, you know!" Ben informed her mildly.

"How did you do that?" asked Nina in a fluster.

Max had gone to the window and was prodding the crystal, he even placed his face right up close to find the answer, which wasn't there. He turned back questionably, only to see the Elan sitting on Phoenix's outstretched arms.

"My dear Paragons, have you not worked out what we are yet? Who I am?"

The group frowned at their lack of recognition.

"A ghost?" someone suggested.

"A dream?" someone else asked.

"Hallucination?" Was added to the suggestions. None of which appeared to be right.

"I know one thing! We are all gullible idiots!" Ben was trying to work out the illusion; she'd tricked them into thinking one could get **in** through a **closed** window. "And can you stop talking into our minds and start talking **at** us?"

Phoenix smiled at his naivety. *"I cannot. It is all I know — it is all I have ever known."*

He replied hastily, "Listen, we are all very confused here, and clearly we aren't quite as bright as you seem to think we are, Phoenix, so...you carry on, continue to talk in riddles and tricks...let's see how far we get, shall we?"

"On the contrary, my dear Paragons, I play no tricks, and you all display the best signs of completion we have ever had within the Galaxy. You are set for greatness! Possibly far beyond my expectations."

That shut Ben up.

"Completion? That sounds ominous!" Nina murmured to herself; no one else seemed to notice.

Suze had been watching this entity. She bent to retrieve the book from where it'd fallen and walked slowly to her; she dared to touch Phoenix on the hand. The others gasped at this slightly troubling sight.

Searching deep in the eyes of the being, Suze tried hard to understand, and said steadily, "What does all this mean?" She lifted the book, opened it, and read a part out loud... **"After which thereafter, only the integration of other life forms in need and/or in threat of extinction shall continue to proceed entry."** She closed the book.

Phoenix's eyes connected to them all. *"The words tell the story; you must work that out for yourselves. It is the only way to truly know; this, in turn, will not bring such intense fear to you at the very moment of your understanding."*

"Another cryptic clue then?!" Max responded dryly. "Why the blank pages in the back of the book? Do we have to keep notes, draw pictures?"

Phoenix looked at Suze.

Then Suze said, "I know what you are. You're the light, aren't you, Phoenix? But **who** you are, I have no idea and what these words mean, I don't know that either."

Phoenix had spent a short time in the house with her Paragons. She told them about light and energy.

She had said, *"I am Light energy yes. Everything is energy. Light is energy, and energy, cannot be destroyed...but it can be changed, and manipulated. For instance, heat, light, even sound and thought can be destroyed but the energy behind it, the energy it possesses, cannot; it becomes absorbed, altered; it may then begin as something new."* She lifted her arms, *"All particles bear energy, their motion, the kinetic energy and their mass; even a particle at rest is a form of energy too."*

She then went on to say how she'd travelled through the crystal.

"Light energy travels through materials that are transparent; the air, fine material, water, glass, or crystal..." She gestured to the window. *"...and as you know, even my thoughts!"*

Suze nodded her understanding to that last point, while the rest simply listened to her words, scratching their heads, as she continued to educate them. In comparison, they looked like a bunch of primitive monkeys listening to a super-intelligent teacher.

Phoenix continued, *"...and, even through time and space. But our light does not experience 'time' at all. And it cannot travel through dark, nor can it travel through solid matter. But remember, dear ones, light can overcome darkness."* She paused for a moment to allow her last comment to settle, then continued...

"Light travels very, fast — in fact, in an instant!" Phoenix could see they were struggling. *"Allow me to put this into perspective for you. The speed of light travels at*

six hundred and seventy-one million miles per hour, that's, one hundred and eighty-six thousand miles per second."

She watched them with interest as they took in those figures, except Ben, of course. He was now nodding at her comments, like he suddenly knew exactly what she was talking about, yet he'd only overheard a conversation in the London underground years ago.

"Now rest. You need not attend the Essence's arrival this Darkentide. I suggest you explore tomorrow. Do not fear what you see; try not to let doubt take shape. Just know that you are in the light and safe with the forest. It will lead your way; it will also protect you." She started to fade, her human-like form dissolving in front of them, but before she vanished completely, she said.

*"Everyone, read through the book again, until it makes sense, because it **will** make sense to you; you just have to allow it. Remember your dreams. Remember the Essence ceremony."*

Phoenix wished them a Good Eventide, leaving them perplexed, and disappeared in a blaze of light, back through the window.

The group remained in the bedroom for a moment, simply gawping at the space where Phoenix had been standing, before turning to leave themselves.

Max didn't; instead, he steadily walked to the window, tapped the crystal again and frowned as a purple spark shot from his fingertip and out the window; he put it down to her static.

They all gathered in the kitchen after that and once again sat in silence for a bit longer.

"So, she...and the other Elites are made up of light. Did I hear that right?" questioned Max, studying his finger — his tone was one of reassurance.

"I guess so," replied Becky. "Now we know how the Elan got in the house that night and let the dog come to us Suze...they must have come straight through the window and unlocked it from the inside? If they are light too?"

"Nice..." muttered Ben in distaste. "We are in a lightbulb! How bloody comforting!" He lifted his arms and let them fall heavily to his thighs.

Max turned to Suze, "How did you even know? I mean, how did you know she was **just** light?"

"Do you know how utterly stupid that sounds?" bellowed Ben — no one replied to him because they were waiting for Suze's reply.

As everyone watched her with quiet curiosity, Suze shrugged slowly and explained how she'd guessed.

"It sounds unreal, I know. It just reminded me of something in the past. The colours, the magic. For a long while, before we got to the centre of London, me and Bay would go to a very old church, on the outskirts; it was so pretty, though damaged and derelict. It had a secret door in the floorboards inside, behind the altar...we slept down there at night with a few others. But before we went down, I used to watch the sun as it set. The broken windows had sharp glass shards sticking out at all angles; they reminded me of colourful teeth." She smiled at the memory and continued...

"They were that old stained-glass stuff — anyway, the sunlight filtered through those pieces of glass making a kaleidoscope shaft of colour, like a rainbow — when everything else was still dark inside, walls all ruined and broken...crumbling," she paused as if remembering, "it was like a sprinkle of warm magic, it made me feel special; like I was being shown something that no one else had ever seen. I wish we'd never left it, but we did."

"Wow, the light passed through the glass and not the wall..." Max noted, "Very clever Suze!"

"I guess so," she agreed.

"That sounds so amazing," Becky said with a smile. "All that nasty stuff happening not far away, but there was still a little piece of beauty nearby."

"Yes, but it didn't last long. The sun passed us in minutes — the light faded inside the church because, as Max said, the walls didn't let the light shine through, you see."

"Nice story, but it only explains about light or energy!" Ben stated. "Nothing else on our list!"

"Nor the blank pages!" offered Max.

Nina had been at the kitchen window looking out, not joining in the conversation, but did say,

"So, if she's light and everything's energy and it can't be destroyed — does that mean **she and the other Elites...and** the Essence and Elan live forever?"

"And what exactly are the Elan?" Max asked. "And the Essence, too, where do they come from?"

Nina wandered away from the group to the conservatory, set on being alone with her own thoughts; her mind was racing...

Yes, what was the Elan Vital, and what exactly was the Essence?

How could anyone possibly be just light?

Because no one can live forever! Can they?

Leaning against the crystal window, a nauseating sensation enveloped her, causing her to clutch her throat and swallow hard. It was as if an invisible magnet was pulling her attention towards the depths of the forest — Nina's heart grew heavy. A vibe had permeated the air, leaving her with an unshakable sense of dread.

Noticing that all the Elan had vanished, she stood up straight, surveying the tree line carefully.

In the abruptness it had come, the feeling disappeared again, leaving her feeling anxious.

Chapter Twenty-Two

Talk of The Stygian

"Thank you all for gathering so swiftly. I have something rather urgent to talk about. It is about the Stygian." Phoenix stood before the others and bowed her head. She turned away, not knowing how to inform her Elites of the impending danger. The Stygian had been around forever and no life form could keep away from its grasp. Yet now, with knowledge and plentiful light on their side, she had strong hope that they would prevail.

"Dear Phoenix, I knew there was something amiss. What ails you? Are we still wholesome? The dark is not at all in any sector, is it?" Amber asked sympathetically.

Amber was the newest Elite, given existence just a few thousand years prior. And although she had learned quickly, her naivety was sometimes worrying. She was the only Elite that Phoenix sometimes felt apprehensive about, but she also knew, the other Elites had gone through the very same concerns and learning curves, back in the day, whilst harnessing their light.

"I am not sure, Amber."

"Phoenix, I am aware of your worries. You are hard to read, and your shield is strong, but the gifts you blessed us with become stronger by the day. I must mention, the recent Essence delivery felt far more negative than usual." It was Sage; no one could keep anything from her.

Phoenix said, *"I say sorry to you all; I have kept this in the light and from you for a while now. I can only hope our Paragons, in all sectors, can cope with the Stygian, as I fear it is near."*

"The Darkness? It has found us, Phoenix?" River enquired placidly.

"It may have River, yes; in fact, I am sure of it — but just a minuscule part of its entirety. The scouts are near; I can feel them. Although the main mass of Stygian is millions of light-years away, I doubt it would take too long to get to us if it wanted. We must prepare the new Paragons for this."

Sol stepped forward, "Phoenix, we are the light. We are the strongest and fastest of all elements, far too strong now; the darkness cannot filter its way through us."

"Indeed, sweet Phoenix, Sol is right. We will not lose our light, nor let the negativity in. We cannot lose you either. We are one." Amber told her. With those wise words, it appeared that Amber was indeed up to the level Phoenix had hoped for at last.

"I will never lose my light, Amber. There is no fear to be had there; I have had a billion millennia to encompass and control it, live it. I do not fear the darkness. Yet the Stygian is becoming stronger in time. You must be aware of this. It simply means the new Paragons must fight with their light as well; I had hoped this would never have to happen. The energy in this galaxy is the strongest in the universe for billions upon billions of light-years."

River then asked, "Do you think they will blaze for us? I know Sectors 1 – 2 and 3 know who they are — who we are and why, but Sector 4 Paragons do not know; they are not fully in the light yet."

But Phoenix was sure in her words, "I trust they will yes. No one wants darkness in their lives anymore, do they? I have just made contact with them; I have shown them our light energy in a different way."

Sage said, "They must learn of their good fortune first, Phoenix. We already feel a change coming from them, do *we not? They know more now that the tools have been seen."*

Sol wanted to know, *"What of Marinas and Avianas? Are they infected also?"*

"I will be addressing them shortly to enquire," Phoenix replied. *"There is no need to concern the Paragons of Sectors 1 – 2 and 3 as yet, I believe this intrusion to be just within Sector 4."*

Chapter Twenty-Three

Paragons Exploring

Day 8

On the morning of the eighth day, the Paragons were in the conservatory with their dog, waiting patiently for the Flourishing to finish. No one was ready to be eaten alive by their suits just yet.

"Ok, let's go!" ordered Nina, swinging the door wide open and sticking her head out to check. "It's stopped."

"So, what about when we get in there?" Becky pointed at the forest. "It'll be dripping off the branches!"

"She's got a point!" Max reflected. "Let's just wait a bit, til' the sun dries it up, yeah?"

"Whatever!" exclaimed Nina.

"Now that's a good point. Where is the bloody sun? Still not seen it!" said Ben, pressing his face to the crystal.

Suze brushed up behind him, "Who knows, I've never seen it either!"

After a few hours of pacing in the house, they finally made their way out across the lawn and walked deftly into the trees. The lawn was still wet and dripping but, surprisingly, hadn't activated their silver suits. The dog disappeared to play, tailed by six Elan Vital, who'd spent the whole night in the same room as Suze and him.

They stood in silence, peering through the branches,

watching for threatening movements. The smell of damp soil and undergrowth filled everyone's nostrils; the woodland smell was thick and lush. Their eyes trailed upward to the tall, strong trees that rose far above their heads, a fine mist resting in the canopy; multiple rays of glistening sunlight shone through the gaps, twinkling like the pillars of a pearlescent palace.

A group of Elan fluttered from the foliage and swirled around and up, climbing like colourful vines on the thick tree trunks, while others sat idly next to budding leaves as if observing the Paragons.

They walked onward into the forest. More Elan gathered and formed a string of lights that hung down, gently swaying from the branches like lanterns, creating even more illumination.

The Paragons were now able to see their footing much better. The forest floor was covered in soft green moss and surrounded by mushrooms, grasses, wildflowers and ferns, like a splendid, sumptuous carpet. But the way was clear, just as Phoenix had told them. No excuses to trample on any of these little pieces of magic, because before their very eyes, a pale crystal pathway emerged from under the thick layer of moss; it twisted and turned through the trees like a giant snake in the jungle. All the while, little ultraviolet lights escorted them inquisitively.

Following the path and almost forgetting where they were, they laughed loudly, skipping, running and clambering at times as the land rose and fell. Little holes sprouted water while Elan played joyously in their environment.

The dog appeared, barked and shot up a bank with no trouble at all. He sat at the top, waiting for his pack to make it. Instead, they were helping each other up the steep, slippery rise; it seemed to be the best option — they were unable to stop giggling all the way.

Nina fell flat on her face halfway up; no amount of control could stop her from sliding back down on her stomach; she just lay at the bottom and laughed uncontrollably. But Max and Ben went back down to help; they unceremoniously hauled her all the way up to the top. By then, everyone had burst out laughing at the messy ordeal.

After brushing themselves down, they explored some more, meandering through this special place, twisting and turning. Until they came across yet another beautiful sight that simply took their breath away.

They wandered closer, and as they approached, all they could see were blue flowers with tiny little bells hanging from thick green stems. They blanketed the entire area; the smell was intoxicating. The Elan sprang up from chunky leaves beneath and flitted about with excitement.

Nina had roamed further along the crystal path; she could not wait to see what was up ahead. The little bell flowers accompanied her, edging the pathway that then split into multiple options to tread.

"OH!" she gushed. "Will you just look at this!"

As they joined Nina, all gathering behind her, a roaring gush consumed their hearing. Before them were three waterfalls, varying in height from just a few feet to at least twenty. They watched in awe as the water fell — tumbling over silky rocks, through the overhanging foliage, tree roots and mossy areas, filtering its way to a large crystal-clear pool. Their ears were marred only by a continuous, strong rushing sound; the spray accumulated and dispersed in clouds. Elan rested on rocks, some at the water's edge, dipping and fluttering.

Suze crouched silently to touch the water with her fingertips as it rippled to the shoreline — careful to avoid getting her suit wet.

Instantly, from far below twirled a swarm of light that ascended from the depths, getting brighter and brighter, Suze pulled back just as a swarm of Elan Vital surged through the surface, twinkling in the sunlight; the droplets of water swept up with them and fell in splendour, like a shower of Opal and Topaz.

Bailey jumped straight in, paddled in a circle, and headed back to the shore — shook himself dry, and in the process, soaked his pack.

"Oh no, thanks, Bailey!" cried Ben. "Watch out for the man-eating suits!" he warned the others; they started to run in all directions.

"I'm sitting for this!" yelled Nina over the tumbling sounds of falling water and plonked herself on the moss.

They waited and waited, yet nothing happened.

"Maybe it's because it's not actually raining?" Beck wondered aloud. After another ten minutes or so, they all agreed she was right.

"Well then, if that's the case…" Nina sprang up with a smile and shoved Max, who toppled headfirst into the water; Nina promptly jumped in after him.

Max bobbed up briefly. "Jesus, Nina, I can't swim!" He splashed about like a crazy man and started to go down again.

"Shit sorry I…" But before Nina could finish, or even start moving towards Max's disappearing head, a plume of Elan had encased his legs and was now supporting him from below; his head neatly surfaced and maintained its position.

"I nearly drowned Nina!" He blew water from his mouth. "I could've died just then! Luckily, it's not too deep!"

Nina was mortified.

In the meantime, the dog had jumped back in and gone off somewhere, while the rest had waded across the shallow edges and were now swimming as best they could, the rest of the way to be with Max.

"Max, I'm so sorry. Please forgive me." Nina was at his side, holding his arm. "I wasn't thinking straight at all, and…you'll be surprised to know that I can't swim well either. I don't know what came over me or why I jumped in!"

He stared at her hard, ignoring her apology, "That's twice you've tried to bloody well kill me, Nina!"

Surprisingly, his suit started to fill with air, it puffed out like an inflatable toy; he slowly tipped backwards, until he lay flat — bobbing about on the surface.

Everyone sniggered.

The Elan repositioned underneath him, then pushed him gently to the shore. Where, quite abruptly, his suit deflated like a popped balloon.

Suze watched in amusement, "Ooo, it must be our superpowers, let's give it a go!" she suggested and started off, then stopped, flipped over and lay floating on her back. She craned her neck up, "The only time I've ever been in water like this was when I was hiding from someone. I held my breath for ages!" She flipped back to her front and swam the rest of the way — clambered up the other side, wiped the droplets of water from her silver suit and waved to the others.

"I didn't balloon!" she giggled.

"That's probably because you can **swim** Suze!" Max spat.

"Sorry, Max," Nina told him again.

Becky vanished, and so did the dog.

"Wooo hoooo, over here!" She was standing on a small wooden bridge that spanned a stream, waving her arms. And as the whole group wondered why they hadn't seen it before they'd got in the water, the dog trotted past Becky, closely followed by his new Elan gang.

Max rolled his eyes.

Onward they went, exploring the deepest parts of the forest; it was indeed a vast sector — they came to realise they'd possibly only touched a small section of it so far.

The trees changed; there were large Firs, Oaks, Elms, Palms, Cherry Blossoms, berry-filled Rowans, Ash and many more, all living together in the same environment. Plants of all kinds, luscious and alive. And as they became ever more observant, rope bridges, caves and caverns — more flowing water and pools, huge rocks and boulders, all areas ordained with colourful, healthy plant life. And still, hundreds upon hundreds of Elan flashed here and there, in the sky and on the ground, climbing up and down trees and peeking from holes in the dark, rich soil, to which Bailey could not resist the smells and his urges to dig.

In the distance was a mountain range like no other, its tips hazed by low silvery clouds. Rising high and swooping down, only to rise again and again. Trees grew in abundance, yet here and there, great craggy rock faces protruded, jutted out and abruptly dropped off, giving way to waterfalls that gushed in a slow motion. The sunlight struck the water droplets, creating spectacular rainbows, curving from one side to another. Elan flew around and about, diving through the falls and out again; some hovered at the top, while others appeared to cling to the vertical sides of the mountains.

To their far left, nestled amongst the greenery and dots of deep pink, they saw a tremendous pale blue light; it seemed to pulsate as if in time with a beating heart. On further inspection, they noted it was a cave, where thousands of Elan Vital dashed in and out of its entrance playfully.

Curiosity took over, and the Paragons made their way to it. On their way, the group noticed they were being watched from afar by two bright security orbs. Becky waved, but they vanished rapidly.

Sometime later, they arrived in a dense part of the forest; it seemed to close inward, encompassing their bodies; the darkness was unsettling, with no sunlight able to peek through from above.

Yet a hug of pure beauty appeared just around the corner in the form of tall, thin trees and a trickling stream with waters that rolled gently over small boulders. Amid this beauty were huge pink roses — they lifted their heads in great blooms, quivering; the group stood gaping at their splendour. Tiny flowers grew close to the ground beneath, nestled amongst their greenery, shimmering with a lively light. The fragrance was heavenly, delightfully engulfing them, and the scent just grew stronger; a lingering trail of perfumed petals filled the air with heavy sweetness.

"Come on, let's go see." Nina encouraged them excitedly. They continued, finding a smaller path branching off to the right.

Yet all Elan had vanished.

Hovering ahead was just one. It seemed to be beckoning them to follow it with little bursts of light. It darted on as they approached, leading them along an ornate path.

The foliage was becoming thicker still, and creeping plants weaved through multi-coloured petals, finding anything they could to hold on to. Vines curled in luminous displays, flowers and leaves knitted amid the throng in a tapestry of nature — until they came upon a stunning archway adorned in an array of vivid hues.

Suze immediately recognised this scene from the cover of the book.

"We need to go this way; we need to follow that Elan," she whispered.

"It's just like the book cover!" Becky acknowledged.

They tentatively fumbled together under the arch of many colours, not wanting to leave anyone behind. The dog was close to their heels.

Then they saw it.

As if intricately carved from the mountain, the crystal cave appeared, bathed in light; a blue glow rippled and shimmered at its entrance. The haze coming from it shone on the surroundings outside. Emotions flooded over the group; its size was overwhelming.

The Paragons stepped in and were immediately captivated by the sheer brilliance of the crystals that adorned every surface inside. The cave was ablaze with light, which filtered into the cracks above, across the walls and ceiling, and hues of purple and silver danced, creating a kaleidoscope pattern.

A sense of awe washed over them.

The air inside was crisp and cool and carried a faint scent of earth and minerals. They embraced the silence; it was broken only by the soft echoes of their footsteps, the distant trickling of slow-running water and, now and again, hollow drips of water falling from above; the echo flowing back created a fusion of the utmost clarity and harmony. The group ventured in further — soon to find the source of the sounds.

"Watch out!" shouted Max, swooping his arm in front of Becky and Suze. "That's a sheer drop! Look!"

Indeed, it was. Tousling gently, far below the overhanging cliff-like structure, on dark rocks, through cracks and crevasses, the water flowed. Only this wasn't like the clear waters they had played in at the waterfalls. This slow-flowing water was a shocking fluorescent violet-blue, almost the same colouring as the Elan. It meandered over the solid levels and pooled thereafter in a magnificent, luminous lake. Mist rose soothingly, drifting upward and rolling steadily over the cliff edge in gentle plumes; the freshness took their breath away.

Ben secretly wondered if this was the moment their suits would activate and drag them into the blue depths. But again, nothing happened.

As they peered tentatively over the edge, they could see wide beams of light to their left and right filtering through possible gaps in the cave ceiling. Elan frolicked there on the surface like damselflies over a summer pond. The dog roamed, sniffing happily, his ears pricked and tail thrashing like a large creamy feather.

With their vision adjusting to the halation, it became easier to see the large crystal-like stalactites hanging majestically from far above and stalagmites rising like glistening white towers from below; they gasped in unison.

Then Suze noticed, "Look, some steps going all the way down, shall we go in?"

"No! We shall not!" Max replied at once, catching Nina's eye. He then turned to make his way back to the cave entrance, and the rest followed. "That's an accident just waiting to happen!" he mumbled.

Becky stopped and looked back. "There's something so importantly special about this cave," she finally said. "Can you feel it Suze?"

"Yeah, I feel sad too, don't you?"

Becky nodded.

They both jumped as Max hollered from the entrance. "Come on, you two, we need to find our way back yet, we've been out long enough!" The two girls slowly made their way out of the cave.

Instead of immediately turning right, to go back the way they'd come, the others stood motionless on the edge of another steep rise — looking out at the sensational view. Suze and Becky joined them, while the dog paced back and forth along the edge; then he started barking. But they hardly noticed because sweet aromas of soil, cool waters and damp forest were drifting upwards, mingling with the clean air and garnishing it further. In the far-off distance, a golden mist rippled, rising vertically into the sky in long, gleaming, silky shards.

Far below, crystalline waters flowed through the colours of the forest. Elan Vital gathered in dense masses, whirling round like vivid blue snowflakes caught in a blizzard — creating a hue that lit their surroundings. Petals and leaves seemed to blush with vibrancy and delight as the Elan hurried in all directions.

To the group's left, was a vast area of soil; they realised this was where the intense earthy smells were coming from. It was edged with a multitude of flowers in all colours; they swayed calmly in the breeze. Scattered about this brown area were large grey stones, gathering warmth and glistening in the light.

Bailey barked continuously.

"Shh, Bay!" Suze told him. He stopped with a whine.

"How did we not notice **this**!" gasped Becky in awe.

"I wonder what's being planted down there!" Suze quizzed.

"Do we have time to explore a bit more, d'you think?"

Max shook his head, "No, Nina, we don't. Let's go now before it gets too dark, and we lose our way back."

Ben nodded.

So that's exactly what they did; they went back.

While wandering back through the forest, they found themselves able to retrace their steps, finding the return route easily enough. The forest was cloaked in an otherworldly allure, enticing them to explore further, but they knew continuing to the house was a far better option.

The Paragons felt good overall, if not somewhat bewildered; life was seemingly safer than on Earth! Of course, this was all very abnormal to them and would have been for anyone else too; the Elites, the planets, the crystal stones and cave, the Elan, and spheres, not forgetting the dreaded and sinister Essence — all of it!

Sure, they kind of understood they were not on Earth any longer, which certainly raised many more questions, all of which, none could answer at present. They'd been told they were safe and should fear nothing here — but something still didn't feel right.

Was it the enormity of the place? The enormity of the situation? Surely none had accepted this as real, had they?

As they walked on, the Elan Vital seemed to whisper, perhaps secrets, perhaps telling tales of forgotten times, endless love and joy, or warnings, their lights beating rapidly like little wings in a new rhythm of life. Each moment spent within the forest's embrace promised to reveal more hidden marvels as if the very essence of the woodland was teaching them, sharing their knowledge.

Suddenly, Becky stopped, letting the others overtake her. A blanket of uncertainty engulfed her; every hair on her body stood on end, and she shivered. Just steps in front of her, Suze stopped too; she slowly turned to face

Becky behind her.
Their eyes locked.
A wave of unease washed over them. The atmosphere felt heavier, a far cry from the airiness just a few moments prior. The towering trees seemed to close in, casting long, menacing shadows that danced in the fading light. A sense of foreboding crept up their spines as if the very essence of the forest was conspiring against them.
Had they done something wrong? Or been somewhere they shouldn't have been? It was like in a trice, the forest held a grudge. How could the forest, once a place of beauty, transform into an area of unease so quickly? Like the very soul of the forest had been tainted, leaving behind a lingering sense of melancholy.
Suze was anxious as she sent a thought to Becky, *"What is it?"*
Becky considered the question slowly before replying. *"Uncertainty?"*
"Yes. Dread too." Suze took a moment to scour the foliage, the branches and Elan. A slightly shaded area caught her eye.
Becky watched her, then said, *"Listen."*
"I feel something. What is it?" Suze questioned.
"Danger?" she replied, unsure.
Without thinking, Suze extended an arm straight out in front of her and twisted it over so that her fingertips pointed up, then bent the elbow slightly. The centre of her hand was glowing, tingling with warmth. Tiny white dots appeared — swirling in the palm of her hand, soon to form a solid mass, like a ball. Then, without notice, a beam of light shot up from her hand and disappeared through the canopy. She didn't feel shocked when this happened; it almost seemed like a natural occurrence to her. Instinctively, she turned her arm back over again and shone her light straight into the dark, shadowy trees, like

a torch. They both peered at the illuminated area.
Nothing.
They were pulled from their conversation.
"Oy, you two daydreamers, get a move on! It's gonna get too dark soon!"

Becky had clasped Suze's hand just at the right time when Nina had spoken, dousing her light. Thankfully, she'd then turned away and moved on with the boys; no one had seen anything.

Nina, however, had glanced back at the girls, sensing something between them. She watched them closely and, unable to hear their conversation, she turned away again, satisfied that all was well.

Becky waited for a moment to be sure Nina had walked on. She studied her hands and placed them together curiously, then looked at Suze briefly for approval of her intention.

Suze dipped her head in agreement...

She gently separated her hands.

Between her palms formed an arc. It sparked with the brightness of forked lightning. Light energy crackled over the curve in thin white strands, throbbing back and forth from one hand to the other. Her body jarred at the sudden shock, and the arc blinked out, just like a switch had been flicked.

She said, *"Our powers? And...we aren't even near the crystal stones?"*

"Let's keep this to ourselves, for now," Suze replied. *"I've no idea how to explain this one!"* They hurried on to catch up with the others.

Chapter Twenty-Four

In Light of a Faded Seal

"Thank you for attending. I have news which affects all of us. I must inform you of this...the Stygian is definitely among us. It rests somewhere in the forests of Essencia, here in Sector 4; it lies in waiting since it cannot move at speed, before perfecting its timing. It has been seen close to our new Paragons, who, I must add, are not fully transpired yet. However, at least two are showing signs of illumination already!" Phoenix stood proudly and spoke calmly, addressing her companions: Aqua, Overseer of Marinas, and Luna, Overseer of Avianas.

She continued. *"Do not let its concern find a way into any of us, your Paragons or your Elan Vital, one slight void in our light and it will try to absorb us all."*

"How did this happen, Phoenix? Are we not fully with the light? Your light is the strongest; therefore, so is ours. How can anything so dull penetrate us?" Aqua asked, his deep blue eyes darting. Before mentioning, *"I believe it has not reached Marinas."*

"Nor Avianas," Luna added to the conversation, with her exquisite feminine softness.

Phoenix thought for a moment. *"I am positive it would have entered during a recent Essence transfer. Sage noted a deeper negativity than we usually encounter. The Stygian sent out millions of scouts hundreds of thousands of years ago, as you are aware; they will be filtering for light, and when it is found, they will proceed forth without hesitation."*

"Albeit slowly." Luna trusted.

Aqua took his hair in one hand, twirled it around in his

long fingers and deftly tied it into a knot on his left shoulder. *"What is your command for us, Phoenix?"*

"Firstly, I will initiate the Birthing process earlier than usual — tomorrow's tide; it will be only their ninth day, but they are progressing well enough to handle the Birthing. The Essence entry will have to wait for now, until River has inspected the portal for damages; it may need to be resealed and relit. The Essence comes through it encased with terror and negativity; therefore, within the realms of possibility, the seal may have been marred and, therefore, damaged and faded, just enough for the scouts to find an inkling of light. You must promptly and thoroughly check the seals in your portals on your return."

Luna stood, her moonlight eyes searched Phoenix's and asked, *"Do you require any assistance here? To help and guard while your Paragon's birth?"*

Phoenix turned away, lost in important thoughts and decisions; her companions waited patiently. She then turned back again to face them.

*"You must return to your planets at once — see that the Heads of Security Galax and Crest inspect the portals personally in all sectors and repair them if required. If they are sound, and **only** if your portals are sound, you may both send one Elite back to Essencia for support. They will then stay with us until the process of the Showing and the Birthing has been completed."* She nodded at her plan. *"Remember, if your portals are compromised, you will need to remain on your planets."*

"Certainly, Phoenix," Luna promised, bowed, and left gracefully at speed; a trail of soft pinks billowed behind her.

Aqua approached Phoenix, *"You, we — are strong. We are one light, the brightest and purest that has ever evolved in this universe. We believe in Us."* He paused, bowed, and at the speed of his own light, swiftly left too, fast enough to leave a bright wake of dashes behind him.

Chapter Twenty-Five

Raven & Orcus

Day 9

Security O-2 made his way to the house of Sector 4; it was far too early for the Paragons to be awake, but his orders were to be there for when they woke.

By 6:42 a.m., there were sounds of movement from within. He drew closer, and since he'd been told not to enter the location, he waited at the edge of the decking for someone to appear.

Suze wandered through to the conservatory half asleep, along with the dog and a few Elan Vital, following closely behind. Rubbing her tired eyes, she made her way to the central crystal door, with the intention of letting the dog and Elan out, and the fresh air in. She felt for the latch, opened the door a crack, and then recoiled at the sight of the security orb hovering above the decking.

She stared at it.

Its golden hue brightened in greeting.

"I wish you a pleasant Waken Paragon Suze. I come with an important request for all. Please do not be alarmed, you may fully open the door if you intend to do so. I will not approach."

Suze paused for a moment, and Nina shuffled in, stretching.

"What's **that** want?" she asked, yawning.

Turning to Nina, who by now was directly behind her, she sleepily replied, "To tell us something…" She swung back to the orb. "Am I right? Is that what you said? It's a bit early, I'm not awake yet."

"*Good Waken, Paragon Nina. Indeed, it is. Listen carefully...*"

"Yes, Ben, the cave we found yesterday. We have to go back there soon."

"For what reason, Nina?" he asked firmly. "It's miles away!"

"I literally have no idea!" She shrugged.

Max recalled the request, "Right, ok, so two Elites will meet us around the side, on the patio and escort us to the cave?"

"Yes, perhaps because we'd never find our way back there." Becky giggled.

Suze nodded.

"Ooo, sounds important," Ben smirked. "Escorted by 'the light.' We are, after all — **The Paragons**!" He used his theatrical voice, then added, "Well, what are we **waiting** for? Let's go get it over with!"

"We're **waiting** for the Elites…on the patio." Max offered, shaking his head.

"Alright, well, let's go wait for the Elites, on the bloody patio then!"

Suze was tired of Ben's childish mannerisms at times. "Grow up, Ben. Let's go."

So, they all filed out of the house. The dog was nowhere to be seen, but by now, his pack wasn't quite as concerned for him as they'd been nearly ten days ago.

As they rounded the house to the right, they noticed no one was waiting for them.

Were they early? The orb had said 'soon.' They stood grumbling and bickering for five whole minutes, wondering if they'd heard the golden ball wrongly. Left off guard, they continued to disagree with one another until...

"*Greetings, Paragons of Sector 4. No, you did not hear Security Orb-2 incorrectly.*"

The group was standing with their backs to the voice and became quiet immediately. They knew, just by the vocal tone, that it was not any of the Essencia Elites that had greeted them at the crystal stones a few days prior. This voice was different; this voice sounded like the air itself.

Slowly, they turned.

There, standing before them were two very different beings.

She spoke again. "*Greetings, Paragons. I am Raven. I am in joint command, also, advisor and healer to one and all on the planet Avianas.*" The entity gestured to the planet to the group's right. To which they side-glanced briefly and at first, not taking a great deal of notice. "*It is pleasurable to finally meet you.*"

The Paragons simply stared at the beings.

The one that called herself Raven was striking and not at all like the Elites on Essencia; although she appeared to be the same height, slender, same kind of facial features, that was about it.

Her hair was the blackest of black, with just a shimmer of deepest blue and was accentuated by her olive skin. It was plated from three places: one from the crown to the very tip; it was only when she tilted her head to the side, letting it swing lightly behind her, that the length of the braid became apparent. The two shorter plates on her temples were adorned with feathers of different colours.

Her eyes were again totally different, still slanted and wide like the other Elites, but hers were pure black and rather disturbing; there was no telling where the iris could be. Nearly everything about her was black or at least a very dark shade of blue.

Her flowing gown was deep blue too, edged with gold, as were the sleeves, but these were decorated with tiny fragments like finely chiselled onyx, with many angles for light to reflect upon. When she moved her arms, the feathery trimming below danced gracefully, reminding them of the wings of an exotic bird. She was utterly beautiful and terrifying at the same time.

She spoke again.

"We are here to escort you safely to the cave; we have important news for each one of you. But first, I will introduce Orcas." She stepped back, allowing him to speak.

"As you know, my name is Orcus. Welcome to the EMA Galaxy. I'm the mentor for our areas of Marinas, I am a Master Empath, Clairvoyant and Clairaudient, and Healer of the Elan and Essence." He paused, pointing to the other planet. *"I trust the Elites of Essencia are keeping you well?"* He dipped his head tenderly.

"Err, well…we…" Nina frowned but could not finish. They couldn't help but stare at Orcus's appearance.

In comparison, Orcus was rather less impressive than Raven and the other Elites, but still quite disturbing and different.

His white hair was pulled back harshly from his sharp features and slicked down to the nape of his neck; from there, it was tied in a tail, with another length of hair to secure it from underneath, wrapped round and round. It then cascaded down his back in delicate waves to the floor. His skin was silver and shining like a thin film of water had settled there, yet his unmoving lips were black. His eyes were also black — unnervingly, the irises were white and stark; his lashes blinked softly. He wore a silvery robe, made from a material like that of the Paragon's suits, and under that, a long smock of the same colouring.

He quietly observed the Paragons, their eyes darting over his appearance. *"Ahh. Please forgive my attire, I have come directly from the oceans of Marinas, where I was giving advice and checking on our new Elan."* He extended his whole arm this time, gesturing to the planet the group had first seen, once thinking it was the Earth's moon — he circled his arm a bit to ensure he had their attention. But the group barely took their eyes off him, never mind noticing what his arm was doing.

Raven interrupted their thoughts. *"Let us be on our journey."* She gave a polite smile and turned away; the Paragons became embarrassed and fidgety, trying hard not to stare any longer than necessary at Orcus.

They followed the Elites across the lawn in a daze, like obedient puppies and entered the forest. Suze and Becky felt anxious; the feelings they'd experienced the other day had been real. They still hadn't mentioned anything to the others about their 'powers', nor the fact that they had spoken with just the use of their minds.

Nina was a bit agitated. "Wait, what...? Hang on a minute!" she remarked quietly. "Suze?"

Suze slowed down so Nina could catch up at her side.

"Did you see what they did back there?"

"I think I know what you mean. Yes."

Becky overheard them. "There's **Elites** on those planets too? And more Paragons as well, maybe?"

Max and Ben stopped, turned and acknowledged they'd heard the very same thing, before continuing.

As they stepped further in, the little Elan Vital lights began to gather and follow. The dog appeared from the foliage, covered in more soil and more Elan.

The trees seemed to bow ceremoniously as the group approached, quivering and shaking their leaves to fall delicately on them. Up ahead, the Cherry blossoms waited, then shook just as they passed beneath. It was like a marriage, confetti in beautiful shades of pink and the purest of whites fluttered down with blessings of love.

A marriage to the forest, perhaps.

"It's so beautiful!" gasped Suze.

They walked on for ages.

"It's **so bloody far** away! How come it's taking so long?" grumbled Ben.

"It's a fair walk," offered Nina, holding his hand. He was totally surprised by her forwardness but ever so grateful for her friendship. "Come on, I'll pull you, you big girl!"

"Ha bloody ha…" he smiled.

They must have walked over tough terrain for far longer than they had the day before; it certainly wasn't the way they'd come, anyway. Most of them were flagging while the Elites shepherded them, one up ahead and the other behind.

"How come it's taking so long, Raven?" Nina shouted.

"Just a different route, keeping within the light areas," she replied.

Suze's and Becky's eyes met; they felt sure it was because of the odd feelings they encountered yesterday.

Raven continued to speak, *"Dearest Paragons, you are feeling weary?"* Although she was the one way in front, it sounded as if she was right there next to each one. *"Will you allow us all to assist you? To take you there?"*

"You are taking us there!" Max called out.

"You have misunderstood Raven's suggestion," Orcus announced. *"Allow me. Please be still and observe; you are in no danger; we only wish to help."*

"Oh, for crying out loud!" exclaimed Suze. "I'm sure someone's said that before now."

Orcus stood in the pathway and spread his arms wide, creating a white arc of light that spanned from one palm to another.

They were all startled — overwhelmed, they stood frozen to the spot. This was all too familiar for Becky, and she gasped aloud. Suze touched her softly on the arm to quieten her before she said anything else.

In a flurry of brilliance, a thousand or so Elan joined them, emerging from trees and undergrowth. They gathered around the Paragons, edging closer and tucking themselves beneath their bodies. The Paragons stiffened; their stomachs contracted into tight little balls as they began to experience the unnatural feeling of floating, soon to be lifted in a blinding glow; they were effortlessly hoisted gently upwards.

Bailey sat waiting patiently.

And in a warm, loving embrace, they steadily moved forward. The group at first had been unnerved because all they could see was the forest floor, leaving them behind, but as the Elan continued to gather, the ground below vanished in their light.

Gliding through the forest in a soft beam of luminosity and weightlessly suspended mid-air, they finally found themselves in a state of pure tranquillity. Elan Vital enveloped them tenderly, casting a serene ambience that erased all the aching from their limbs, along with any doubts from their minds. It was a moment of blissful escape from the constraints of the heavy hold of gravity and concern. The beauty of a thousand lights shimmering and twinkling around them was truly uplifting — in more ways than one.

The Paragons became aware of the low-frequency hum; it seemed each Elan wanted to speak, whispering explanations and reassurance, but none could understand.

It would become a moment that would be etched in their memories, a testament to the power and persuasion of what appeared to be pure magic.

Chapter Twenty-Six

The Showing

Raven entered the cave first and dipped her head in greeting. Orcus followed his companion.

Out of nowhere, the three security orbs had arrived and taken their place at the entrance, where they would remain throughout the process.

The horde carrying Elan dispersed, bringing each Paragon down to the ground so gently that they hardly noticed. They then gathered behind in the foliage, but the Paragons remained outside, not daring to enter until they had to. Bailey ran straight in without a care in the world.

"Shit...!" flustered Suze quietly, "That dog will be the death of me!"

"Ah, you are here. I trust your journey was safe. With no unexpected delays?" Sol questioned Raven, who was now fully inside the cave.

"Yes, Sol, entirely safe, no sign of threats at all," she replied, turning to usher the Paragons in with a wave of her hand; her voice echoed sweetly to the entrance like a flower blooming in spring; they could imagine petals unfurling, tiny buds appearing.

But they didn't move.

"What do you mean no signs of threats?" Max bellowed over. "I thought we were safe here!" They could all hear his voice echoing deeply in the vast mouth of the cave too.

Ben pushed through the group, chest out, and walked straight in. He was about to spout a remarkable cursing but simply couldn't. Something was very different.

"What's going on?" he inquired. "What is all this?"

Hovering over the cliff, above the pooling blue waters they'd encountered the day before, were tall crystal cases, twirling slowly in mid-air. They were not empty — each filled with a blueish substance that resembled the movements of ribbons caught in a breeze but seemed to ebb and flow like water.

Just then, the rest wandered in, mouths agape and eyes wide.

"What in the hell..." Nina strolled closer, "...are they?"

The Elites remained quiet, yet Phoenix ushered them further in.

There was something else in each of the cases, blurred images, pale, unmoving, hard to define amid those watery movements.

With a sense of dread, they all tentatively neared the cliff edge. None of them could take their eyes off the cases, each one trying so very hard to work it out.

"One – two – three, four, five? What are those there?" Nina pointed.

Soon, fear began to flow freely from the Paragons; it was something that had been expected and was natural for humans in this state.

In an immense tidal wave, their emotions crashed upon the crystal walls; the atmosphere inside became heavy with the weight of their apprehension. Every nook and cranny seemed to reverberate an echo in the surging terror that spun like a tornado — wishing to ground everything in its path. For the Paragons, the cave had now transformed into a place of tremendous unease, where the day before, they had just sensed sadness, along with an unforgettable feeling of specialness. They spun on their heels.

Phoenix placed an order. *"Raven, Amber and Sage. Please form the light shield at the entrance. Then extend it totally inward."*

Negative energy called fear hampered their thoughts and decisions as all five scattered in panic, not knowing which way to turn or run — none made it to the entrance. They were trapped.

The sight of this upset and troubled the Elites, but it was the very last time it would ever have to happen.

With the light shield now in place, preventing anyone from escaping and, more importantly, anything else from getting in during the ceremony, it began.

"Initiate captivation. From our core, it is the most effective and will stifle their confusion," Phoenix commanded. All the Elites became still. Opening their mouths wide, they sang one harmonious note; had this been at any other time and a moment of peace, the chorus would have been a simply beautiful sound.

In a golden mist, the note vibrated, sending energy waves of sound and light towards the bundling group. With that, a sudden bubble formed and began gathering the Paragons together to hold them at bay.

They became petrified, literally.

Their bodies felt like stone as they stood motionless, immobile, resembling lifelike statues. Unable to break free from the paralysing grip, every muscle in their bodies tensed, and their hearts pounded; all they could do was stand there watching from within the bubble.

"My dear Paragons, settle. We have captivated you only to save your growing light from damage." Phoenix told them.

The group tried to speak.

But only their thoughts were free.

Sol spoke next. *"Welcome to the Showing. You will not remember, but you chose to come here; you were not forced."*

Sage said, *"You will remember soon, but for now,*

your light is still marred by the recollection of who you once were. Please allow yourselves to relax a little more, bathe in the light we gift to you." She stepped back and allowed River to speak.

"Your final conditions had to be right. You were given the option to join us, and you all chose to do so. Once you had been prepared for the journey, we then set your bodies in the controlled-time unit within our vessel; we effectively suspended time. We can only sustain this state for ten days. After this, a natural bodily process will most likely exceed the limitations for character transfer. We then brought you here to the EMA galaxy, where we looked after you until your light began to show."

Amber softly offered, *"Your bodies laid in timeless situ, while your personalities were absorbed by your new light, and your characteristics transferred."*

Ben's face was red and screwed up; he had been about to shout something unpleasant before being paralysed.

In a moment that surprised the frozen Paragons, Suze spoke. If the rest had been able to move, the shock on their faces would have shown, yet this was an impossible task, so these physical emotions were kept hidden.

"What does this mean? I don't understand any of this!" she asked.

The Elites brightened with the sense of knowing, and smiles gradually formed on their faces, while mumbled thoughts began to fill the bubble as the others tried to speak.

Becky spoke. *"Suze and I found ourselves talking this way and spilling light from our hands on the way back to the house yesterday; it came rather naturally. Answer Suze's question, please!"*

"Yes, you and Suze will have naturally acknowledged the light before anyone else." Raven told them, then turned to Phoenix, asking, *"I believe their qualities are*

highly empathic?"

"Yes, you are correct, Raven, but they have much more to give."

Nina. *"Hello, you two? And you didn't tell us?"*

Ben. *"Ohhhh, for crying out loud! Again?"*

Max. *"Well, it seems appropriate since we can't bloody move at all!"*

Nina. *"Hang on, go back a bit! Can I just ask, **what the hell happened to our bodies? Because we are clearly ...still in our bodies**!"*

Sol intervened. *"Paragons, please, remain calm; we need to begin your birthing process a little earlier than usual."*

Max tried to halt this 'process' happening altogether and kept talking. *"What...wait? Would you like to elaborate a bit on that? We've already **been born** Sol!"*

*"**And, we still have our bodies**!"* Nina pointed out.

Sage tried to comfort them. *"The next step will come as a shock to you all. You are soon to witness your lifeforms before your demise; this is called the Showing. Please know that you are in a better place."*

*"Demise? As in **DEAD**, demise?"* Ben's thought was quickly lost in words and sentences as the rest started chattering.

"What?"

"...Zombies?"

"Are we ghosts?"

"Oh my God, you killed us?"

Phoenix reassured them. *"My dear Paragons, you are much more than those things, and we did not end your lives. You are the pure essence of your former self. A part that will reveal great strengths and abilities, ones that you never believed could exist."*

*"Former selves? We **are DEAD**?"* Nina babbled in disbelief. She was angry and confused. She knew if she'd

been able to move, she'd have pushed each Elite over that edge and made a run for it, leaving the beings stranded in the depths below.

"*How? That's preposterous!*" stated Becky, wishing she could pat her legs to feel the firmness of her body in her silver suit.

As if Sage knew their thoughts, she told them, "*Please, listen to us; there is nowhere else to go, and you chose to be here.*" She paused, glancing at Phoenix, who nodded, then Sage said. "*We will now release your holding. Please remain calm. Do not try to run, it will only result in more petrification.*"

The barrier holding their new Paragons suddenly burst into a spectacular array of colourful, glittery light.

After checking themselves over, the group bunched closely together. Bailey then circled, ushering them nearer to the Elites, a dog gathering lambs for slaughter.

But Nina couldn't contain herself. "What do you mean by our demise?" she demanded, thankful she could speak with her mouth.

"Demise means dead, doesn't it?" Max stated aloud.

Ben turned to him. "Don't you think we'd know if we were dead? How can we possibly be **here** if we are **dead**? Like you said, we've been born already! They are lying."

"We can't be. We simply can't be. Why would you say such a dreadful thing?" Suze sputtered, hoping the Elites would start making sense.

"Maybe, just maybe, our dreams were talking to us, Suze." Becky rationalised.

Nina was beside herself; how could this lot be so dumb?! "They were **just dreams — Beck!**"

No Elite tried to answer the questions and comments that were coming in volley. Instead, Phoenix ushered them to the edge.

"*Please come closer, I promise all will become*

clearer, my friends."

"You want us to jump to our deaths?" Ben complained agitatedly.

"We do not wish you to do that, only to look!" Amber told them.

"Yes, get close and you'll shove us all over!" Nina insisted; she saw Sage make eye contact with her.

"Not one will push another anywhere, Nina."

Nina shuffled on the spot; she knew Sage had heard her thoughts from the bubble.

With that in mind, Becky was the first to take a glimpse over the edge, followed by the dog. He brushed closely on her legs, making her jump.

She heaved inwardly; her hand shot to her mouth. Suze joined her and silently stared down.

"What is it, Suze? Beck?" ordered Ben. When no one replied, he marched to the edge. Max and Nina followed.

They peered over; their eyes slowly dropped to the waters below. They had been so preoccupied that they hadn't noticed the cases had vanished, but their contents had not.

Chapter Twenty-Seven

The Birthing

Resting peacefully and floating on the surface were five still bodies.
Their bodies.
The anger that had bounced from wall to wall earlier had now slipped from those surfaces in waves of sadness, shock and quiet disbelief.
The Elites gave them a moment.
A sense of hopelessness and sorrow consumed all, leaving them in a subdued state of despair. The fragility of their human life settled in their souls like a rock in a bottomless, silent void, bringing only hollowness and suffocation. In that vacant moment, they tried so hard to register those five floating bodies from Earth's past, but they were simply too numb to put anything into words. Emptiness ebbed through them as they grappled with a huge sense of loss.
In one harmonious voice, all seven Elites spoke — an aria of the utmost beauty.
"Welcome now to your Birthing."
A tear slipped from Suze's eye. *"What about my dog? Where is my dog?"* Her voice shook with grief and heartache; she couldn't see him in the water.
"Do not fear, Bailey was birthed in these waters very early on," Sage told her.
Suze turned to find him; he was doing the same old thing, sniffing and then rolling. She remembered seeing the 'fireflies' for the first time, when Bailey had reappeared from the trees, he'd leaned on her leg; his wet body soaking her jeans on the lawn. He'd been covered in

bits from the forest — and probably wet from this water, but then he was always wet. The water magnet.

"It is why he has never been afraid. His soul has always been pure; he did not need to wait long for his characteristics to transfer." Amber told them all. Suze dimly recalled the many times he'd just disappeared happily, bouncing, being goofy and running off to play with his Elan pack. It could have been any of those times, and she'd never known.

She turned back to the bodies.

All eyes fixated on the lifeless forms floating on the surface of the water below — seeing their bodies motionless and completely devoid of any signs of life was indescribably distressing.

The Elites waited on.

How could this be?

Nina held her hands up looking at the palms, she flexed her fingers, examined her nails then pushed her hair away from her face, but not before holding the length of coppery hair to the side and staring at it; her eyes dropped to the bodies in the pool; she decided that she was real, and they were not.

Becky hugged herself and bundled closer to Suze.

Could it be that they were now mere shadows, entities trapped between the realms of the living and the dead? Their bodies submerged in what? A pool of water creating eternal life and light? Or perhaps this was a twisted dream from which they still couldn't wake up. They tried to make sense of it all, battling with the finality of existence floating below them.

"But first…" Phoenix started, *"…please listen. We know your abilities are coming forth; you have used them already and noticed them in short bursts during your time here. Your light is stabilising deep inside your spirits."*

Sol said. *"You will have noticed your light, flickering*

by your sides, at your feet, hands and fingertips. This is all very natural for beings of light; you should not concern yourselves over this."

Each and every Paragon remained quiet, keeping their own thoughts to themselves. They all secretly knew what the Elites meant.

Nina recalled her fingers, as did Max, along with his glittery breath. Suze remembered seeing the light from the soles of her feet and managed to produce a torch from her palms of free will. Ben knew he'd seen something but had said nothing to anyone. And Becky had created a White-Arc of Positivity, which she would soon release to be something that was not expected of her just yet, nor for a long time to come, and then there was her apple, the coloured bite marks. Not only that, but they also knew how quickly they had healed — no food or water had been consumed for well over a week now.

They were indeed changing.

Sol explained the process while the Paragons stood in quiet consternation. They were to descend the crystalline steps together and enter the water, where they would stand close to their physical bodies. He then went on to explain that any leftover energy that wished to complete the cycle would automatically transfer from their bodies to their new light forms. It was also a time to bid farewell to their old life and embrace the new.

Ben piped up, totally confused. "What energy? Where's the light you're going on about?" He brought his arms up so wide and quick that behind the backs of his hands followed a streak of silver that split into thousands of minuscule stars. He cried out in utter disbelief as the starlight danced around him, swooping to join his body again.

"There it is, Ben. Right there!" Suze told him. The others stood staring at him.

"Right…so, then what happens to us, eh?" Nina cut in, unconvinced. "Is this going to hurt? Do you really expect us to **believe** this shite?"

Sol ignored her questions, telling them they would receive knowledge of their demise and the choices made; all would come forth, and all would be revealed.

But Phoenix answered some questions; she pointed at Ben. *"You have nothing to lose and everything to gain — as you can see, you are already in the light."* Then turned to Nina. *"You will experience no hurt, nor will you feel pain, only a distant knowledge of the scars you once knew. And yes, you will soon believe this, Nina."*

Ben stared at her in horror and back at his hands, the pit of his stomach reviewing the reality of their situation.

"Are we in Heaven?" asked Becky. She'd said it so quietly, it was as if she was on the brink of finally accepting the consequences or fate of her 'choice'.

Phoenix shook her head. *"No."*

"You are the abductors, then? No one else was ever coming for us, were they?" Suze questioned.

Raven finally spoke, *"Dear Paragons, remember, you chose to come here, you were asked the questions, and you then chose to come."*

"The questions in the book…" Becky finally noted.

"Hang on, I have other questions!" Max told them suspiciously, "What happens after we go down there? Do we get to come out, alive?"

Phoenix answered him, *"Alive in a different sense, yes. You will feel more alive than you have ever felt or have ever been before."*

It was all getting too much for Nina; she couldn't

accept the words of the Elites and why should she?

"In a different **sense**? **What the hell does that mean?**" she retorted.

Becky understood far more. She walked slowly to the top of the crystal steps and turned, looked back at Suze, who then followed to stand beside her; they held hands like little sisters and waited, as if about to embark on a journey to somewhere secret, somewhere only they knew.

Phoenix repeated, *"You have nothing to lose and everything to gain."* Then added, *"You must trust in me and the light; you must venture to the pool without our force, without our pressure and by your choosing."*

"What about the suit?" Ben stammered. "It'll close up, won't it?"

"No."

"This is insane! You want us to believe this crap?" Max argued.

"Yes. We have confidence in you — you will remember your choices once you touch the waters, which in turn, will set your spirits free."

With that last comment, a sense of awe and wonder trickled over Becky and Suze, and they slowly ventured down one step at a time into the shimmering pool. Firstly, their toes touched, and with the next step, their calves entered, then thighs, torso and neck; they wanted only to move forward, further into the warm depths. The water seemed to hold the secrets of eternity, promising a life without end. With each step, they could feel their heaviness lifting, replaced by the buoyancy of the silky waters.

Suze turned to the others on the ledge above. "Come in; this water's good."

The rest studied the girls as they continued wading through the pool to the far side and their bodies; Becky seemed to tread water and swim in parts, but Suze was taller and walked slowly. They seemed joyous, with no emotional pain or physical hurt, just laughing and splashing each other like children in an exotic pool of paradise, as the waters lapped around their necks and cheeks.

"Ohhhwww...!" That was all Nina could manage. And watched them motionless.

Max hollered down. "I can't swim! I can't save you; get out! Ben, go get them out for Christ's sake!"

"Oh, bloody hell!" he croaked and stealthily negotiated the steps; he went straight down and straight in, nearly bumping into a corpse. He cringed. However, on closer inspection, he found he was right next to his old self, floating quietly there on the blue surface. He didn't even go to fetch the girls. After a few minutes of looking at himself, he touched the cheek of his buoyant body.

"You do not need to worry about sinking; the water will keep you afloat should you not be able to touch the bottom." River suggested.

Max clearly couldn't count on Ben for help.

He crossly stomped over to the steps, hesitated, then took them two at a time, shouting, "Get out now!" But slid on the last step and ended up in the water, where, after a mild panic, he firmly placed his feet on the bottom of the pool.

By now, Becky and Suze had reached their floating bodies and stood beside them, gazing blankly.

Max was on his way to the girls and waded past Ben, who never noticed him going by. He was completely entranced by the sight of himself — still and cool to the touch.

On the way, Max stopped; his eyes could not miss his own self there, peaceful and bobbing gently.

Nina was shouting angrily from the ledge.

"That's right, you lot just leave me up here! I can't

rely on any of you!" she huffed.

Edging closer to the steps because she felt tempted to follow, she spotted her body, empty and alone. Nina felt sorry for herself; her coppery hair floated effortlessly in the water around her face; it reminded her of fire.

A surge of compassion rose from the pit of her stomach; it wanted to console, soothe and reassure the body; she reluctantly made her way to it.

The Elites gathered on the edge above and watched them closely.

After a few moments, the pool's luminous glow filled their hearts with a sense of purpose, along with an intense thirst for knowledge that they somehow knew would span across an endless age.

The boundaries of time and mortality became blurred, and a profound sense of interconnectedness with one another and the universe enveloped them. Warm waters lapped gently around, and a distant recollection of sadness, death and destruction passed through their minds, though never stopped long enough for consideration.

Then, memories of their choices were recalled.

They saw the bright, all-encompassing light that had flooded down on them. A strange entity was speaking, soft lips moving slowly, forming words they could now hear. It had said…

"My dear one, I am your Waken and your Darken. You are dying; let me help you. I can offer and promise a life everlasting, a life in the light, full of love and nurture. You need not suffer this pain and endure this hatred any longer.

Everything started to become clear as the information on their past was fed to each; the group had finally begun to understand — each one witnessing the very moment they'd fallen.

The voice continued...

"Hear me now and give me your answer quickly. I am in search of a life like yours. One of kindness and compassion, with a will to lead, defend and empathise.

You have only a short time to make your choice. But I will assist, should you find it difficult amid the confusion of your death.

Listen.

Will you agree to live in and with the light? Understand you will be fed my knowledge slowly, to educate you, to ensure your light may grow firmly in my positive environment."

"Yes..."

"Do you agree to gift your light and use your light to heal and protect, to enhance and calm?"

"Yes..."

"Do you agree to oversee and encourage my other life forms thereafter? Those that are also passing, those that are in danger of extinction."

"Yes..."

"Know that I will give you your life eternal."

"Ok..."

"Do you wish to come with me? To help me preserve life forms from my torn world?"

"I do..."

The entity had received her answers.

They all now knew that on the verge of their deaths, they had indeed agreed to leave.

The entity nodded, smiled warmly and said, *"Then allow me to assist you to the vessel, where, once stable, you may depart this world peacefully without further pain. Do not be afraid any longer. I bless and thank you forevermore."*

They remembered being lifted with kindness toward an airborne vehicle.

They felt the panic, where once it had tried to close in — it was now a million miles away, just hovering in the distance.

Their bodies were paralysed as they entered a brightly lit craft, soon to be placed gently on a surface that moulded around them, like a mother's womb protecting her unborn child.

An intense whooshing had then deafened them, their consciousness dropped abruptly, and they took their last breath, before entering a quiet, bleakness.

Their Birthing into full light was almost complete.

The Elites watched on, patiently waiting. The water below bubbled, flickered and swirled with lighted colour, because the last of their consciousness, characters and personalities were now leaving their physical bodies forever.

In a tremendous blaze, they rose above the pool. Lifting with utter gracefulness, where they hovered momentarily, their light grew brighter, and a multitude of colours that developed in vivid flashes helped to cast away any shadows that dared to linger. All five were bathed in gentle radiance and were destined to shine brightly, to leave a lasting imprint. From this moment on, the Paragon's presence would become a pillar of positivity, gifting and illuminating the life forms around them.

They had transcended, passing beyond the limitations they had once known.

Chapter Twenty-Eight

Colours

Phoenix extended her slender arms, inviting them to join her and the rest of the Elites.

As the Paragons lowered themselves and stepped onto the ledge, they were, at first, nothing more than a pure column of white light. The vibrant hues they had risen with followed them in twirls — a thousand rainbows began dancing and rippling across their newly acquired forms. A new kind of rainbow had finally dawned in Sector 4. Ethereal beings of solid positivity and illumination, all experiencing a considerable shift in their essence, no longer feeling fully bound by the restrictions of their previous forms, radiating strong energy that set them apart from the mundane world of planet Earth.

Standing beside Phoenix, they could see a smaller ball of creamy gold light, although it wasn't as small as the Elan Vital and certainly not as large as the gold security orbs.

It began to circle the Elites and then rushed to Suze.

"Bailey! Oh, Bailey, there you are! I can see you!" she gushed. His pale golden hue burst with love as she melted herself into him. For a small moment, they became one. But he soon materialised and, in true Golden Retriever style, dashed off exploring the edges of the cave once again.

"Well done, dear Paragons, you are brightly beautiful, how do you feel now?" Phoenix asked. *"You have transcended; you are no longer reliant on your physical state, you are — pure light."*

Suze gasped. *"I feel weightless..."* She spun to her

right and very slowly ascended to the ceiling of the cave, scattering particles that spread outward in little waves, before she came spiralling gently back down again.

Becky then said, *"Me too, I feel free…"*

"It's like… Like…I am whole again. I didn't believe you, and I'm sorry!" stated Max.

"All is well, Max," Sol reassured him.

Nina. *"I feel like…I…think…I've just turned really intelligent!"* She was finding it hard to describe her feelings, but it just didn't seem to matter that she couldn't.

"You are gaining the knowledge, Nina; you will understand more and more as the Wakens pass." Amber assured her, then said, *"Dear Paragons, you will not lose your sense of humour, nor your quirky traits at all; any doubts left behind will diminish in time."*

They turned to Ben. He had been very quiet until, *"Where have my arms and legs gone?"*

Sol answered with a smile. *"You can slip into a human form; you only need to think it, Ben. This will perhaps take a few tries before you manage it. Once you're happy, your energy will 'save' having programmed your state to shift at will."*

Sage told them all, *"I will help you if you wish; this is where we will see your colours."*

*"Can I **slip** into any form?"* He inquired amusingly.

"You will only be able to shift to a male human form, Ben," Raven told him, then added, *"…and like the others on these planets, they can only ever be the form they once were — if they wish to show themselves; however, this very rarely happens."*

All was quiet for a moment as they absorbed that last piece of information.

"Hang on one minute! Have I still got my clothes on?" Nina quizzed.

River answered her, *"Nina, clothes were part of physical beings. Your coverage here was not meant to last; they were only there to help you feel safe or somewhat familiar after passing, and to protect your growing illuminations until your Births were completed."*

"I'm...naked?" she sputtered; her light shuddered.

Becky was already materialising her human form. She appeared in a blaze of red particles.

Her skin was pale. Her big, slanted eyes were squeezed tightly shut in concentration before softly opening — unveiling deep maroon irises, with flecks of silver washing throughout; her lashes fluttered like wispy black feathers on her now blushing skin tone. She smiled at her Elites with full, pale pink lips.

Becky's hair was astonishing; maroon in colour with flashes of bright red and silver weaving their way through the length. She managed to dress her form in a long flowing gown like those of the Elites, it sparkled with red dots like small chippings of Ruby and Garnet. She twirled, leaving a spiral of glittering particles of light in her wake.

She touched her hair in awe. *"A bit longer, don't you think?"* With that, it grew at her command and stopped behind the knees. With a flick of her hand, the hair began to plait itself, and like a thick rope, it lay gently on her back.

Suze was soon to follow; her colour matched that of her best friend, a shimmering mellow glow of creamy gold. Her hair was now platinum blonde with glistening strands of amber and highlighted with pure gold tints — she ran her fingers through the soft length. Her gown materialised; long, light and airy. On its surface shimmered millions of specks of the purest brilliance.

She looked at her fingers, wriggled them over her head and as she did so, her hair lifted, turning itself into a loose but pretty knot at the nape of her neck. She faced Becky with soft beige, slanted eyes...her irises sparkled, complementing the golden streaks in her hair.

Becky was stunned. *"Oh, Suze! Look at you! How glorious you are!"*

Nina found it a little harder. But soon her form, along with her coppery fiery colours, haphazardly began to take shape. She continued to struggle alone.

Meanwhile, Ben's piercing green eyes appeared next; he was disturbing to look at, but as he took hold of the change, the brightness faded, becoming soft. Calm shades of light-filled dots took over, creating a camouflage pattern. He chose to wear coverings that resembled trousers, not quite ready to don a dress!

His hair had vanished; there wasn't one single strand on his head. Nina and Max were too busy adjusting their forms to notice, but Suze and Becky watched him closely.

He rubbed his bald head, mystified. *"I've found my arms and legs but lost my hair now!"* he mused. *"Sage, please help...? Something fitting...and like what I had before...?"*

Sage smiled, glad to help her Paragon Ben. She pursed her lips, kissed her palm and blew it towards him. And in a flurry of sage greens and neutral tones, Ben's hair took shape. Curls, curls and more curls, shiny and healthy. And, of course, the odd strand of silver wound its way through. Suze and Becky nodded their approval, so Ben smiled widely.

"Nina, please ask if you need assistance." Sage offered, but Nina wasn't listening.

Max had by now managed something...it looked to be some kind of all-in-one attire. He abruptly flicked himself into his new form with a shake of his head. He was the richest deepest of violet-blue they had ever seen; even his skin seemed to radiate the glow, particularly around his eye sockets, now encasing his black irises — the whites of his eyes shone a delicate violet shade. His hair fell loosely at his temples in flashes of blues and silvers; he was a stunning translucent shimmer — he nodded at his attempt and was happy.

In the meantime, Nina had lifted her arms, twisting them like flames from a fire; she undulated her form in writhing waves of leftover frustration. Promptly, her arms dropped to the sides, and she became perfectly still. The others watched her with anticipation.

Slowly, her hands turned upward, and her arms lifted once again in an altogether more controlled and purposeful manner. Nina's palms met above her head — she paused again. Then, swiftly swept them downward in a strong fluid motion. On the underside of her arms fell any remaining confusion, raging like angry fire and molten fluid, which then fell and dispersed instantly on the crystal ledge.

Sage was about to intervene, but Nina had taken full control. She lifted her face and erupted into a pillar of beauty like a dormant volcano that had suddenly awoken. Her skin was tanned and looked like it had been kissed by the sun itself. Fiery orange particles surrounded her, perhaps mirroring the intense passion that burned in her soul. And as her gown appeared, began a soft, drifting material that danced effortlessly about her.

They gazed at her in awe, a formidable, steadfast, strong-of-heart being.

With the newfound brightness, they crafted a display of radiance as they tested their powers. The air around them danced with hypnotic swirls of colour, blushing their new reality, woven with threads of pure light, like spiders casting their silken webs to the sun.

The ceiling above became a surface for their magic, as they painted rainbows that curved, flourished and twirled with every stroke. Sparks of excitement filled the cavern, revealing just the very beginnings of their hidden abilities.

The air crackled with energy as their light sent small lightning streaks overhead, where rainbows intertwined and spun, energising the crystals above.

Now, the Paragons understood almost everything, along with the choice they had made, and the promises they had been given at the beginning of their end.

The mouth of the cave served as a grand stage.

A sea of Elan Vital had assembled to herald the birth of their new Paragons; their sheer numbers were a testament to the significance of the completion of Sector 4. Joy and exultation filled the air, as the Elan revelled in their full arrival, with every leaf, branch, blade of grass, flower and rock, awash with their pulsating ultraviolet glow.

"Congratulations, Paragons." Raven smiled.

Sol told them. *"The knowledge of your powers will come forth very quickly, I suggest you become familiar with harnessing these abilities. The nature around will help and guide you."*

"We will need these soon, won't we? We felt the darkness, didn't we Suze? How did it get in?"

"I have felt it too, Beck," confirmed Nina. *"I didn't know what it was until now."*

Max and Ben listened on while Bailey's creamy light rolled around the cave.

Phoenix filled them in. *"Yes, Becky, we will need help from you all. We did not envisage this happening on your arrival. Hence, we said, you are not here to be intentionally harmed or to be taken advantage of. You are not here to serve us, nor are you here to fight and struggle. Nina, we believe small amounts of negativity gained access from a compromised area in the portal, where the Essence enters."*

The Paragons became acutely aware of the dark energy that lurked in the shadows, stalking the very light they had come to embrace. It filled them all with a sense of urgency, a call to protect and nurture these light forms, along with the incoming distraught souls — now that they had come to understand.

They knew dark shadows, although weak, were creeping ever closer, threatening to engulf everything in their path with negativity. So, they accepted their brilliance and talents with gusto, ready to wage a battle against the forces of the Stygian scouts.

With unwavering determination, they vowed to join forces and converge their light with the other Paragons in Sectors 1 – 2 and 3; there would be twenty of them in all, along with the Five Elites from Essencia, Orcus from Marinas, and Raven from Avianas.

They vowed to illuminate the darkest corners of the sector and restore its harmony. With that, the Paragons calmly acknowledged their quest and left the cave at the speed of their light.

Chapter Twenty-Nine

Let the Battle Begin

And the day came. The Stygian scouts infecting Essencia were on the move, unsatisfied with lying in wait any longer. Their thirst for light set the masses in motion to take their moment of glory. Some Elites were gathering on the lawned area, near the tree line.
"*Are we truly ready for this? Are we capable?*" Max asked, approaching Sol. "*Of course...we want to help; I just think we don't want to let you down. Am I right, you lot?*" Everyone else agreed, shimmering in a blush of brilliance.
"*Why do you doubt yourselves? You have all practised and performed perfect Light-Arcs, Ground and Sky-Bursts, along with gifting and nourishing. Your very aura lights the way.*" Sol circled the group. "*You have even shown us light arrays in showers that Paragons from the other sectors have not. You are magnificent; a truly balanced, wholesome group.*"
"*We are with you, Sol. All the way.*" Suze assured him. "*The knowledge of our abilities is taking time to settle, that's all.*"
Bailey whizzed back and forth like bolt lightning, emitting a trail of glitter.
Sage spoke, though she was nowhere to be seen just yet. "*Have faith, you are all splendid, and surprisingly so soon, you all have the traits of an Elite.*"
Phoenix materialised in the garden. "*Dear Paragons of Sector 4, I am certain you have **no** damaging doubts; it*

is only in your complete awe of circumstance that you question yourselves."

Amber, River and Sage joined them, along with their security orbs.

River informed. *"Our Paragons from Sectors 1 – 2 and 3 are arriving now, Phoenix."*

"Indeed." She masterfully held out her hands to the Sector 4 group. *"I wish to introduce the other Paragons of Essencia..."* With that, she swooped her arms wide.

Fifteen brilliantly white orbs streaked down from the sky, creating long flashes of light behind them; they came to an abrupt halt beside the Elites, where they began to materialise.

The new group gazed upon the arrivals. Each one was adorned in their own unique palette of colours that mingled and intertwined with the next, a boundless creativity in this breathtaking galaxy. Undeniably, they were all as magnificent as one another.

Deep within the labyrinth of towering trees, the Elan Vital had taken refuge, finding solace in the farthest corners of the forest. Each individual huddled next to another, forming a collective, merging to create bundles of ethereal beauty, and emitting a powerful glow that they hoped would shield themselves from the clutches of darkness, a barrier to repel the forces if any dared to approach until further help arrived.

The dance between light and darkness unfolded within the depths of the forest. The dark negative energy, driven by its insatiable hunger for light, came alive, and prowled through the intricate network of branches and leaves, then drifted upward, searching for a better view.

It pushed on up, through the branches, mingled in the canopy and emerged above it like a huge, angry storm cloud.

Yet, unbeknownst to these savage scouts, not only had the Elan Vital and Elites established a stronghold, but now, there were more formidable Paragons and one dog of Sector 4, and they were lit and ready.

The umbra descended from above, transforming the clearest of skies to dense shadows and tumbling gloom; a sense of unpredictability flowed in the chaos. Billowing shapes of wild, untamed darkness clashed with itself while preparing to dominate.

The Elan Vital became caught up in its fury and was dragged up and away. Their only hope was to keep their beloved light protected, bright and firm.

All the Elites spoke at once, seven voices, sang in perfect harmony. *"Paragons, bring forth your light. Gather the positive and guide it to the core of your very being! You are the light. We are all-powerful. Await the instruction to discharge."*

And as the wind began to rise, to twist and turn, thrusting their colours about in a chaotic fashion, fifteen Paragons from the other sectors rushed to stand in front of Sector 4's. And proceeded to gather themselves.

With every ounce of their beings, the new Paragons nurtured the burgeoning power within them. They gathered and moulded it — controlled and directed it. Bailey started his dash again, round and round, his creamy glitter almost lost in his speed, circling them all and never stopping, once.

Like seedlings reaching for the sun, their light

expanded and flourished amid the raging winds, radiating an aura of pure glory. They continued to channel the energy; their very essence vibrated with an electrifying force, ready to burst forth with an unstoppable surge. As they embraced their true potential, the light within them grew into a magnificent blaze, pulsating with this new energy that was both awe-inspiring and untainted by darkness.

Reaching for the skies with an air of authority, the dark scouts grew; adorned with brooding grey clouds and filled with impatient haste. Like the fingers of a thief, wispy, blackened tendrils extended downwards and outwards, as if trying to grasp hold of something — anything from the light below.

"Now!" the Elites ordered, their voices resonating on everything in the vicinity, leaving behind a perfect note that continued, never stopping or wavering, until the end.

With that, a battle between the forces of darkness and light erupted with breathtaking intensity. In a myriad of colours, the Paragons and Elites coordinated their power of light and began to unleash their abilities, holding nothing back, causing the air to ripple further, like disturbed waters in a torrential storm.

"Becky, your Arc please," Sol instructed. *"Send it up, create a barrier between the scouts and us."*

Becky brought her hands together and began opening them slowly, controlling the curve. Once established she mindfully threw it into the sky, setting it wide and strong.

Sol then turned to three other Paragons, each from different sectors. *"Paragons Finn, Cassy and Ren, prepare your Arcs…to assist Becky's."* All three deftly created their Arc and waited for the signal to release.

As the Stygian scouts were descending on Becky's Arc of Positivity, the impact was so forceful that the ground shook beneath them. The collision was ferocious.

Particles of both light and dark scattered in mighty waves; the explosive raw energy ran rampant.
"Finn release — then get your Prism ready!"
Finn thrust his Arc up and away; it hovered neatly under Becky's. Then he shaped his body for his ultimate creation, the Prism. He formed pieces of pure light and placed them overhead — they fused, creating a huge, almost transparent pyramid-shaped object, edged with precise angles and smooth, flat faces; it spun wildly: he summoned his White-Arc of Positivity, ready for his next order.
"Zeena, Seb, Kane, start uninterrupted Sky-Blasts!"
These Paragons from Sector 3 complied in an instant.
Ren and Cassy were waiting patiently, holding their own White-Arcs steady between their palms.
"Cassy — Ren release!" River directed.
They both launched their Arcs to meet Finn's prism. With a synchronised motion, the Arcs collided with it, refraction occurred, and instantly, rainbow shards escaped, shooting out at all angles. Becky held her own Arc firmly to protect the Prism.
The seven Elites stood strong, casting wide rays like stoplights to keep the scouts at bay while the battle took place; they were accompanied by Bea and Elsie from Sector 1 and Lily from Sector 3.
Two Paragons from Sector 1 joined forces, merging, becoming one huge blaze of purest white. Working closely together, they caused an explosion so bright it could blind human eyes.
Nina's passion ignited with the devotion of her inside protector. She Ground-Burst, her hands shot downward, unleashing a fiery eruption that bounced thunderously. The wave of energy was so strong that it knocked a few Paragons off their feet, but the rising aftershock was worse; the blackened clouds above took full force,

undulating and writhing, yet still trying to penetrate the Arcs and Finn's Prism.

Ben and Max steadied themselves, feet apart, on bent knees, and with the skill of master artists — in unison, they discharged a Sky-Burst towards the layer of negativity. It penetrated through the Light-Battle above and hit the darkness — an upsurge so dense in energy that the scouts visibly recoiled.

Suze used her newfound ability of Light-Showering. She sent her lambent shower straight through the Arcs, swooping it round to hang over the darkness. Once it was positioned above, she allowed it to pour relentlessly in torrents of luminosity. The scouts unleashed outrage. Determination was high and so hurtled resentment downwards in droves, its malevolence seeking to extinguish the brilliance of all light beings.

"Cassy...watch out!" Someone yelled. It was Paragon Ava from Sector 2; she could not leave her position — she was holding the dark horde at bay with her rapid violet Bolt-Bursts.

Against the gleaming odds and forward warning, Paragon Cassy from Sector 3 was hit hard, her pale pink light all but absorbed by the negative force; she was failing fast, a mere flicker. Sage flashed to her side in an instant and gifted, while Bailey left circling his pack and headed straight for Cassy, he appeared to sit on her — his creamy glitter melted into her hue.

Out of nowhere, another, smaller white orb appeared and dashed about them.

Nina, who had also seen Cassy's energy taken, gifted her a shot of light. A fiery blue surge darted towards her; it mixed with her colour, creating a purple haze. And in this instance, Bailey and the smaller orb darted off to circle the perimeter together.

The Light, with their never-ending determination,

launched a relentless assault, striking with all their might from every possible direction. Their synchronised attacks created a pattern of power, shaking the very foundations of darkness.

Luke from Sector 2, drove a Blanket-Wave outward in pale shades of green, a swell of battering lustrousness. It ripped effortlessly through the entire lower areas of the forest, breathing freshness and life back into the dimming foliage and Elan Vital.

As their blows intensified, the malevolent force began to falter, its grip on the light weakening with each push.

"Grace, catch!" yelled Carter-S2.

Carter effortlessly juggled five silver Molten-light orbs, each presenting shiny, pure and smooth. As he skillfully manoeuvred them, tiny sparks danced along the edges. With a fluid motion, he tossed two of them towards Grace, who caught them effortlessly, one in each hand, swiftly launching them towards the straggling scouts. Zeena, Seb and Kane continued with their powerful Sky-blasts.

Gradually, the tendrils of darkness started to recede like recoiling serpents, briskly retreating, unable to withstand the onslaught, and fading away in small explosions of ultraviolet. Possibly having been caught off guard by the positive strength, it seemed several areas of negativity made wise choices and turned to the light, forever able to live without fear and confusion. And as for the rest of the mass, it simply vanished, allowing the light to reclaim its territory.

Just like a curtain being drawn back from a blackened window, the once obscured sky was now able to reveal itself. An atmosphere filled with serenity, a pristine space of clear blue, with a silvery aurora borealis calmly shimmering.

Chapter Thirty

The Knowledge of Truth

Over the coming days, as the pieces of the puzzle fell into place, Sector 4's minds were flooded with a torrent of understanding. The knowledge they had accumulated was forming a solid picture, shining a path of clarity. The abstract concepts of light, dark and energy that were once shrouded in mystery now stood proudly before them in vibrant hues. The Paragons could at last make sense of the intricate connection between these forces — how they intertwined with the very fabric of all existence, along with the effects they had on all life forms within the universe.

Perhaps the most surprising revelation to them was the identity of Phoenix.

She was their Mother Earth and had risen from her own ashes, radiating an aura of strength and resilience. And since her cries for help, 'The Noise', had gone unheard, she departed; although she did not abandon her life forms, only her dying planet. The echoing energy of her urgent request for help remained on Earth for aeons to come.

She'd undergone a remarkable change, a total and complete transformation full of courage and hope, for the second time in the history of the universe.

In a moment of splendour, Phoenix Elite-1 was born.

She rose, fragmenting her earthly spirit into separate entities, resulting in a band of powerful life forms and a brand-new galaxy, consisting of three enormous worlds, crafted by positive energy alone. The light. Her galaxy pulsated with the power of an unfathomable number of shining stars.

Phoenix had brought with her many things, including the essence of Earth's plant life; all species from trees and flowers to seaweeds and corals to adorn each planet's sector, ensuring the best environment for the Elan Vital, and maintaining worlds that were as familiar to them as possible.

Planet Essencia: For all life forms that chose regular temperatures with a selection of land and water needs. Including saline water and fresh water and a vast variety of plant life.

Planet Marinas: Mostly aquatic life forms, seafaring birds and animals, a planet full of oceans and islands — split for warmer and colder climates. Including fresh water and varying plant life.

Planet Avianas: Mostly inhabited by avian life forms, though others chose to inhabit this world too. A world of water and earth, split for warmer and colder climates. This world also included saline water and fresh water, along with a multitude of different plant species.

The enigmatic mystery of the Essence and Elan, a notion that had eluded their thoughts, now revealed itself as the reason behind the creation and innovation of a new galaxy. The dreams they'd shared had shown just some of the creatures that were on each of the planets, but as they'd been told, they rarely materialised into their past forms, preferring to keep within their Elan Vital light; unless, of course, they wished you to know exactly who, and what they were.

The once-feared Essence, who arrived as mere dark shadows, shrouded in despair, writhing and terrorised after falling from a disc above the canopy, were the souls of selected earth species — where they could gather after being promised a life everlasting; they would be preserved forever. Animal souls of water, earth and sky, who found themselves in peril or on the brink of extinction. Human souls with all hope lost and were dying. All arrived in complete confusion, most not remembering their choices.

There were two choices to be made: to leave the earthly planet upon their deaths and then choose a planet where they could exist forever within the light.

Once the choices were made, these desperate forms had boarded the Light-Vessel and had been contained; their essence would then be transported to the Mother Illumination, where they poured through the portal. Here, emotions of terror and anxiety took hold, so they were subdued for their own safety — in preparation for the Arrival of the Essence ceremonies at Darkentides.

The Elan already inhabiting the planet knew what to do. They gifted their light and positivity, which would be absorbed by the Essence, who would then find peace at last as Elan Vital.

Chapter Thirty-One

A Gathering of Paragons

On the day of the Light-battle, all Paragons from Sectors 1 – 2 and 3 had left. But a day or two later, they returned to Sector 4 for a social gathering.

They discussed topics for hours, like how long they'd been on the planet — what abilities they came by — tending their sectors and Elan Vital — even venturing into how they'd died.

"I'm so impressed by that prism you made, Finn; how did you do it?" Ben gushed, bursting into mellow greens.

"Easy enough with practice. Took me quite a few tries before I got it, though. I've had time; S-2's arrived in 2001. What year was it when you came?"

Ben was so shocked by the time that had passed between S-2 and 4's arrivals that he was lost for words for a while.

"2243!"

"Cool, what was it like?" Finn asked.

Ben recalled. *"Not in the least bit 'cool', mate! You're better off here, trust me. We all are!"*

Finn smiled, waving him to follow. *"Come over here, I'll show you the prism."*

Suze sat chatting with Zeena and Kane from S-3 and Renshaw from S-1.

Zeena said. *"Suze, I simply love your eyes! Did you **make** that happen, or did it **just** happen?"* she mused. Her olive skin shimmered with a fine layer of gold dust, enhanced with glints of fuchsia pink.

"It just happened; I was thinking about Bailey at the time." Her Ivory irises sparkled. *"I don't mind, beats*

being covered in his hair — I'm now covered in his glitter!" Suze watched on while Carter S-2 played with Bailey and Zeus, his little West Highland Terrier; they darted back and forth after silver balls of light, and then she added,

"Now I know what that little ball of white light was zooming about with Bailey!"

Kane smiled as he recalled the white and creamy flashes circling at them at the Light-battle. He questioned Suze's Light-Showering; his alabaster skin tone was textured with small veins of frosted blue. His pearlescent eyes studied her closely.

He said, *"I've never seen that before. No one in S-3 has ever done that! I can see why the Elites chose you. How did you do it?"*

"Nor S-1! Well done." Renshaw complimented her. *"You should show us."*

"I don't know, Kane; I found the ability while practising after my Birthing." She shrugged, then added, *"I can show you Ren. I'm sure I'd be able to do it again."*

Renshaw smiled widely.

Grace and Ava from S-2 and Bea from S-1, were with Nina over at the tree line, making intricate patterns with light particles, and Becky talked with Cassy, Lily and Seb from Sector 3, while they inspected the Elan.

"To think these little sparks of light were once living beings, with feelings and worries, struggling to survive in a world that had no hope."

"They still have feelings, Beck," Seb told her, moving closer. His pale sky-blue mingled briefly with Becky's red shades, scattering mellow silvery Magenta dots about them. *"They experience love and joy; they just don't remember the worries and fear they felt as a physical being."*

"Oh, I don't know, Seb...they seemed concerned when the dark scouts were roaming near them," Lily added, gently closing her lids, covering acute gold eyes.

"Perhaps it brought back a memory." Becky wondered. *"Cassy, are you feeling better now?"*

"I am, thank you," she smiled, *"I fully recharged that same Darkentide."*

Which left Max with Elsie, Amos and Alby, all from Sector 1.

"So, we were all homeless, even before the wars took hold? All of us — on all the planets?" Max directed his question to Elsie, her bright human form shining cyan in the sunlight; her hair floated like the waves of a gentle ocean.

Elsie nodded quickly. *"It was such a shock to us when we came here in 1917. We were the first Paragons on this planet. We didn't adjust as quickly as your sector has."*

Amos and Alby nodded together, glimmering in their white brilliance, with eyes of pale pink. Max found out that they were albino twins, a proficient team when paired together. They had died together too, in late Victorian Edinburgh, after a devastating gang attack on the prejudices of their appearance.

Combined, their powers were unstoppable.

*"**We** didn't birth until..."* Amos started...

"...the 12th day." Alby finished. *"Renshaw was ill, he..."*

Amos took over, *"...he couldn't cope. The Elites said he had forgotten his choice..."*

Alby told him, *"...but that he would settle...and he did, on the 11th day."*

Amos continued, *"Our physical bodies had almost deteriorated until nothing could be done! Ren felt..."* he gave way for Alby to speak.

*"...he felt bad about it, he always tries to make up for

it still, but…"

"*We forgave him long ago.*" They said in unison.

Nina was on the lawn near the trees, questioning Grace, Bea and Ava.

"*So which planet was the first?*" she asked them.

Ava twirled her lilac and silver streaked hair in both hands, placing it gently on her left shoulder, "*They were all created at the same time, it took a thousand years or so, Phoenix had the determination and good reason!*" she replied, then added, "*The Essence started coming aeons ago, then, the first sectors in the galaxy were given Paragons in 1917.*"

Nina couldn't believe her ears; her muted fiery orange quivered.

"*And every planet is complete now.*" Bea grinned, amused by Nina's reaction; her skin looked like liquid honey and glistened in the waken light.

Then, Grace said, "*I know it all seems quite unreal, Nina, but it's all true, and our reality is real.*" Rose gold particles wafted from her form like tiny shining leaves falling in autumn.

"*Unreal!*" Nina managed. They giggled together.

Most of the day had gone by in a blink, and the Paragons needed to return to their own sectors for the Essence ceremonies that Darkentide.

And with promises to share the light again in the near future on the planet Marinas for regular Light-Gathering celebrations, they soon departed.

The Paragons of S-4 watched on as the fifteen starlit orbs ascended, then stopped way up above the silver haze before splitting into three groups and shooting off around the planet to their sectors.

Now left alone in their sector, the sky was beginning to dim, and where once the Darkentide had filled them with fear, it now heralded a sense of giving and joy.

"I actually do have a question that no one has answered yet, and I simply haven't found the knowledge of it..."

"What question is that, Beck?" Suze asked her.

"Well...where did our bodies go?"

Nina gave a burst of light. *"We can ask about that soon enough; I haven't thought about our physical bodies for a while now."*

"Yeah, it hardly seems important, really. I was just curious, that's all."

"Where's the dog?" quizzed Suze.

Max looked around. *"Mmmm... Good question."*

Ben materialised to his vaporous form and lifted slowly upward, looking for Bailey's creamy flash. He scanned the forest and the Palm trees, the Aloe vera and the herb garden. *"Over there, looks like he's digging again!"*

"So, we get to meet the other Elites soon, then," Max said. *"I wonder if they look as odd as Orcus does?"*

"Who knows! We shall see...I guess we should get ourselves ready for the Essence, you lot," said Nina and started to wander off. The rest followed.

Becky zipped ahead of her friends, *"This place is so special."* She spun in a twirl of reds. *"It's like that old-timer's story...the one, back in the ancient days...what's it called? You know...when the animals all gathered!"*

"Ohhhh, I know...erm, what was it called?" stuttered Nina, trying to remember.

Max said, *"It was Noah's Ark! Except now it's Phoenix's Arc!"*

Epilogue

The Paragon's days turned into weeks. During this short time, their balance became whole and unified; individual powers and abilities surfaced, becoming stronger. They were now light beings; radiance flowed effortlessly, working together in waves of positivity. The word 'negative' and its meaning were all but lost in this place, leaving no room for it to take hold. However, a distant memory remained.

No longer did they need food and water as sustenance, nor did they need the facilities or confines of the house. Sector 4 was their home, a playground of love and light — it gave them everything they needed.

From the day of their Birthing, a monumental surprise had been given. The enormous crystal stones they had each chosen in the beginning were now their refuge, a place for resting, recharging and gathering light energy during the Darkentides; they just entered them, mingling their particles with those of the crystal.

The little house had now completely vanished. It had all been a simple light illusion, just like the food they'd eaten, the wine they'd drunk, the showers they'd taken, the clothes they'd worn and the wounds they sustained during the moments of trying to escape — all set perfectly in place for their physical familiarities.

Phoenix had chosen a formidable group to help care for and guide the life forms in the EMA galaxy.

There was still so much left to learn; they had even more Paragons and Elites to meet — bearing in mind they had already encountered Raven and Orcus.

And they had questions still left to be answered.

What of the blank pages in the 'Earth' book?

Where were all their bodies now that they had birthed? Could the Elan move from one planet to another?

Did it ever snow here? They hoped not!

And where was the sun? The daylight came and went — a Waken and a Darken…a sun appeared to rise and set somewhere over this planet just like any other sun would, yet no one in Sector 4 had ever seen it do so.

Was there a moon, too?

They guessed these questions would all be answered 'in good time'.

Meanwhile, they prepared for the upcoming Light-Celebrations on the ocean planet of Marinas.

About the Author

Laura, originally from Milton Keynes, now lives in Derbyshire with her husband, Carl. Together, they enjoy walking their two Golden Retrievers, Bailey and Daisy, working in the garden and being in nature.

Not only does Laura have a passion for singing and performing with her local community choir in concerts, but she also has a deep interest in the paranormal, such as Bigfoot, UFOs, ghosts, and the power of positive energy and thought patterns. She has diplomas in The Law of Attraction and Parapsychology — Proofreading, Editing and Reiki healing level 2 and works in the comfort of her own home as a freelance book cover designer, typesetter and editor.

Her passion for positivity, along with the unexplained, has led her to delve into the wonders of the universe. Influenced by the plight of our awe-inspiring planet Earth, Laura felt compelled to tell a tale that explores a different harmony between humanity and the environment.

Through her storytelling, Laura aims to extend the possibilities of our thoughts, challenging perceptions and igniting the imagination of her readers. Encouraging them to embrace the unknown with open minds.

'The Arc' is Laura's first novel; she is currently working on the second book in this trilogy.

Website www.lauracosbyauthor.co.uk

https://www.instagram.com/lauracosby.author/

https://www.facebook.com/AuthorLauraDCosby/

Stock image source © <a href='https://www.123rf.com/profile_virtosmedia'>virtosmedia</a>, <a href='https://www.123rf.com/free-images/'>123RF Free Images</a>

Lauracosbyauthor.co.uk